Second Chance Books

By Carina Gaskell

Map illustration by Jamila Geronimo (@poppylovae)

Book cover illustrated by Ksenia Nosova (@sennydoesarty)

Editor: Julian Baet

Content Warning

This book contains mentions of suicide, terminal illness, death of a parent, infidelity, leaked nudes, physical violence, pregnancy complications, addiction, and drug use. A more detailed breakdown of how these subjects appear in the book (whether past or present, on-page or off-page) can be found on my website, linked at the end of this book.

Please read with care.

To Nic,
without whose love and support this book would not have been possible.
May you recognize the love you have given me so freely
transformed into the pages of this book.
I love you eternally.

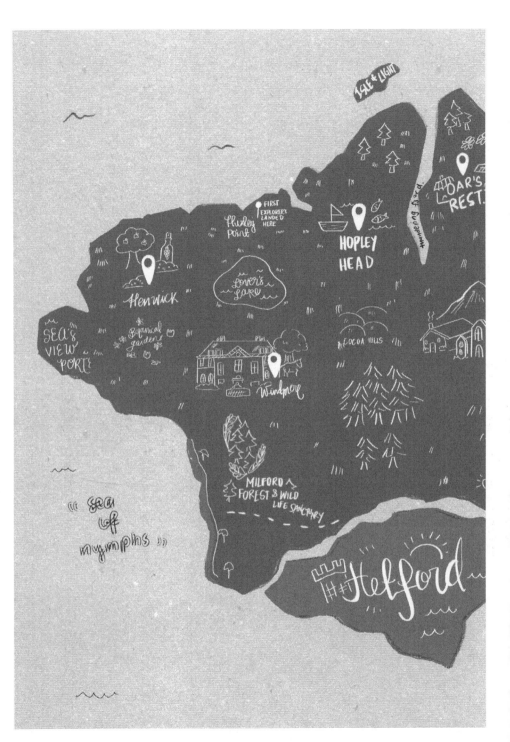

Cerulea
Weepy Hills
OXLEA
LONG ROAD
Chetham
Newbury
CINEMA
ROLLER RINK
BEACH
COASTLINE
Royaume Beach
east cerulean sea

Nell

SOS.

My older sister, Kate, could not have chosen a worse time to send me that text. I'm in the middle of an important meeting with my boss and the rest of the acquisitions team at the real estate development company I work at. As an assistant, I'm supposed to be paying attention. Taking notes.

Not stressing out about my sister, who could either be in mild distress or dying.

SOS? That could mean anything. Is it SOS—I need help picking a dress for date night? SOS—I forgot Mama's recipe for kaldereta? Or SOS—I'm bleeding and need to be rushed to the hospital ASAP? Because she knows I can't drive. I don't even have a license—or a car, for that matter. The best I can do is call a cab.

I send a quick reply as discreetly as I can.

NELL

????????????????

1

When I look up, my boss, Jane, is glaring at me. Her vibrant red hair, curled in loose waves, makes her head look like it's on fire. Sheepishly, I set my phone face down on my lap, ignoring it when it begins vibrating with a call.

I'm restless with the desire to pick it up. Ever since the doctor broke the news that Kate's pregnancy is considered high-risk, her husband, Henry, and I have been on equally high alert with regards to her health. But if I excuse myself from this meeting—for a personal call, no less—I may as well consider myself fired.

Jane takes these meetings seriously; she demands one hundred percent from the team, regardless if you're an agent or an agent's assistant.

I dutifully put pen to paper, jotting down an agent's update (*Roger Fitzgerald—still uninterested in selling his property; pulling out assigned agents for the time being*). Under it, I list everyone's subsequent ideas for resolving that issue.

Offer him discounted prices for a new apartment? (No idiot is going to take money from us just to give it back.)

Bump up the asking price by an additional three percent? (We're already offering him millions. No way.)

I console myself with the fact that—whatever Kate's problem may be, be it a fashion emergency or worse—Henry will be there to take care of her.

I have never met a more dedicated and loving partner—or person, even—than Henry. I credit him with restoring my faith in love and diminishing my pessimism and disdain for romance.

Had he not married my sister, I probably would have never had the guts to pursue Creative Writing in college. My dream of working for Clover Press, the most prestigious publisher in all of Cerulea, on top of writing romance novels as a career, would have remained just that. A dream. But because of Henry, it's an actual path I'm steadily working towards now that it's the summer before my final year of university.

I'd probably still be working in Vanguard Properties, as I am now, but instead of just a means to make a living and pay my tuition, I'd probably take Jane up on her offer to turn me into her protégé. An agent-in-the-making.

Can you imagine? *Me?* Selling properties and developing them for a living? You may as well ask a fish to ride a bicycle.

As soon as the meeting ends, I check my phone on my way back to my desk to see if Kate has replied.

Nope.

Nothing.

Just one missed call and then radio silence.

"Is everything alright?" Jane asks. She stands in the doorway of her office, one hand on her hip, the other on the doorframe.

"Huh?" I blurt out. "Oh. Yes. Sorry."

Jane inhales deeply, her shoulders rising as if she were gearing up to lecture me. I steel myself, ready to apologize for my earlier distraction. Instead, Jane exhales slowly and relaxes her shoulders.

"If you insist," she says. She glances at her wristwatch before turning back to me. "Have today's minutes in my inbox before you leave. This Roger fellow is a major pain in my ass."

"Yes, of course," I say, but I don't think she hears me. She shuts the door to her office and I slump down into my seat, worrying about my sister.

I shoot her another text.

NELL

Kate? Is everything OK?

KATE

NELL

Are you sure?

KATE

Don't worry about it.

Now I'm really worried.

My shift could not have ended any sooner.

I take the bus from Hetford, the capital city where I work, to Oxlea, the town in Central Cerulea where I live with my sister and her husband in a yellow terraced house.

Usually, I spend the hour-long commute from the office to decompress. I read a book or listen to music. Sometimes both, as long as there are no lyrics to distract me from the words on the page.

But today, I call my sister incessantly. She picks up on my third try.

"Hello?" Her voice is the same as always, soft and gentle, if a little strained. If I thought I'd pick up on any signs of her distress over the phone, I thought wrong.

"Kate," I say. "What happened? What was the emergency?"

She chuckles. "It's nothing. I just—I thought we were out of garlic. I was going to ask you to bring some on your way home, but I found more in the pantry. It's fine."

I sigh in relief.

Kate *loves* cooking; before Henry, she dreamt of opening her own Filipino restaurant called *Kusina*.

"K for Kate," she said.

But all that's been set aside in favor of starting a family, which she and Henry have been working towards for the past year they've been married. She's four months pregnant now and already beginning to show.

"I'm making adobo," she says.

"Pork or chicken?" I ask.

"Pork. Just how you like it."

I smile, even though she can't see me.

I have the best sister in the world. We weren't always close; she's nine years older than me and left home at sixteen, but ever since Mama died three years ago and the state put me in Kate's care, we've been closer than ever.

"I'm on my way home," I tell her.

"I know."

"Is Henry back from work yet?"

"He's..." Kate trails off. "He has some stuff he needs to take care of."

Oh?

Kate must sense my concern because she's quick to clarify.

"Work stuff."

That shouldn't surprise me; as a doctor, Henry worked long shifts, sometimes leaving in the middle of the night to care for a patient. But ever since Kate got pregnant, I guess I thought he'd slow his roll. Be around more, especially given the circumstances surrounding Kate's pregnancy.

"Anyway," Kate says, "dinner should be ready when you get back. Please be safe. Call me in case of emergencies."

I snicker. "Can I send an SOS text instead?"

"Very funny," Kate says dryly.

"Love you," I say.

"Love you too, Nell."

I hang up feeling lighter.

I enter the house and hang my keys over the console bearing a vase of flowers, before kicking off my shoes and setting them aside.

Kate and I owe the concept of inside and outside clothes to our Filipino heritage: neither of us can stand the idea of wearing dirty shoes in the cleanliness of our home. Forget about wearing outside clothes to bed, either. It's pambahay all the way.

It took Henry some time to get used to, but after maybe the fifth time we yelled at him, he got the memo.

"Kate!" I call out. No response. "Kate?"

I turn left into the living room but it's empty. I cross into the kitchen, from which a fragrant garlicky aroma emanates. On the stove, a pot of adobo is boiling, threatening to spill over. I hiss under my breath and slip on an oven mitt to transfer it and let it cool.

"Kate!" I call out again. Thank God the stove doesn't run on gas or the house could have burnt down.

I rush upstairs when I still hear no response. It's not like my sister to be so irresponsible and inattentive to details, especially when it came to food.

I find her in their room, curled up in a fetal position on the bed, staring absently into space. There's a dark patch on her pillow, damp from where her tears fell.

My blood runs cold.

"Kate." I fall on my knees on the floor next to her, hands pushing her hair away from her face. "Are you okay? Are you in pain? Should I call Henry?"

Her face screws up at the mention of his name. She lets out an agonized groan. Her tears start up again and fall in quick succession.

Panic constricts my throat. "Kate. Tell me what's wrong. I can't help you if I don't know what's going on."

She rolls onto her back, her palm cupping the bump on her stomach. I breathe heavily, giving her the time to sob first and then collect herself. In the meantime, I scan her body for any external signs of pain: a scar or a welt or a blood stain but find none.

"Kate," I plead, my voice breaking.

"He left."

"What?"

"Henry. He—He's not coming back." She chokes out a sob and buries her face in her hands. I can tell it was hard for her to even say. As if verbalizing the truth cemented it as real.

Even I can't believe it. Surely she's talking about a different Henry? The Henry I know—the Henry she married—would never leave her. He'd never walk out on our family, especially now that they were expecting.

But I look at my sister and I know it's real. This is happening. This is our truth now.

I have never heard Kate wail like this, not even when she left home, that night she and Mama fought harder than they ever had, the fight to end all fights, or the day she picked me up from school after Mama took her own life.

Henry is gone. He's left us behind.

Whatever faith I had in love crumbles all over again.

I want to pry. I want to ask Kate to give me all the gory details. The "how's", the "when's", and then maybe, together, we could figure out the "why". But I know it's delicate. The wound is too raw. All that matters right now is my sister and her baby and the pain that is surely detrimental to their health.

I crawl next to her onto the mattress and scoop her into my arms, not caring about our own rule of no outside clothes in bed. I stroke her hair. I rock her back and forth the way Mama used to do to us when we were younger, the way Kate did to me after she broke the news in her apartment that she was now my legal guardian.

We lay there until the sun goes down and the streetlights outside switch on. Until her staggered breaths even out and calm.

"Where is he now?" I ask the dark, in case Kate doesn't want to reply.

She sniffles. "I don't know. Gone."

"Just gone?"

"It's not like I asked about his plans," she scoffs.

I squeeze my sister's hand. "I'm sorry," I say. That was careless of me.

She breaks out into a soft sob, as if she's afraid I'll hear, even though her tears dampen my shirt.

"I don't know what I'm going to do," she says, sitting up to face me. "Does this mean we're getting a divorce? *Should* I divorce him? Where do we go if I do?"

Henry was the sole breadwinner of the family. The house was under his name, a gift from his parents when they wed.

I shush her and wipe her tears from her face. "Don't worry about that," I tell her. *Leave that to me.* "We're going to be fine, okay? Everything will be alright."

"No, it won't. Nell, he left. I mean, he was practically *gone* our whole marriage, always busy at work, but now he—" She buries her face in her hands. I can hear her heart breaking all over again.

I don't understand it. I don't understand *him*, and I don't think I ever will.

Mama spent her whole life hopping from one relationship to another. Kate and Henry swore they'd be different. That they'd work hard through the good and the bad.

It was in their vows, for God's sake.

Where the fuck has he gone?

"Kate," I say softly. I peel her hands from her face. Tuck her hair behind her ears. "We're gonna be okay. Remember? Us Garcia girls stick together." A mantra Mama had taught us. There was nothing we can't get through so long as we were together.

"The baby—"

"I know," I say, nodding. "It's gonna be okay. I promise. We'll figure it out."

"There's so much bills, and the doctor's appointments. I don't have a job. I don't know where I'm going to get the money to pay for everything." She's hyperventilating now, her mind seemingly spiraling from one bad situation to worse.

I won't lie and say I'm not worried about the same things. Us Garcia girls stick together, yes, but us Garcia girls also seem to be doomed to live a life of financial insecurity.

My whole life there never seemed to be enough money to get comfortable. There was only ever enough to stay afloat, but just barely. We were always scraping the bottom of the barrel, just getting by. It wasn't until Henry that our conditions improved, and his family knew that. They made Kate sign a prenup, as if my sister was marrying the guy because of his money.

Fucking assholes.

"Kate," I say, cupping her face and forcing her to look at me. "Everything will be okay, Katie, I promise." I don't know *how*, but what I do know is that I will do everything I can to make this better. I'll pick up a second job, drop out of college, give up my dreams of becoming a published author for a cushy gig flipping properties.

Kate sniffles. I can tell she doesn't believe me, but she wants to. That's a start.

"Are you hungry?" I ask. "I can reheat the adobo for you."

"Fuck."

I wave her off. "I let it cool before I came up here. Don't worry."

Her shoulders relax.

"Yes? Hungry?" I prod, hopeful she'll let me take care of her for a change.

Kate nods. Relief washes over me. I get off the bed and help her up to her feet. I rub circles onto her back as she shuffles into her house slippers.

My head still spins with the news. Henry *loves* Kate. He adores her. Anyone with eyes could see that. Even his greedy, selfish family could see that.

So how could he just leave? After everything. And why now? I didn't even know they were having problems. I never would have guessed. The last time I saw them together, they looked as they always did, like they just tied the knot a minute before I laid my eyes on them.

Everything's going to be okay, I tell myself. *Us Garcia girls stick together.*

There is a way out of this. I just can't see it right now, but it's there. It'll show itself to me. It'll make itself known.

Or I hope so, anyway. We've been through so much, Kate and I, that I'm worried soon enough our luck will run out.

Just not any time soon, God. Please.

Tom

Ever since the new apartment complex in town opened three weeks ago, there's been an influx of new customers at Second Chance Books, the bookstore where I live and work.

They've got a sheen to them, these newbies, their bright eyes like neon signs telling the world they're not from here but are ready to make this place theirs. It's a stark contrast to the weary look most locals wear on a day-to-day basis, knowing as well as I do that we're all steadily being priced out of our homes.

These implants stick out like sore thumbs, their manner of speaking and dressing so out of place in Newbury, but especially Second Chance Books, with its dusty wooden shelves so full of worn paperbacks we've had to start stacking them on the floor. Getting around the store feels like being in an obstacle course. If you're not careful, you'll knock a stack and there will be a domino effect that will bury you in books.

One such customer is leaving the store as my boss, Roger emerges from his room in the back to look out the window.

This has become part of his daily routine. He stands by the window and looks out at the street, first left then right. Then he glances at his wristwatch before turning to me to say, "No sharks today," as he has over the past two weeks.

The sharks are real estate agents from Vanguard Properties trying to convince Roger to sell his property. Almost all the other stores around us have been bought out by Vanguard, their buildings knocked down into dust and rubble, turning our once lively street into a shell of its former self.

"Maybe they're regrouping," I tease. "They're clearly no match to your strong will."

Roger presses his lips together in a polite smile. Those jokes used to get a laugh out of him. I don't know what changed.

The other day, he asked me whether it might be time to close up shop. To take the offer of millions and "explore new horizons."

I told him he was out of his mind.

Second Chance Books is not for sale. Not now, not ever. And I'll do whatever it takes to remind him of that.

The rest of the day passes by in a blur. I don't leave my spot behind the counter where I ring up customers unless to go to the restroom or have lunch. Before I know it, Roger and I are setting up for the weekly book club meeting: sweeping the shin-high platform-as-stage, arranging the round wooden tables and chairs in orderly rows.

Book club at Second Chance Books isn't like any other; instead of reading the same book and discussing it as a group, people are invited to share passages from their latest or current read, which has morphed into some members reading their own writing or even singing songs, which Roger says falls under poetry. He's been trying to get me to perform ever since he learned I was in a band in school. He even convinced the members of the book club to chip in to buy me a new guitar, and then a keyboard.

I've managed to get away with not doing that by offering to play background music or dramatic accompaniments to whoever's reading. But Roger, unlike the sharks, never knows to leave things well enough alone.

"Have you got anything for us today?" he asks.

"You ask me that every week," I say.

"And you never say yes. You've been here five years. You have to get up on that stage at some point."

I sigh. He's dropped hints of song requests before in the form of loaning me vinyl records from his collection: The Beach Boys, Billie Holiday, The

Velvet Underground—he has quite the music taste. I just don't think I can handle that many eyes on me, judging me, perceiving me.

"I'll consider," I say.

"Like hell you are. We're coming up on the book club's anniversary."

"And I told you I was already working on something for it," I protest. I've been scheduling interviews with some members for a mini documentary on the club and its history, both to commemorate it and strengthen Roger's resolve against the sharks.

Roger doesn't care though. He never listens to me. He always has to have his way.

"Here," he says. "I'll put you after Bobby." He signs my name for me on last week's sign-up sheet, bumping Walter, one of our newest consistent attendees, down a slot. That puts me in third.

"Roger," I warn.

He checks his wristwatch and then wiggles his brows at me. "I'd get to practicing if I were you. An hour should be enough, no?"

I settle on Mazzy Star's "Fade Into You." A classic, and one that I already knew how to play and had memorized the lyrics of. My acoustic guitar's leaning against the shelf next to the platform, ready to be picked up when it's my turn.

I stand by the refreshments table as people spill into the store. I love how Second Chance Books looks at night, with the warm ambient lighting and dark wooden everything. Members, both old and new, come to greet me.

Mildred, one of the members who's been here the longest and helps cohost the book club, smushes my cheeks and greets me with a kiss on each side. She tells me she's looking forward to my performance, which means Roger has already called up everyone he knows to tell them the news.

Everyone takes their seats but I'm too jittery to sit. I stand there, trying to make myself useful: pouring wine into paper cups for whoever asks, nibbling on the cheese and crackers laid out for guests.

It's a full house. Fuller than it's ever been. More and more people arrive, and when all the seats are taken up, people stand in rows in the back, their new faces outnumbering familiar ones almost ten to one.

What will they think of me?

They'll clap, of course, to be polite. But what if my voice cracks? What if I miss a note? There's a couple whispering to each other by the door, the woman's bright red hair catching my eye, and I imagine what their conversation might be like after my performance.

"He should stick to selling books," the man will say, pleased with himself when the woman laughs.

"I never want to hear that song again," she'll reply, to which he'll insist they should listen to the original to drown out their memory of my rendition.

Louis gets up onstage after Mildred's introduction. His permed curls are slicked back, and on the bridge of his nose rests thick black glasses. He reads a passage from Stephen King's *On Writing*. He shares his thoughts, which tend to veer off-track, so Mildred limits him to fifteen minutes of stage-time max. When he finishes, there is a smattering of applause. He reclaims his seat just as Bobby, a hulking mass of a human teddy bear, steps onstage.

That's when I see her. A face new to this place but not to me. Her honey-brown hair is tied up in a neat bun. Loose strands frame her rosy cheeks. She tiptoes from behind someone's shoulders, trying to catch sight of the stage.

Our eyes meet. Hers brighten. She grins and waves.

My mind goes blank. My chest is pummeled by the heavy fists of my longing.

She looks the same as always, if a little more radiant. I feel her magnetism pulling me towards her, almost forcing me to my knees as if there was no better response to her presence than to worship her.

But I can't. I *won't*.

I've let myself be drawn to her flames before, and like Icarus, all I got were scorched wings.

Bobby wraps up onstage. I can hear Roger introducing me. Everyone's eyes add to the weight of her gaze.

I can't breathe. It's as if someone had stuffed my ears with cotton, muffling all the noise around me.

She sticks her fingers in her mouth and whistles. It sounds hollow in my ears.

They're clapping, all of them, for me.

I should get up there, strap my guitar to my chest and just play. Make Roger happy and be done with it. Then after, I should go and say hello to her. *What's up? How are you doing? I haven't seen you in so long.*

There's so much I should do. If I were a better man, a braver man, I'd have done them already. Instead, I turn on my heel and flee. I lock myself in Roger's room and don't leave until book club is over.

I try to ignore the obvious disappointment on Roger's face when I emerge from his room hours later. Quietly, I stack the used paper cups and throw them in the bin. I carry the tables back to their place. I rearrange the chairs.

Roger approaches me and hands me a tiny sheet of paper, seemingly torn from the back of a worn paperback.

"What's this?"

"A girl left you her number," he says. "Some girl named Paulina."

I stare down at the sheet. There, her unmistakable print. Elegant and precise in its strokes, divulging its author's confidence.

Roger wiggles his brows at me. "I'd call her if I were you."

But you're not me.

I clench my fist around the sheet. It crumples in my palm.

Roger grunts as he sits himself down. "Do you want to talk about what happened?"

Oh, nothing. Just the fact that a girl from my past—*the* girl from my past—is now back to haunt me.

"Stage fright," I offer.

Roger sighs. "Next time, then."

I nod. "Next time."

Nell

The Vanguard Properties headquarters is a dazzling all-glass five-story building, a paragon of new Cerulea: sleek, modern, and so clearly affluent. It's flanked by older Victorian architecture and would otherwise be described as tacky had the contrast not been by design. It's one of the first things they tell you as a new hire: the building serves as a mirror to Cerulea, forcing its citizens to confront the country's need to modernize.

I just like that every single floor and room is air conditioned, from the hallways to the bathrooms.

I swipe my keycard in the elevator and ride it to the fourth floor, just in time to start my shift. All week, I've been hesitant to leave Kate alone to go to work, but each day she'd insist she was feeling better than the last, and even though she didn't look like it, I had no other choice but to go. We need my income, now more than ever.

"Oh, good. You're here," Jane says when I arrive at my desk. She's sporting an animal print blouse tucked into a red pencil skirt that matches her hair—professional attire only in form but not style. No one else in the office can get away with that, but the C-Suite guys love Jane because she's efficient and effective, so they let her get away with almost anything. No red tape stands in her way.

She beckons me into her office and orders me to bring the NEWBURY: FITZGERALD file. I find it easily, given I've been alphabetizing the documents in my file cabinet the past few weeks. I set it down in front of her and stand back, awaiting further instructions.

While seated behind her desk, Jane flips the folder open. She stares at the first page, deep in thought. From memory, I know it contains Roger Fitzgerald's profile, the subject of last week's meeting, as well as notes from agents who have tried to convince him to sell his property to us.

"This man," Jane finally says, "is a pain in my ass."

Ah, so it's that kind of morning. When work is tough, I sometimes double as Jane's unwilling therapist. At least I don't have to do much but stand there and ask questions like, "He still won't sell?"

"No," Jane says. "I went to their stupid book club meeting with my husband, thinking maybe I can talk to Roger myself, but the man is *famous!* Everyone swarmed him to get a minute of his time. No wonder he refuses to sell. I have half a mind to commit arson just to get him out of there."

I imagine Jane inside the secondhand bookstore pictured in the NEWBURY: FITZGERALD folder. She's such a modern woman, I can't imagine her not sticking out in a place as cramped and cozy-looking as Second Chance Books.

I remember when I first found out about it. My heart clenched at the knowledge that I'd be playing a role in shuttering a bookstore, no matter how small. After all, bookstores have always been my refuge from reality. When times got tough, I could always wander into a bookstore, inspect the shelves, and remind myself that there is always some place I can run off to, even just for a while. Even if it's between the pages of a book.

Besides, good or bad, every book has an end. Happiness might not be permanent, but the pain won't last forever, either.

I've had to teach myself to forget about Second Chance Books every time we discuss the NEWBURY: FITZGERALD case. In its place, I imagine an empty plot of land.

"Maybe don't do that," I blurt out. Jane glares at me and I realize she was just exaggerating. Even after months working for her, I'm still not used to not taking her literally. It's gotten me in trouble a few times before, but thankfully nothing too bad.

Jane sighs exasperatedly and flips the folder shut. With her elbows resting on her glass tabletop, she massages her temples and says, "I'm running out of ideas. Wes *desperately* wants that piece of land, no matter how many alternative options we give him."

Wes is Wesley Grant, CEO of Vanguard Properties. Despite how close Jane is to him, I've never met him before. I don't think I've even seen his pictures. The guy values his privacy, I'll give him that.

He has some fanatics in the office, mostly the other boys my age who were desperate to climb the corporate ladder and become rich themselves, but I've also overheard some employees talking about how they preferred when Wesley's father was in-charge. Having only worked here under Wesley's reign, I can't exactly give a fair opinion.

"Did you know," Jane says, an incredulous look on her that tells me that whatever she's about to say, I'm not meant to see coming. "Even with the ten percent commission, no other agent wants to take him on. Ten percent, darling. That's over triple the standard rate. That's—what? At least a couple hundred thousand Cerulean crowns?"

My jaw drops. How could anyone say no to that much money? I could pay back all my student debt with that money, cover all our bills at home, and take care of any and all of Kate's medical fees.

"Wesley wants to break ground by end of summer. There's no way we're convincing that stupid old man to se—"

"What if I try?"

The words are out of my mouth before I can stop them. Before I've even given them much thought. But the longer the words hang in the air between us, the more it starts to take shape, to become a viable option.

This is our Way Out, and if I get this right, Kate, the baby, and I will be taken care of.

Jane stares at me, mouth slightly agape.

"I—I mean," I begin to stammer. "I know I'm not, like, an agent or anything, but you've always been going on about taking me under your wing. Not that it's annoying or anything, I didn't mean to say you were going on and on and o—"

Jane grimaces and holds up a hand. "Yes, Eleanor, I get it."

I clench my fists and bite my lip to shut myself up. On top of forgetting not to take Jane so literally all the time, I also talk too much when I'm nervous.

Come to think of it, my boss might be a saint, considering what she's had to put up with me.

Jane folds one hand over the other and leans forward. "So you've given my offer more thought?" The offer, of course, is to be her protégé.

"Yes." *No. This is the first I've even seriously considered it.*

"And you want *this* to be your first project?"

"You said no one is up for it. I figured I'd be a team player."

Jane levels me with a severe gaze. It's as if I've been placed under a microscope, my every fault and flaw magnified and displayed for her to pick apart.

I start to sweat. The ends of my cropped hair scratch at my neck, making me itch.

She can see right through me. She knows I'm in it for the money.

But then again—*who isn't?*

Finally, Jane relaxes. "Well, I always say—no better way to get started than to jump straight into things."

"So, you'll let me?"

Jane shrugs. "It's worth a shot."

I dig my nails into my palm to keep myself from squealing. *Don't get too excited*, I tell myself. *We're not out of the woods yet.*

"And the commission," I start, letting myself trail off so I don't have to explicitly ask if it'll be mine.

"You convince Fitzgerald to sell," Jane says, "and the commission is yours."

My spirit soars. Jane holds out the folder for me to take and dismisses me with an order to review the file and pitch her a plan.

"You get a day off to execute it," she says as I'm walking out the door. "And please try not to come up with anything too lavish. The man and his assistant know how to run a bill, judging from the last time we hosted them at the resort in Hopley Head."

I heard about that. Roger and his assistant had steaks and lobsters for dinner every night, amongst other frivolous expenses.

I promise Jane I'll keep my pitch fiscally conservative and return to my desk.

She has no idea what she's just given me: a Way Out, a map to the light at the end of the tunnel, whatever you want to call it.

Kate and I are going to be okay. We're going to be *more* than okay.

Tom

One of Roger's strongly held beliefs is that a new day heralds a new beginning. It doesn't matter how badly you fucked up the night before, whether you raised your voice at someone you love or acted cowardly. When the sun comes up, you get a new chance to make things right. To apologize. To be brave.

I wish I could say I'm the exemplar of that belief, but alas. At lunchtime, I spot Paulina crossing the street towards the store. I duck under the counter. I have approximately fifteen seconds to get the fuck out of here before she arrives. I crawl towards the door behind me which leads to stairs that go straight up to my flat, feeling every bit of pathetic as I look. I just about get the knob twisted when the bell over the store entrance rings, signaling Paulina's arrival.

Roger emerges from his room and gives me a quizzical look. I stick my finger through the teeny tiny slat in the doorway, cringing when the door creaks open.

Roger clears his throat. With a shake of his head, he proceeds to the center of the store and greets Paulina. I make my escape, still on all fours, just as I hear our standard greeting:

"Welcome to Second Chance Books! How can I help you?"

I stumble up the staircase, my chin nearly slamming on a step from my panic. I lock my front door behind me and press my back against it, my chest rising and falling in quick succession as I try to steady my breathing. Now that she's back, any hope of writing last night off as a nightmare flies out the window. I can't even comfort myself with the implausible idea that she hadn't seen me. We met eyes. The look on her face had gone straight to my stomach.

It's not possible. There's no way I can still be attracted to her all these years later, right? Surely this is just a holdover, or my surprise at seeing her again after all this time. There's just no way…

Fuck.

I double-check the lock on my door in case Roger gets ideas, then cross the studio to peer out the street-facing windows. When she leaves, I'll see her from here. I chew on my thumbnail, arms crossed over my chest.

Come on, come on, come on.

After what feels like forever, she emerges from the store. I drop down to my knees in case she looks up. I peer over the sill and watch her leave.

There she goes, her statuesque figure shrinking smaller and smaller until it disappears.

I wait a few more minutes before I return downstairs. Roger's doing his crossword puzzle at his usual table. He quirks a brow at me when I reclaim my spot behind the counter.

"Do you want to explain to me what that was?" he asks.

I swallow hard. I rack my brain for an explanation. Something that doesn't make me sound as stupid as I must have looked.

I come up empty. I guess that just means I'm stupid—*fact.*

Roger sets the newspaper down, his fountain pen holding it in place. I'd asked him before, why he wouldn't just use pencil, and he said it's a lot more thrilling that way, having no method of erasing his mistakes other than striking it out, forcing himself to reckon with it eternally (or at least until he recycles the page). "So, if last night was stage fright, what's today?"

I open my mouth, but nothing comes out.

"Thomas, my boy," Roger says, impatience dripping from his voice. "The lovely girl from last night came back today because you still haven't texted her, even after she so kindly left you her number. And not only did you not have the decency to show your face, you would rather make like a cockroach than say hello. Around here, we call that *stupidity*."

I exhale an exasperated sigh. He's right, of course. Where usually I'd be inclined to defend my honor, I have no excuse in this scenario. I acted stupidly. No, *cowardly*.

Roger gestures for me to take a seat across from him. I oblige. He levels me with a piercing gaze, one I've come to know throughout the years as expectant. An *'explain yourself while you have the chance before I come up with an explanation for you and run with it'* kind of gaze.

Where do I start?

Roger knows all about my history at this point. My family background. How I ended up here and why. But I could never bring myself to name the cherry on top of it all. The final straw, my own personal shame.

"Do you remember," I start, "the night you and I met? When I ran away from home?"

Time had dulled the sting of this truth. It's just another story now, one I tell the world about myself like the first song I learned on the guitar or how my shoulders would ache from hours of piano lessons and improper posture.

Roger folds his arm over the table and leans into it. *Go on*, his eyes tell me.

I believe that certain things happen to us that mold us into the person we're meant to become. A trial by fire that results in a rebirth, a phoenix rising from the ashes.

I remind Roger of my genesis. Of the night my father was inducted into the Conservatory of Music's Hall of Fame for his contributions to Cerulean arts and culture. Of sitting at the table with my stepbrother, both of us dressed in stiff suits and uncomfortable brand-new leather shoes.

"I told you about the girl," I say. "Greg's girlfriend."

Greg was—*is?*—my stepbrother. He's less man, more Neanderthal. He walked into any room like he owned the place *and* the people inside it.

That night, he wouldn't stop snickering at something on his phone while the sons of my father's bandmates laughed along. Finally, Greg's phone circled the table and reached me. And there she was: a drunken Paulina, undressing on camera.

I don't remember what I said anymore. Only how I felt saying it. Years of pent-up anger flowed out of me, and when Greg snorted and told me to *chill*, I reared my fist back and threw the first punch. My knuckles connected with his nose with a sickening *crunch*. My father was onstage giving a speech. He'd cut it short when Greg tackled me and began pummeling my face in retaliation.

The night ended early for us. On the ride home, my father was dead silent. Greg and I both held ice packs to our faces. My stepmother, Yvonne, kept glancing back at us in the backseat. Or, well, she glanced at Greg. She glared at me.

When we got home, my father lasted the short walk it took to his study—a room full of musical instruments rather than books—before he exploded. I can still hear the echoes of his rage reverberating somewhere in the back of my skull. That kind of anger coming from your father never really leaves you.

He didn't care that Greg had beaten me to near-pulp. Only that I initiated. That I humiliated him. He said I was grounded. That I had to quit the band I'd started with my friends, because clearly they were a terrible influence if I was going around thinking I could punch people.

He threatened to cut me off. To disown me. I figured I'd make it easier for him.

Greg didn't get the same reprimand. Apparently, it was fine to beat someone up as long as they threw the first punch. *Self-defense or whatever.*

After my dad sent me to my room, I paced. Back and forth, back and forth, for maybe a good hour. I couldn't sit still. I had to let Paulina know.

I changed out of my shoes into sneakers and climbed out of my window, still in my tux. My coat caught on a branch, and I still remember the sound of the fabric tearing. I didn't care. I ran all the way to her house with a crater-sized hole in my coat.

I threw pebbles at her window, the way I always had since we started hanging out two years before, when we were fifteen. We watched a movie where the guy would get the girl to come out for late-night rendezvous that way—I don't remember which movie it was anymore—and she said she thought it was romantic. I never had the courage to ask her out, but I'd hoped—stupidly—that she'd get what I was trying to do, pebbles and all.

Obviously not. She started dating Greg a year after that movie came out, and as far as I was concerned, they'd been going strong ever since.

I still remember the look of confusion on Paulina's face when she poked her head out her window and saw me standing there, breathless and wild-eyed, talking a mile a minute.

I told her about Greg. About the video. I reassured her I'd only seen a second of it—that a second was more than enough.

She asked if I was drunk. She wouldn't believe me when I said no. She wouldn't believe me about Greg, either.

In what will go down as the most pathetic last-ditch effort strategy of all time, I told her I loved her. Her face screwed up before she frowned. I wanted the ground to open up and swallow me whole. Even now, just remembering, I want to crawl out of my skin and disappear forever.

"Tom, *no*," she said. "We're just friends."

Yeah, I got that.

I said sorry, so she did too. Kept saying it, over and over. Asked if I wanted to come in for a glass of water, at which point I started getting angry because I wasn't drunk. I had not a single drop of alcohol in me, but she wouldn't believe me.

So I left. Crater-sized holes in my coat and my chest. I started walking back home, trying not to cry, partly because it was humiliating enough without the rest of her street seeing me sobbing, and also because my face was starting to swell, and it fucking hurt.

I couldn't bring myself to go home, though. I didn't want to see my dad, or Greg, or Yvonne. I didn't want to apologize for my actions and make up with Greg. I'd sooner puke out my own guts and eat them back up than do any of that. Even now.

I ran aimlessly until I actually puked into someone's bush on an unfamiliar street, then carried myself to the nearest bus stop. I rode it to the station and then took the midnight express to the farthest stop, a five-hour drive from home, where I passed out from exhaustion and woke to an old man shaking my shoulder and asking me if I was hungry.

Since then, this bookstore has been my home.

Roger sighs when I finish telling my story, names and all.

"Thomas," he says, "you know what I always tell you. It's best to leave the past in the past." A wave of relief washes over me. So he gets it. He knows why I acted the way I did. Why I hid and refused to show my face.

But Roger doesn't stop there. He says, "At the same time, I don't think it's healthy for you to try and keep running from it. Far be it from me to claim to understand the way the world works, but if she's returned, it must be for a reason. Wouldn't you prefer to know what that is than to live the rest of your life wondering?"

I draw in a deep breath. When Roger doled out morsels of wisdom like this, there was no arguing. I know what must be done; I only need time to scrounge up the courage to do it.

Roger patted my hand and offered me an understanding smile. "No matter where you go, there you are." He winks at me. "I don't remember where I heard that, but what a quote, eh?"

Nell

There's not a lot of information online about the book club at Second Chance Books, but given what Jane has told me, it must be a community staple, attended by long-time locals and new residents alike.

Studying the NEWBURY: FITZGERALD file, I notice that all the other agents missed that key detail about the bookstore. You can't put a price on community, especially not one built on something so distinctly human as the love for stories. I would know.

Even before we learned to write, we were telling stories, building communities through them, forging friendships and identities and using them to figure out our place in this world. If I was in Roger's place, I wouldn't want to give that up for money, either. Millions in Cerulean crowns won't replace the joy of geeking out over books with likeminded people.

But it can make it possible.

Quick research shows me that there's an underfunded public library in Newbury. With Vanguard's connections, it can be revived. The local government can even commission us to renovate it.

It makes perfect sense: once Roger is secure in knowing his beloved book club will carry on, albeit in a different venue, he'll be more likely to agree to the sale.

Of course, my plan hinges on Roger being more attached to the club than the store, which is why I added a contingency plan of our helping him donate his books to the library and any excess to nearby schools.

Jane loves my idea. "Inspired," she calls it.

"I don't know why we didn't think to ask you sooner. You're a bookworm, aren't you?"

I remind her that I'm currently studying English literature and Creative Writing in St. Catherine's in Hetford, the oldest university in all of Cerulea. So, something like that.

"Divine," she says. "I'll send this over to the top. Can't be making promises we can't keep. Once they give us the go ahead, we'll send you out to Newbury. Good job."

I leave her office gleaming from her praise.

In anticipation of the C-Suite's approval, I busy myself with taking care of Kate: going to her doctor's appointments, helping her make dinner, doing the laundry so she won't have to. Even though her doctor's given her a clean bill of health, we've been advised to err on the side of caution. No overexertion, lots of rest.

Come the following week, I take the first bus out to Newbury. It's an hour's drive so I've brought a book with me to read—Daphne du Maurier's *Rebecca*—but I can hardly focus. All I can think about is what awaits me at Second Chance Books, whether I've got what it takes to convince Roger to sell—"to do the impossible," as Jane put it when she gave me the go signal.

What happens if I fail? What if I lose my nerve, apologize for the inconvenience, and thank Roger for his time, then leave potentially even worse off than when I arrived? What repercussions will I face were I to return to the office bearing bad news?

Will Jane fire me? The other agents will certainly have something to say. I'll be the subject of breakroom gossip. That is, if I'm lucky enough to be allowed to stay long enough to hear it.

I can't imagine a worse time to start doubting my own plan.

Oxlea's oolite limestone buildings give way to sloping grass fields dotted by sun-dappled trees. We cross a bridge and Newbury comes into view. A burgeoning seaside town split in half by Vanguard's touch.

We hit the end of the newly-paved road, and as the bus grumbles along old asphalt, the shiny new buildings—apartment complexes, boutique hotels, restaurants, a single night club—are succeeded by construction sites and then the old Newbury, all red brick and two-story Georgian architecture.

I alight at the bus stop, anxious as ever, and take in my surroundings.

High Street is empty; most stores have closed permanently, including the pharmacy I'm standing in front of. A construction permit is taped to its window. FOR DEMOLITION.

Soon, there will be no memory of it even existing.

I imagine what this place might have looked like in its heyday. Who I'd have to have been to be the girl that gets her prescription refilled at some place called *The Apothecary*.

My phone vibrates in my pocket.

JANE

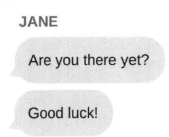

Are you there yet?

Good luck!

I thank her and let her know I've arrived. Then I cross the street towards Second Chance Books.

My breath catches in my throat when I see its wooden façade, presumably once a dark green, now mellowed and sweetened by time. There is a table out front displaying further discounted books.

Through the big glass windows, rows upon rows of shelves stand across a familiar-looking boy behind the counter, his chin resting on his palm. It looks to me like a stand-off: man vs. literature, and the books outnumbered him 10,000 to one.

Where have I seen him before?

I had prepared for this moment. I even thought, perhaps foolishly, that I was the best person for the job, being an avid reader and a student of literature myself. If there was anyone who would understand Roger's unwillingness to let go of his bookstore, it would be me. My pitch proved that.

But nothing could have readied me for the reality of what I was about to do. In the face of online retailers with low overhead costs and dwindling numbers of indie booksellers, I have come to represent the wrong side. My circumstance has robbed me of the luxury of choice.

I steel myself and enter the store. Its aged and well-worn door welcomes me with a gentle push. The scent of old paper and sandalwood fills the air.

The familiar-looking boy sits up and regards me with a small smile. But he's not just any boy. Up close, I recognize that handsome face, those sharp features that soften when he smiles. I go weak in the knees for that smile. I melt, like hot chocolate.

Thomas Whelan. My childhood crush, my dream boy—in the flesh after nearly ten years.

"Hi," he greets, clearly not recognizing me. I don't blame him. We'd only known each other less than a year before we parted, and back then I'd always worn my hair long. But oh, what a year that was. "Welcome. Can I help you with anything?"

I gulp. "Just… looking." I make a show of inspecting the shelves. I disappear behind a row to collect my thoughts.

Holy shit. I was not prepared to run into Thomas fucking Whelan today.

He still has the same head of chocolate brown curls, the same pale complexion that brought out the rosiness of his cheeks and lips. I'd crushed on him my first year in Cerulea, when my mother worked day shifts cleaning houses and sang in jazz bars at night. Sometimes I'd accompany her to the mansions she cleaned and imagine a life where we lived in each one.

Who would I be? What would I be like?

I was a shy kid, but when Tom noticed me watching him practice on the grand piano in their living room, he'd invite me to sit next to him. I'd watch his hands go over the keys, struck by wonder at the melodies he played. I'd always wanted to play the piano, but lessons were too expensive. When I told him this, he began to teach me.

He was the gentlest boy I've ever known, and for a while, I thought he was proof that love existed. Not the kind that consumed you, no. The unconditional kind. The kind that just was and expected nothing in return. He was the reason I was a sucker for the childhood friends-to-lovers trope. Because of him, I always liked the idea that someone can know all of you—every single you you've ever been, good and bad—and still see the best in you enough to love you.

Time, of course, had been the superior teacher. I know now—especially after Henry's departure—that love like that doesn't exist. Not outside of fiction, anyway.

Tom and I managed to perfect the "Heart and Soul" duet when my mother was fired, accused of stealing his stepmother's pearls. Turns out Mama noticed his stepmother hardly used it and 'borrowed' it for a date. I was too embarrassed to stay in touch. I was grateful when we moved away, far from his reach.

But surely it can't be him? Just a lookalike? My Tom's the son of a rockstar; there's no way a rich boy like him would be working at a secondhand bookstore. The Tom I knew must be partying on a yacht right now, celebrating the success of following in his father's footsteps (I'd be lying if I said I didn't keep a lookout for any up-and-coming Cerulean artists, on the off chance that I'd see his name listed there).

My line of thought is cut by the sight of Roger stepping out from the back shelves, dusting his hands on the side of his trousers.

"Oh, hello," he says. His hair is grey and slicked back. His beard takes up the entire bottom half of his face, making him look like Santa Claus, round belly and all. He's much shorter than I expected, nearly eye-level with me. "How can I help you?"

"Are you Roger?" I ask.

He grins. "Depends who's asking."

I extend a hand. "I'm Eleanor. But you can call me Nell."

His hand is soft but his grip firm. "Are you here for the job opening?"

I open my mouth to say no, but he cuts me off. Gestures for me to follow him out of the shelves as he speaks.

"I'm getting too old to be stocking the shelves myself. It's gotten to the point where I just shove them wherever, which isn't good for organization and makes browsing that much harder for our customers."

I try to speak again, but he hardly gives me space in the conversation to say anything.

"Tom can't do it because he's already manning the counter, and he's got so much on his plate as it is."

"Wait," I manage. "Tom?" Just saying his name makes my stomach flutter, like admitting to a deep, dark secret held closely to my heart.

"Uh-huh. My boy over there." He points to the boy behind the counter, who lifts a hand to wave at me despite the confused look on his face. Roger beams with pride, and I'm hit by a realization that I've been given a key, though the door which it opens, I don't yet know.

How many agents have used Tom against Roger?

"Roger—"

"It's a simple job," Roger cuts me off. "We're open from 9 to 5, except on Thursdays when we have book club, so we stay open later. Although sometimes those hours vary depending on how many customers we have. It shouldn't be your concern, though. I just need you to sort the shelves and help Tom out with whatever administrative work needs to be done."

"That's nice and all, but—"

"The salary starts at twelve crowns, which I know isn't a lot but it's over the minimum wage."

I pause. Twelve crowns for eight hours totals nearly 3,000 a month. If I take this job, that's extra money in my bank account to help Kate with whatever she needs.

"Are you interested?"

Fuck it. Why not? Every agent before me has tried the direct way of getting Roger to sell. Of simply asking and then feeding him corporate-approved lines when he says no. If I work here, I'd get to know him better than any profile written up by any agent's assistant. I'd know what makes him tick, what he thinks of Vanguard Properties, why he doesn't want to sell, and what he wants more than anything in the world that I'm sure a fat paycheck from Vanguard could afford.

My pitch will be a hell of a lot stronger once I tailor it to fit the exact kind of person he is.

I force myself to smile. "Absolutely."

Roger claps his hands together. "Brilliant. When can you start?"

I purse my lips and shrug. "Any time."

"Can you start today?"

I glance at Tom, whose gaze weighs heavily on me. He appears to be studying me, as if he senses my dishonest reasons.

I push the thought away. I have to stay focused. Childhood crushes are not going to stand in the way of my plan.

"Sure," I nod. "Just tell me what needs to be done."

Nell

To my surprise, Jane loves the idea. She cackles on the phone when I step out of the store, claiming I need to inform my sister that I was starting immediately.

I can practically see Jane wiping the tears from her eyes as she says, "Oh, brilliant, you clever, clever girl. I can't believe we've never thought of that before." She must pull her phone from her ear because her voice is distant as she calls out for one of the agents named Duke and tells him the news. I can hear Duke laughing in the background.

"Alright, Nell," Jane says. "How long do you think it'll take?"

I chew on my bottom lip. It would be beneficial to extend my stay at Second Chance Books for as long as possible, but I know that doing so would be detrimental to an even bigger payday with Vanguard Properties. So I try to strike a balance.

"I don't want to be too obvious," I say. "Could I have two weeks to settle in?"

Jane considers on the other line.

"That's alright," she says. "But I expect progress reports every week. And don't forget—we want construction to begin by the end of summer, so worst case scenario, you have until then. Although preferably we don't cut it too close. There's a lot of paperwork that needs to be done and... well, you get it."

"Absolutely. I won't let you down."

"And you'll have to find yourself a replacement," Jane adds. "In the meantime. I'm assuming you won't be reporting to the office as frequently."

"I—"

"Never mind. I'll have my niece come in. Don't worry about it. Focus on the goal."

Guilt and panic swirl in my chest. I push them away. She doesn't need to know I'll be double-dipping, and anyway, if she was in my position, she'd probably do the same thing.

Plus, I gave her a chance to say no. If she said no, I could march back in there right now and tell Roger the truth. But she said yes. Anyway, whatever Roger will be paying me is a mere pittance to the money he'll get from the sale. He'll be so rich, he could buy the house next door to Tom's and rub shoulders with Tom's father, *the* Mick Whelan, of Double Helix fame.

Jane ends the call and I take a moment to text Kate I'll be out late. Then, feeling proud of myself, I send her enough money to settle our bills in advance. With my new job, we won't have to worry so much about only making ends meet.

When I return to the store, Roger has excused himself to prepare for an errand, which leaves me with Tom.

"So," I say.

"So," he echoes.

I bite the inside of my cheeks. *Just out with it, then.* "I'm sorry, but you look super familiar. You're not Tom Whelan by any chance, are you?" I already know the answer, but I don't need him thinking I'm some creepy stalker, especially if he doesn't remember me.

His rosy cheeks turn scarlet.

"No kidding. Is it really you?" I ask.

His jaw tightens but he says nothing. He must think I'm one of his father's superfans. God, no. I could never bring myself to listen to another Double Helix song after his parents fired my mother.

"It's me," I say. "Nell. Remember? Eleanor?"

Tom's eyes brighten with recognition. "Garcia?"

"Yes!"

"Holy shit. Nell!" He rounds the counter and pulls me into a tight hug. His arms are strong. He smells like flowers with hints of citrus, and I find myself taking a deeper inhale than is probably acceptable. When he pulls away, he grips me by my arms to hold me in place. "I can't believe this, I—"

"Of all places—" I interject.

"What a small world!" We laugh, and finally, he releases me.

"What are you doing here?" I ask. "Aren't you supposed to be living it up on a yacht right now?"

He furrows his brows. "What gave you that impression?"

I gulp, suddenly sheepish. It's one thing to notice someone's wealth, but another to comment on it.

He chuckles, saving me my grief, and shakes his head. "I get seasick. But you—I can't believe *you're* here. The last I saw you—" He stops, his smile faltering for a split second before lighting back up. "It's good to see you again. Wow. I can't believe this."

Me neither. I still haven't decided whether this reunion is a good thing.

"Hey, I guess we'll see each other more often again, huh?" Tom says. "Are you still playing the piano?"

I shake my head. "You?"

"I have a keyboard upstairs. Do you remember—"

"Heart and Soul?" I chuckle. Sometimes, when I come across a piano, I catch myself miming the motions of playing it on imaginary keys. "How could I forget?"

His eyes sparkle when he laughs. I see traces of his younger self in his boyish smile. Still handsome as ever. I used to think God pulled him straight out of a fairytale and brought him to life just for me. I don't think that anymore, obviously, but he still looks as princely as I remember.

"Remember when we used to pretend to be in a jazz bar like your mom?"

I cover my face, cringing at the memory. Mama was my hero; whatever she did, I wanted to do, too, so I convinced Tom to sing jazz covers of famous songs with me. In my defense, it made sense: we were both the children of musicians, except his dad was more famous than my mom would ever be.

"Do you still sing?" he asks.

I shake my head. "I did a short stint pretending to be Disney princesses for children's birthday parties, but that's it."

We spend a few more minutes catching up before I excuse myself to inspect the shelves, see what work I've got cut out for me. Tom, unwilling to end our conversation there, accompanies me.

"Don't you have work to do?" I ask.

He gestures to the empty store. "If anyone comes in, we'll hear them."

I can't argue with that.

As we stand in front of the first row of shelves, I catch him up on the better part of my life: Kate's pregnancy and my impending graduation from St. Catherine's next year. He tells me he'd taken up a degree in History but dropped out his sophomore year, just a year before I entered university. Roger's still on his ass about it and wants him to go back.

"So you live here now?" I ask.

"Yeah."

"What'd your dad say?"

He shrugs. "He doesn't mind."

"And Greg? Your stepmom? How are they?" I wasn't the biggest fan of those two. Greg was always so rude to me and my mom, and his mother wasn't any better. Even before the pearl necklace incident.

Another shrug. "They're fine."

"And Roger's... your uncle?"

He shakes his head. "Just my boss. But honestly, sometimes it feels like he's my annoying grandfather, you know? He's always in my business like, do this, do that."

There. An opening. "He must really care about you."

"I guess," he mumbles. He reaches a hand out and traces the dusty spine of a paperback. He flips it open and I catch sight of a handwritten dedication on the front page.

My heart clenches. Each book in this store holds stories beyond their pages. Dog-ears, reminders long forgotten; testimonies of love and friendship whispered in inscriptions.

"How long have you been here?" I ask.

"Couple years now. Five this year."

"Oh, wow. Do you like it here?"

He nods. "I mean, I've been here a long time. It's my home now."

Fuck. Guilt creeps back up on me, and this time it's harder to push down. I nod my head in as nonchalant a manner as possible while muttering,

"Cool, cool, cool, cool, cool," under my breath. I scan the shelves as an awkward silence passes between us.

My eyes light up when I see it: a worn paperback copy of my favorite book of all time, coincidentally a book Tom had gifted me for my birthday early on. It's called *Elara of Everton*, a Young Adult fantasy romance novel.

I pull it out from the shelf and hold it up to Tom. "Do you remember this?"

Tom blinks at the cover, nose scrunching up as he reads the title, and then laughs when he recognizes it. "Didn't I get you that for your thirteenth birthday?"

I nod. "I couldn't wait to turn sixteen."

"Man. Remember how much we wanted the leads to end up together? You started writing fanfic—" My hand shoots up to cover his mouth, eyes wide as if warning him not to speak further. Tom holds his hands up in surrender. Tentatively, I lower my hand. My skin burns where it touched his lips. I wipe my palm on the side of my legs as inconspicuously as I can.

"Do you still write?" he asks. "I was always on the lookout for your name when we'd get new stocks. Nell Garcia. Or Eleanor. But I guess I didn't account for you using a pen name..."

It's strange, to learn that someone you've been passively keeping up with has been doing the same for you.

I tell him about my capstone project due this coming school year. Seniors in my Creative Writing program are expected to submit a polished manuscript, typically a collection of short stories or poems, or a play, a screenplay, a novella, or even a major portion of a novel with the rest of the book outlined in detail. The me from a few months ago was feeling ambitious so I requested to write a romance novel in full. It took the department some convincing, but they eventually agreed, telling me that *if* I don't finish in time, the outline is still an option.

I've been brainstorming ideas, ways to write a romance novel without having experienced romance myself. It turns out, despite all my pessimism, I'm still a staunch defender of romance as a genre. It was the only place in which Happy Ever After could exist for me now, after all.

"So you want to write love stories," Tom says, brow quirking.

"Why'd you say it like that?"

"Like what?"

"Like you're judging me."

A laugh bubbles out of him. "I'm not judging you, Nell."

I put *Elara from Everton* back into the shelf and pull out a romance novel, which just so happens to feature a shirtless man with a sculpted chest, staring fiercely at the camera so that it feels like he's looking straight at me. I cringe inwardly but push on.

"This," I say, holding the book up to him, "is no less valid than..." I scan the shelves and pull out an Ernest Hemingway paperback. "This."

Tom's gaze burns holes into my skin. He doesn't say anything, which for some reason prompts me to keep going.

"Okay, this?" I hold the book up to his face.

"Taming the Bad Boy," he says, reading the title.

"Yes. This book. On the surface, it might look like—what, a gratuitous romp, a horny woman's fantasy? Which, sure, it is. It *can* be. That's just as valid, too. There's space for that. Women are allowed to not only think about sex but crave it, too." *Oh my God, Nell, shut up.* This is like a more humiliating version of the Devil Wears Prada cerulean sweater monologue.

"But look deeper and you'll find—well, bad boy romances, in my opinion, are a rebellion against the narrow path that's been prescribed for women. The bad boy represents unpredictability, unexpectedness, the 'wrong' choice who is only wrong in the sense that he is not who society expects or wants for you. Because he doesn't fit the mold of society's idea of a Good Man." *Shut up, shut up, shut up.*

"Romance as a genre centers on the woman's choice. Despite society's insistence that the bad boy is—well, *bad* for her, he turns out to be good because he cares and he listens and he protects, signaling to the reader and the world at large that ultimately, it is the woman herself who dictates what's right or wrong for her."

Tom quirks a brow. He folds an elbow over the shelf and leans against it lazily. Like an idiot, I go on talking.

"Sure, romance novels are often about a chronically horny asshole discovering that women are people who deserve respect only after he falls in love—the rose-tinted glasses term for possessiveness—but men often consume media that brutalize women on the daily. The age-old story of a lothario changing his ways for the love of his life is the least horrible thing I can think of insofar as fantasies go.

"The irony, of course, is that the bad boy trope has become so pervasive that he's now become an Ideal Man that men struggle to live up to. But that's another topic for another time."

I finish my speech, breathless, my face burning, knowing full well I should have stopped speaking a good two minutes ago.

Tom grins. "I missed hearing you talk about books. You should give that speech at book club. They're going to love you."

I avert my gaze, wishing the ground would swallow me whole. "Sorry," I say. "I didn't mean to break into a tangent there."

"Stop. Don't apologize," he says. "I liked it. And you're right. I've never thought of it that way. But it makes sense. If there's anyone who'd get it, it'd be you. You've always been into romance. Like, princesses and princes and stuff. But you always preferred the stories where the princess saved the day."

He remembers that?

"If you told me you've broken a string of hearts since we last saw each other, I would have believed you."

I grimace. "God, no. No love for me."

"No?"

I shake my head. Love and I have a very complicated relationship: as a kid, I wanted nothing more than to fall in love the way Mama did. I used to dream about the day I'd be old enough to have a partner—their gender didn't matter much to me—but then Kate left, and then Mama's penchant for falling in love with the wrong people cost me one of my closest friends, so love seemed safer to pursue in fiction. By the time Henry came back to restore my faith in love, I was too busy with school to have time to date around. And now here we are.

"Why not?" Tom asks.

"It's pointless," I say. "You either leave or get left behind."

"That's not true," he says.

"Yeah, it is. There's a reason they say *'til death do us part.'* Richard Siken even wrote: *'Someone has to leave first. This is a very old story. There is no other version of this story.'*"

Tom blinks at me. "Did you just quote poetry at me?"

My cheeks flush. "You know about Richard Siken?"

He shrugs. "I think Annabel, one of our book club members, has read something of his before."

I tell him Richard Siken's one of my favorite poets and he promises to read more of his stuff.

"But I don't know if I agree with him," he says. "I like to think that when we die, we go back to the same source. God, love, whatever you want to call it. And if we all go back to the same place, then are we ever truly separated?"

God, he's so hot when he talks philosophically at me. I turn away from him and march down the aisle to avoid humiliating myself with my big mouth any further.

"So, is it any good?" Tom asks as he catches up to me.

"Which one?"

"Bad boy romances."

I shrug. "The wealth of options means there's a lot of good, but even more bad. But that's subjective, no? It helps to read the reviews first and to know what you like."

Tom sighs. He takes the book from me and flicks through the pages. He appears to be lost in thought.

"What are you thinking about?" I ask.

"Can I ask you for your opinion?"

I tilt my head to the side. "For what?"

Tom draws in a deep breath. "Well, there's this girl."

Ah. Of course. There is always a girl for handsome boys like Tom, and if it was ever going to be me, it would have been from the get-go. But it wasn't, and it still isn't, so *get it together, Nell.* The jealousy stings, the antidote to which is the reminder of why I'm here: to secure my commission and get out.

Tom pauses, chewing on his bottom lip. I gesture for him to continue.

"She was my close friend. In school."

I give him a look that says, *And?*

"And we haven't seen each other in forever," he says. I blink at him, waiting for him to make his point.

He clears his throat. "She gave me her number."

And? "I don't see your problem."

"How do I know if she's just being nice or not?"

"Did you ask for her number, or did she just give it?"

"She gave it."

"There you go," I say. "No girl gives her number all willy-nilly to someone they don't want to hear from."

"But what if it's a fake number?"

"Girls usually only give fake numbers to guys who are pushy about asking for it," I say. "Were you pushy? Dropping hints?"

"No. I mean—*no*. There's no way she could have—" He clears his throat again. His cheeks darken to scarlet.

Despite the antidote, my heart sinks. He really likes this girl.

"I guess there's only one way to find out," I say. It's probably for the best that it's not *me* he likes. That would make this job even more difficult.

I picture myself cutting the cord, blowing out whatever candle my twelve-year-old self has been holding out for him this entire time. No more of that. *We're done.*

"What do you mean?"

I hold out my hand. "Give me your phone."

Tom pulls his phone out from his back pocket and unlocks it before handing it over.

"What's her name?"

"Paulina. But I haven't saved her number yet. It's—" He pulls a crumpled sheet of paper from his pocket and smooths it over, then holds it out for me to see.

God, he was an idiot. This Paulina girl wrote her number out for him and he's here asking me whether she wants him to call? Doesn't he know that practically the only criteria for men to win in the romance department was to be handsome, and Tom—for all his stupidity—is as handsome as they come? He looks like a young Jeff Buckley, who I knew only because Mama always made me put on her copy of his album, *Grace*, in the little black stereo she kept in the kitchen and which crackled every so often from disrepair. Kate and I could tell whenever her current relationship was ending because she'd put "Lover, You Should've Come Over" on a loop and tell us, if only she could meet a man like Jeff Buckley, as if a man was the key to her happiness.

I've met boys dumber than Tom in college, with body counts up to a hundred, and the only reason I know this is because they make it their mission to 1) brag about it, and 2) shame any girl who even comes close to having that same number. Tom has the looks and the stupidity that should translate into confidence but somehow doesn't; the experience is sure to follow. All he has to do is exist—maybe smile a little, joke a little. The whole damn system's set up so that boys like him are guaranteed a win.

In secondary school, I watched boys of all kind—meek boys, goofy boys, annoying boys (of which there were plenty)—grow along with their pride, comforted by their wealth of choices and their place in a world that tells them it's theirs for the taking. They were carefree in a way that us girls couldn't be; their friendships were shallow, yes, but enviably simple. They doled out their approval to the prettiest girls, or if not pretty, then those they deemed easiest, and the selected girls, the unlucky few, lorded it over the others both explicitly and implicitly, often through exclusion. Very early on we were taught that our bodies and the way we looked doubled as currency, and because the belief that it's a man's world is drilled into us with sayings such as 'boys will be boys,' a man's recognition, then, his acknowledgement of you validated your existence. And if they loved you enough to commit, this I learned from my mother, only then were you worthy of love.

Men got to pick and choose. We had to beautify ourselves to be worthy of being chosen. And only when we're chosen are we real. Before that, we're invisible. And any girl who dares to think otherwise, any girl who considers herself pretty before a man calls her such, is called arrogant, a shrew.

I hated it. I hated all of it. I would rather have my eyes pecked out by crows than partake in any of that. But if I were to hazard a guess, this friend of Tom's that he's been jonesing for since high school has been dying for this chance just as long or doubly so, and here he was, stressing in front of me about whether she might want to hear from him.

I dial her phone number. I save it under her name, then write her a text.

TOM

> Hey, Paulina! This is Tom. It was nice seeing you again. X

"An X?" Tom screeches. "I didn't exactly see her—we met eyes and—"

"Relax." I swat him away. "Since you're not sure if she wants to see you again, we'll leave the ball in her court. I'm assuming you'd like to grab a drink with her to start—coffee, or whatever it is that you like."

"Lemonade," he says.

I resist the urge to chuckle. "If she brings up coffee or something, then you can ask. Or schedule. Whichever."

I hand the phone back to him just as it beeps with her reply. He tosses his phone back to me like it's hot potato.

PAULINA

> Tommy!! Hi!!! So nice to see you again!! Let's catch up soon please!!! Xx

"Double X's," I say. "See? She wants to see you again."

A slow smile creeps on Tom's face. "You're really good at this."

I don't tell him it's just standard conversation: you want something, you communicate it and give the other person the chance to say yes or no. Instead, I shrug. "I guess so."

"What do I say next?"

"Well, you plan with her, obviously."

"How?"

"What do you *mean* how?"

"Like, how do I say it?"

I sigh and hold my hand back out.

TOM

> Are you free for coffee this weekend?

PAULINA

Absolutely! The Drowsy Poet
on Saturday? 9AM? Xx

Another kiss.

TOM

I'll see you there.

I hand Tom back his phone. "There you go. You have a date with Paulina this Saturday, 9AM."

Tom stares at his phone like I've handed him a bar of gold. "You're incredible," he says.

I take a snapshot of his smile and file it away in my head. The next time my guilt threatens to eat me alive, I'll remember this. I might be instrumental in taking his home away from him, but at least I helped him win over the girl he likes.

Home is where the heart is, after all.

Tom

When Roger told Nell we were hiring, I thought it was weird at first because we weren't. Organizing the shelves has been my project for the better half of the past year, but I suppose all's well that ends well. Not only was I reunited with a childhood friend I'd been wondering about for practically my whole life now—when Nell disappeared, my father wouldn't tell me where she went, and I was so broken up about it I wrote my first hyperbolic song about how much I missed her and wanted her back (and yes, it makes me cringe to remember now)—she also helped me face my fears and reach out to Paulina.

Plus, Nell loves books. She's perfect for this place. I can rope her into my project for the book club's anniversary. The more there are of us to remind Roger why he shouldn't sell Second Chance books, the better.

It's crazy to see her again. I look at her and my head fills with this melody. A song that's been playing longer than I've been alive. A song that will keep playing even after I'm gone. I've taken to my guitar every night after work to try to capture it, but I never hear it as strongly as when I'm around Nell.

Nell and I managed to convince Roger to give me two hours off on Saturday morning so I could see Paulina. Of course, Roger asked me whether

I thought it was a good idea first, if I was sure and all, and I reminded him of what he said. That I can't keep running away from my past. That at some point, I was going to have to face it, and then move on.

The Drowsy Poet is on the second floor of a building about a block away from Second Chance Books. Despite its proximity, I've never been here before. A narrow stairway opens up to the cozy, sunlit interior of exposed brick, potted plants, and an eclectic mix of furniture. There's a chalkboard menu hanging from the wall behind the counter. The brewing machine whirrs loudly. The unmistakable aroma of coffee hangs thickly in the air.

I take a seat on the long leather booth lined against the wall. There are a few customers occupying separate tables: a girl with headphones on and poring over a textbook, no doubt cramming for summer classes. Two men in suits talking animatedly about their cryptocurrency wallets. A mother trying to placate her toddler with a bite of cupcake.

My heart thunders in my chest. My pulse rings in my ears. I try to focus on the offerings listed on the menu, trying to decide what to order when Paulina gets here. But I can't sit still. Every time someone walks in, my eyes snap towards them, my pulse quickening and then dropping when it turns out to be just another stranger.

I bounce my leg under the table to rid myself of excess energy. If it were at all socially acceptable to do, I'd pace. Last night, I stood in front of the bathroom mirror rehearsing what I might say, how I'd greet her. Nothing I did came off naturally. I looked like an idiot, so I felt like one, too.

Finally, Paulina arrives. She looks like how one would imagine summer if it was a person: all smiles as her paisley-printed dress billowed around her, arms tanned and swaying, wrists encircled by stacks of golden accessories. She wears a bright white headband that pushes her honey-brown locks away from her face. I would have believed her if she told me she'd just hopped off a yacht before coming to see me. I rise to greet her as her vanilla perfume overtakes my senses.

"Tommy," she breathes. The song in my head stops. All is silent. The nickname goes straight to my stomach. Every memory I had of loving her comes surging right back and stops at my throat where it clogs, and I feel like I can't breathe. She presses her soft, warm cheek against mine before pulling away. "You haven't ordered yet?"

"Not yet," I manage. "I was waiting for you."

She leads me to the counter where we fall in line behind two women in athleisure, one of which was carrying a small white dog with curled fur. It barks at me when we meet eyes, and I jump backwards in shock.

Paulina laughs. "Aw. He's so cute."

Me or the dog?

She reaches out to pet the dog.

There's my answer.

I carry our tray of drinks back to our table and we finally sit down.

"Well, how have you been?" she asks. I take a sip of my iced Americano and fight the urge to make a face. *Yeah, no. I hate coffee.*

"Grand," I say. "You?"

I know she responds because her lips are moving, but I can't hear anything over my heartbeat racing in my ears. I feel it thumping loudly in my chest, as if it recognized her voice and wanted to break out to hide someplace safe.

I manage through the conversation for a good two minutes, taking large gulps of my bitter coffee before I stand abruptly. My head is spinning. I blink rapidly as if to will my vision to still.

"Tom?"

"Excuse me." I speed-walk to the restroom and lock the door shut behind me. I hunch over the sink, knuckles blanching from how tightly I grip the edges.

Get it together, Tom. Remember what Nell said? No girl gives you her number unless she wants you to call. No girl agrees to go out with you if she doesn't want to.

Memories of the last time I saw her flood my brain: the look on her face, the inevitable rejection even I knew was coming.

Deep breaths. In, out. In, out. My phone buzzes in my back pocket, startling me.

NELL

How's it going?! 😍

47

I barely manage to type back a quick SOS in response before someone knocks on the door. I almost drop my phone into the sink.

"Tom?" It's Paulina. "Are you okay in there?"

I pull the door open and plaster on what I hope is my most convincing smile. "Yes. Sorry. Just... needed to wash my hands."

Her brows furrow but she doesn't say anything. Merely rubs the small of my back as I step out and make my way back to our spot.

"As I was saying," she says, touching my hand over the table. Her fingers are cold, and her nails are long and painted a deep red. "I can't believe it's really you. I wasn't sure at first when I saw you that night, but then the old guy—"

"Roger," I interject.

"Yeah, him. He said your name and I was like, *oh my God. That's him.* I've missed you so much!"

As if on cue, Nell bursts through the shop doors, her micro-bangs and some strands of her short hair sticking to her reddened cheeks. She's got a bewildered look in her eyes as she scans the room. When she spots me, her eyes widen.

"Nell," I blurt out. Paulina looks over her shoulder as Nell approaches.

"Hi," Nell greets. "Oh my Gosh. I'm so sorry. I hate to intrude, but Roger sent me to fetch you. There's, like, an emergency at the store, and—"

I shoot up, my knees knocking the underside of the table in the process. Paulina gasps, her hands flying out to steady our wobbling drinks. "Right," I say. "Of course." I glance over at Paulina. "This is Nell, by the way. My co-worker."

Nell extends a hand. "It's so nice to meet you," she says. "I'm sorry again."

Paulina presses her lips together in a thin smile and shakes her hand. "It's fine." I can't tell whether she means it. To me, she says, "Go."

"I'm so sorry," I say, already backing away from the booth.

"Another time."

Nell's hand clasps mine. She drags me out of there without a second thought.

The sand is warm under my legs. Nell and I have gone down to Newbury Beach, away from the crowd of holidaymakers and new residents on the boardwalk, to the far corner of the coast across the Vanguard Properties construction site for a resort that claims it will be finished this time next year.

I hold my head in my hands, my elbows pressed against my folded knees. I tug on the curls on the back of my head, straightening it and then twisting it round my finger, just something to do so I don't focus too much on the all-consuming humiliation I feel over how I behaved at The Drowsy Poet.

Nell sits beside me, quietly watching the waves kiss the shore.

"Be honest," I say. "How bad did it look?"

She drags her teeth across her bottom lip.

I groan. "That bad?"

"You didn't give me time to respond!"

I groan and flop back against the sand. I'm going to be dusting it off my hair and clothes for ages to come, but I don't care. I have half a mind to ask Nell to bury me in it and leave me be.

"I'll admit, I wasn't sure what to think when you sent me the text. If I'd known the specifics, it might have been easier to make up a more convincing lie to get you out of there."

I grab fistfuls of sand and dump it over my stomach.

"Stop that." Nell dusts the sand off my stomach. "It wasn't that bad. It's repairable."

I tilt my head towards her. "Is it?"

"Of course it is. But Tom—"

"Hmm?"

"If you want me to help you, I'm going to need a lot more information. Like a lot more."

I sit up. "What kind of information?"

"You know..." she trails off. "I know you guys were like friends or whatever, but did you guys just drift? What's the story there?" Nell fixes her gaze on me. With the sun setting in a sky swathed with pink, orange, and purple hues, she's bathed in a warm light that brings out the flecks of gold in her brown eyes. I'd never noticed them before.

I heave a sigh and flop back down. I don't have it in me to tell her my sob story. I've endured enough humiliation in one day. I don't need Nell to know I had my ass handed to me by Greg, or that my dad sided with him.

"Something like that," I mumble. "I just panicked, okay? I haven't seen her in forever, and the last time we saw each other... It didn't end well."

"Meaning?"

"Meaning..." I grab another fistful of sand and sprinkle it by her legs. I mumble the rest of the sentence under my breath.

"You're going to have to speak louder than that, Tom."

"Meaning I told her I loved her and she rejected me, okay? There. Happy? Ha-ha. Laugh all you want. I know it's pathetic."

Nell gives me an unamused stare. "What's pathetic is you moping around like this over something that can be easily fixed."

I gape at her.

"Okay. Phone?" She holds her hand out again. I fish my phone out of my back pocket and hand it to her. I don't even bother unlocking it for her; I just recite the code from memory so she can do it herself.

She freezes. I realize belatedly that my passcode has been her birthday since the year we met. I open my mouth to speak, to explain it away, but she quickly recovers and taps open my messages.

She's silent for a good minute. Despite myself, I turn over and ask her what she's up to.

"Saving your ass," she says.

"How?"

She flips the screen over to me.

TOM

> So sorry I had to leave early.
> Can we reschedule? X

PAULINA

> It's okay, I totally understand!
> Xx

I'm free next weekend, same
time? Xx

"See? She double-texted. It's fine. You're fine."

I grab my phone and blink at the screen. "So she doesn't hate me?"

"No, drama queen. She wants to see you again."

I ball my free hand into a fist to fight the urge to hug Nell.

"But—" Nell lifts a finger. "You can't send me another SOS text. You want to be with this girl, you're going to have to *learn* how to be with her."

"Meaning?"

She exhales a sigh. "Meaning you and I are going to hit the books and study what it means to be a good date."

"You've got lots of experience, then?" I ask. "I'm not surprised."

Nell looks at me funny. "No, Tom. I just read a lot of romance novels, remember?"

Oh. *Right.*

"Speaking of. I could use some help brainstorming for my capstone project. I won't go into the details—it's really no big deal, but maybe you can scratch my back, I'll scratch yours? A little quid pro quo?"

I quirk a brow. "What are you talking about?"

"I help you prepare for your dates with Paulina, you share your... boyish insights on romance."

"Boyish?"

"Fine. Manly. Whatever."

I grin at her.

"You and Paulina fit the bill. Kind of. Childhood friends to lovers, and all."

I don't tell Nell that she and I could fit that bill, too.

Nell continues. "The goal is, by this time next week, you will know the do's and don'ts of dating so that you don't make a fool of yourself in front of Paulina."

"So you're saying I *did* make a fool of myself in front of Paulina?" I ask.

Nell disregards my question. "We have a week to prepare. Tomorrow, I'll bring my notes from when I was trying to work on another story. I made a list of all the things that made me kilig, so—"

"What's kilig?"

"Oh." Her cheeks blush. "Sorry. It's a Filipino word. It's like... the giddiness or the exhilaration you feel from a romantic experience. Like, the hand scene in Keira Knightley's Pride and Prejudice."

"The what scene?"

Nell clicks her tongue and shakes her head. "We have a lot of work to do."

Nell

While Tom was on his date with Paulina, I busied myself by brainstorming ideas for my capstone project while sorting the shelves. Everything I came up with seemed too cheesy or cliche, nothing worth writing about. Of course, I know the *real* reason why I've hit a snag: whatever faith in love I'd built up, Henry had destroyed.

Therefore I must say: this is my most ingenious plan yet. It's like three different birds, one stone: helping Tom win Paulina over on the express condition that he helps *me* back with research for my capstone project not only addresses my guilt but also allows me to get to know him better without raising any suspicions. And the better I know him, the easier it will be to get his help in convincing Roger to sell the bookstore.

Love and happy endings might not exist for my family—a fact that Henry had just proven once again—but that doesn't mean Tom can't try his hand at it. Love makes fools of us all, but if he wants to be a fool, who am I to stop him?

Is it manipulative? Kind of. Sometimes it scares me how quickly I came up with this scheme, but most times I remind myself I'm just doing the best I can, given the cards I've been dealt. I have a pregnant sister to provide for and a mountain of bills to pay; with Henry gone and my sister unemployed, it falls on me to buy the groceries and cover the electricity and water bill.

Besides, I haven't even gotten to *talk* to Roger since I started working at Second Chance Books, so it's not like my evil master plan is well underway or anything. Not that my plan is evil to begin with. It's just that Roger's always heading out to run an errand or to meet with some friends, and the day of my first supposed book club meeting, Kate asked me to accompany her to the emergency room because she was having unusual abdominal pains. (Nothing to worry about, the doctor said, but she did advise me to monitor Kate's symptoms if they worsen.)

Tom says it's unusual for Roger to be out this often, but his theory is that because now that there's an extra set of hands to help with the store, Roger has more time to do all the other things he's been wanting to. And I could start convincing him that selling would give him more time to do those things—if only I knew what those things were.

In the meantime, I do my work at Second Chance Books. I go to the back shelves, where I'd begun the tedious task of rearranging all the books in-store and sorting them into proper sections.

Prior to my arrival, their organization system seemed primarily to be just "Stuff It Wherever It Fits", as Roger said, which has resulted in sky-high stacks of novels of all kinds and shelves filled to the brim with secondhand books. This was no good, especially when their clientele consisted primarily of senior citizens likely to break a hip if they tripped on a stray copy of *Fifty Shades of Grey*.

I could glean hints of a former system: three rows of thrillers here, a shelf full of outdated self-help novels there. The romance books—of which there were plenty—seemed to take up two whole shelves, until someone shelved a Stephen King novel in the mix and turned it into a hybrid of horror and romance.

I've been busy with extricating one from the other, though it did cross my mind once or twice to just leave things be. I can't think of anything more terrifying than falling in love and losing yourself to another.

I update Jane on my progress, nothing more than a quick email to tell her I'm working on winning their trust. Her replies are even shorter: *Good job* or *Keep up the good work!*

During our lunch breaks, Tom and I begin our lessons on love. We dissect romcoms, take notes on things that made our hearts flutter and our stomachs flip. We even trade playlists.

I let him go through my notes from watching K-dramas and other romcoms and even Studio Ghibli films. An old friend of mine had gotten me into them, but we don't talk anymore. Haven't spoken in ages, really, no thanks to Mama, and so now the only way I can consume Ghibli movies is from an academic standpoint. I'm there purely to study Miyazaki's storytelling skills and nothing more.

Most of my notes, no matter the film, series, or novel, have a few things in common. Contrary to popular media, I'm not a fan of bad boys. I like when the love interest is kind, gentle, and thoughtful; when they pay attention and notice all the small details about the protagonist.

I tell Tom not to play mind games; will-they-won't-they's are fun in fiction but aggravating in real life. *If you like her, let her know. Don't beat around the bush.*

We watch *10 Things I Hate About You* and *How to Lose a Guy in 10 Days*, both classics which happen to have the number 10 in them.

"At which moment," I asked, three days into our new routine, hot off the heels of watching yet another rom-com, "did he realize he was in love?"

And he pointed out a scene where the male lead got this look in his eyes when the girl did something so definitively *her*, "And it's right then," he said, "that he knows there's no one else in this world for him but her."

We take our lunch at The Drowsy Poet on Wednesday. With Roger out, Tom figured it wouldn't be so bad if we stepped out for an hour or two, so long as we locked the door behind us.

We choose the back corner booth by the window overlooking the street.

"Okay," I say, placing both palms flat on the table. "We've studied the Greats. We know what makes us kilig. It's time to put it to practice."

Tom quirks a brow at me. I don't let his apparent skepticism deter me.

"The key to any date is in being a good conversationalist," I say. "In my opinion, anyway. Think of Benjamin Barry and Andie Anderson's banter. Their chemistry just *pops* off the screen."

"Nell," Tom says, his chin tucking as he levels his gaze with mine. "I wouldn't have asked for your help if I didn't trust in your opinion. You don't have to give me disclaimers."

I blink. I'm not sure what to make of that, so I say, "Okay," again. "But don't just listen to speak. Listen to understand. Too many people fall into the trap of just waiting for the other person to finish speaking so they can reply. Like, yes, it's important to be quick and to be witty, but the whole point is to get to know the other person, you know? And obviously to let the other person get to know you, so just be yourself."

"Do you want me to be witty or to be myself?" he asks. "I can't be both."

"Tom."

He grins. "Sorry."

I wave a dismissive hand. "Okay. Pretend I'm Paulina. We've just sat down and...?" He stares at me blankly. "What do you say?"

"I... Hello?"

I let out a breath. We've got so much work to do.

"How have you been?" I say.

"Grand," he responds. "Oh. Wait. You want me to ask that?" He clears his throat. "Okay. Hi. How have you been?"

"Well, don't be stiff with it, Thomas," I tell him. "Relax. It's just me."

"But you said to pretend you're Paulina."

"Was *this* how you were around her?"

"You're putting a lot of pressure on my shoulders!"

I gape at him. "Because I asked you to ask me how I'm doing?" I throw my hands in the air and fall back against my seat. "You're hopeless."

"Okay, *no*," he says, taking both my hands and flattening them on the table. "Let's start over. How're you doing?"

I narrow my eyes at him. He smiles back at me earnestly. I tip my chin upwards, feigning haughtiness. "I'm good, thank you. And you?"

"Good," he responds. I gesture for him to keep going. He stammers, "I—uh... What... what have you been up to these days?"

"Just work, mainly. You?"

He furrows his brows at me. So, maybe I'm not as good of a conversationalist as I should be. In my defense, I never claimed to be a good actress. At least this way he learns to deal with awkward silences and curt responses?

"The same," he finally says. "What do you—uh—what do you do for work?"

Shit. Quick, think of something.

"I... model?" My cheeks burn.

"You model?" he echoes, incredulous. "Is that what you think Paulina does?"

"Well, she *looks* like she models," I say. "Does she not?"

He pauses, considering. "I don't think so."

"Well, she should. She's really pretty."

She's the kind of girl my mother would have wanted me to be more like, with her ski slope nose and a toned body that she must spend hours at the gym perfecting. The kind of girl anyone would be jealous of, because she seemed to be privy to some feminine secret the rest of us aren't. Or maybe she's just God's favorite.

Tom bursts out laughing.

"What's so funny?" I ask.

"You think a model would want to go out with me?"

I swat at him. "Stop fishing for compliments. Focus."

He presses his lips together, but I can tell from the look in his eyes that he's still amused. I push on anyway. There's no way in hell I'm admitting that I had a crush on him growing up. Over my dead body.

"You see how it's just a back-and-forth, right? Like ping-pong."

He tilts his head to the side. "I've never played ping-pong."

"That's beside the point."

"Is it?"

"Thomas."

He laughs. "I was just teasing you, Nelly. Yes, I know ping-pong. Continue."

But I can't. Not when he's just called me Nelly for the first time in forever, a nickname that, when spoken by the best people, never fails to make me feel all soft and gooey on the inside. I guess twelve-year-old me still thinks Thomas Whelan is the best person ever.

It reminds me of that short story by Sandra Cisneros called *Eleven*, which basically says that when you're eleven—or any age in your life, really—you're also all the years that have come before it. Being around Tom brings out the side of me that's still twelve, the me that still believed that Happy Ever After wasn't just possible for me but attainable. Within grasp.

Twelve-year-old me is in for a rude awakening when she finds out twenty-year-old me is helping her "soulmate" get with another girl.

I clear my throat. "Okay. So. Try to think of something you really want to ask her. You're interested in this girl, so I'm assuming you want to know all about her."

"That's a fair assumption," he says.

"Okay, so ask me something. And by me, I mean Paulina. Me-as-Paulina. Something you really want to learn about me. As in *her*."

Tom draws in a deep breath. His eyes glide over to my left as he considers. The sunshine pours through the windows, illuminating his hazel irises. I used to love looking into them. The twelve-year-old part of me still does.

Finally, he asks, "What's your favorite song?"

I rack my head for an answer. A cool girl like Paulina wouldn't just listen to the Top 40s. She'd have a refined taste that made her even cooler.

I settle on "California" by Joni Mitchell.

"That's on your playlist, isn't it?" He hums the song's opening melody and plays air guitar.

I hate that it charms me, and I especially hate that he doesn't realize that song isn't in the playlist I gave him, which means he's just admitted to snooping on my Spotify account. I decide to play dumb.

"What playlist?"

"The one you—" He falters. "I mean—my friend made a playlist. *Good tunes*, I think she called it."

"*She?*" I exclaim, catching the attention of nearby diners. I make buzzing sounds as if he'd just lost a game and slap the table repeatedly. "Don't *ever* talk to a girl you like about another girl. Come on, man. That's common sense. Start over."

"Wait," he says. "But is 'California' really your favorite song?"

Why are we talking about me now? "Just one of them," I say.

"So what's your *ultimate* favorite?"

That's easy. "'Vienna,'" I say. "By Billy Joel."

The corner of Tom's lips quirks upwards in a small, lopsided smile. "Are all your favorite songs named after places?"

Huh. "Just a coincidence."

When we return to the store, Roger is doing his crossword puzzle in the middle of the room. Tom gestures for me to follow him to the back of the shelves, and though I'm confused, I oblige.

"I've been meaning to ask you," he whispers, "but you weren't there last Thursday."

"Why are we whispering?"

"I don't want Roger to hear."

"Because?"

Tom narrows his eyes at me and clamps his hand over my mouth. "Let me talk, and then you can ask questions later, OK? We have about two minutes before Roger gets suspicious and thinks we're making out back here."

My stomach flutters at the thought. I've never kissed anyone before. Now he's planted the seed of my kissing him amongst the books and it's blooming, its roots digging deep into my psyche.

What might it be like? His lips on mine, my back against the shelves, our bodies pressed into each other. He'd smile into the kiss and it would taste sweet, so sweet, and when I tangle my fingers in his curls, he'll blow a hot breath against my neck, whisper in my ear and say—

"Hello? Nell? Are you listening?"

I blink back my thoughts and crash-land into reality. "Sorry, what?"

"I was wondering if you'd be willing to help me. The book club's anniversary is coming up later this summer, and I'm making a documentary for it. You're so much better with people than I—"

"I'm not very good with people," I say.

"You're certainly better than me."

Roger coughs. "Thomas," he calls out. "When you two are done canoodling, could you get me my other pen, please? The blue one. It's on my desk in my room."

My face burns. "We're not canoodling!" I call out.

"Sure, you're not," Roger replies.

Tom chuckles and pets my head affectionately. His hand is warm and heavy, his mere touch enough to make any girl's knees buckle, much less mine, Eleanor Garcia, who has had a crush on him since I was thirteen.

Had. Had a crush. As in past tense. I can't be crushing on my co-worker in the present.

"I've learned it's best to just let him think whatever he wants," Tom says.

"So? Will you help me?"

I hem and I haw. I'm already helping him with Paulina. Assisting him with the documentary means more time together, which—good, great, I get more opportunities to help him to my cause of convincing Roger to sell. But that's *more* time together, and just the mere suggestion of us kissing has already sent me into a haywire.

It sounds like a bad, bad idea.

"Please?" He pouts.

It's not fair. Why is he drawing so much attention to his lips?

He grabs my hand and squeezes it. "If you help me, I'll do whatever you want. I'll forever be indebted to you."

"I'm not paying you two to make out, you know!" Roger calls out.

I grimace. "Okay, yeah, fine," I say, if only to get Tom to back off.

Tom pumps his fists in the air. "You won't regret it," he says. "I'll be your foot soldier. Whatever you want, I'll make it yours."

God.

"Go get Roger's pen, Tom," I say, wishing he'd leave me alone to hide amongst the books while dreaming of dunking my head in cold water. All these hot and heavy thoughts need to go away, stat.

Tom backs away from me and blows me kisses with both hands. I roll my eyes, but as soon as he's out of view, I bury my face in my palms.

What the hell have I gotten myself into?

Tom

I've been saving up for a new camera the past few months. It's where I got the idea for the documentary.

After Nell agreed to help me, I finally bit the bullet and placed the order. It arrived two days later, a beauty of a thing with its black compact body, built-in lenses, and a tilt-up touchscreen that makes shooting from different angles that much easier.

I got into photography a while back—just as a hobby—maybe about a year into my stay with Roger. We'd gone to his hometown to have a look around, and I was really into the idea of *The Giver* at that time, having finished the book on the train ride over. The idea of memory-keeping and of memories belonging to everyone—I thought it was interesting. It's why I took History in college, before I decided higher education wasn't right for me.

The day after we got back, Roger gifted me a film camera—his own, from his youth. I spent all my money on film and having my photos developed at the studio nearby—another business that closed no thanks to Vanguard Properties.

And then for my 21st, Roger gifted me another camera—a digital camera this time with the ability to shoot videos. I've been using that the past three years, but no more. Nell and I tested this new one out by taking turns filming each other at the store. We did a mock interview where we asked Roger about his thoughts on love.

"All I know," he said, "are two things. One is that love's given freely, not earned. And two: love is not without its risks, but it is always worth it."

Initially, my idea was just to interview the longtime book club members. I had no questions drawn up and figured I'd make them up on the spot.

It was Nell who came up with the idea to show how the many individual lives of the members converge every Thursday for book club, and how it's precisely their differences that have made the club work as well as it has.

What on earth would I do without her? She makes everything better.

I wait for Nell outside the store on our first official day filming the documentary. The plan is to have Roger man the counter in the few hours we're out, but it's also a Saturday, which means Nell doesn't have to report for work after. Just me.

I'm leaning against Roger's ancient station wagon when she appears.

"Wow," she says. "Nice ride."

I snort. "It's Roger's. If you want to listen to music from this century, you're going to have to burn them into cassette tapes."

"How old is this thing?"

He shrugs. "Older than me, probably. He doesn't take it out much, except to buy groceries. He doesn't drive anymore, though. That's my job now."

I open the passenger side door for her, then round the hood to get behind the driver's seat. I switch the radio on and pull out of the curb.

The first person on our list is Mildred, who lives thirty minutes west in Cheltham, a town fenced in by farmlands and known for their cheeses. Every summer, they host a market for their local artists and artisans, and most of everyone I know in Newbury drives up to have a look, Roger and I included.

I've been to Mildred's house plenty of times before so I knew the way.

When there was a leak in the flat, she let Roger and I sleep over for a few days while it was repaired, and I remember her couch being the comfiest couch I'd ever had the pleasure of sleeping on (Roger, of course, got to sleep in the guest room with the queen-sized bed; said he needed it for his back, as if our sleeping arrangements were ever in question).

I've also run a couple of errands for her: home deliveries when she was under the weather—be it books or groceries; and the occasional chauffeuring to and from her weekend visits to the community center, where she dances ballroom with an instructor (she tried to get me to dance with her once—*once*).

Beside me, Nell starts breathing heavily. I glance over, and she's got this thousand-yard stare going on. Like she's here, but not really.

"Are you okay?" I ask, turning the radio down.

Her head snaps to face me. "What?"

"You look like you're hundreds of miles away," I say. "And you're breathing funny."

Her brows knit together.

Shit. Was there a rule about this? Don't point shit out to girls or whatever? Fuck.

"I—I don't mean to pry," I stammer. "I was just worried."

"What do you *mean* I'm breathing funny?" she snaps.

I tighten my grip on the steering wheel. "You know..." I draw in loud, shallow breaths through my mouth. A look of horror passes over her face.

"It's—it's okay," I tell her. "Like, it doesn't bother me or anything. You just got this look in your eye and—"

"What look?"

God, why can't I shut up? I exhale slowly. "Like you're not here. You know. Like you're up there. In your head."

My words hang heavy in the air between us. I'm desperate to fill it with reassurances, or something, *anything*.

"Roger says I get like that sometimes," I offer. Usually when I'm zoning out behind the counter. "It's why I noticed."

Nell doesn't say anything.

Hint taken. "Sorry. I'll shut up now."

"Don't!" she exclaims, startling even herself. "I mean—it's okay. I was just... shocked."

"Shocked?"

She shakes her head. "No, sorry. I mean I was preparing myself for the interview. Or, well, getting the panicking out of the way so I could prepare for the interview. I didn't realize it was that obvious."

Oh.

"Are you nervous?" I ask.

"A little," she admits. "Okay, a lot."

"What are you nervous about?"

She drops her gaze to her lap. "I don't know. Nothing. Everything."

"Mildred's really nice," I offer.

"I know," she says. "It's not that."

"What is it then?"

She's silent.

"You don't have to tell me," I say, worried now that I'd pushed it too far. "I'm just... *here*. If you need anything."

We're quiet for a few moments. Finally, she meets my gaze. "I'm just not good," she says, "with people. Whether I've just met them or known them my whole life."

My chest tightens at her confession. "That's not true," I say. "You're good with me. And Roger."

"No, it's true," she says. "If I'm any good with either of you, that's by chance, not out of an inherent skill or social savvy."

It pains me to know that she sees herself that way. I always thought she was wonderful: a real clever girl, smart and cool and artsy. So much smarter than I will ever be, despite being older than her by two years. Life was more interesting when she was in it, and I can still remember how gutted I felt when she left.

I wish there was something I could do, some way I could show her the way I saw her.

I shift in my seat. "How about I handle the interview today," I offer, "and you manage the camera? You can chime in if you come up with any interesting follow-up questions or tap my shoulder and whisper in my ear if you have any ideas."

I can tell from her expression that she's relieved by this suggestion. "Won't Mildred think I'm rude?"

"No, but I can tell her you're feeling a little shy. She'll understand. And then when—*if*—you feel more comfortable, you can talk to her more. I mean, you came up with the questions after all."

"I'm not a little shy," she says quietly. "I'm, like, *a lot* shy."

"You have no reason to be," I tell her. "But I get it."

She offers me a small smile. "Thanks, Tom."

"Any time," I say, when what I really mean is: *always.*

The rest of the drive over is pleasant enough; when Nell felt better, she switched the radio back on and we compared our favorite tunes. She'd never heard of The Cure, which I thought was ridiculous, so I made her take one of the cassettes from the glove compartment and listen to "Just Like Heaven".

I remember making that playlist two summers ago: I saved up enough money to buy a set of cassette tapes and a tape recorder from the antique shop nearby—now closed, no thanks to Vanguard fucking Properties—and I sat in front of the computer, recording every song I liked so I could listen to it every time I got in the car.

We're on "Here Comes Your Man" by Pixies when we arrive. Nell tells me she liked the songs; I take the track list I'd written from the cassette's case and hand it to her.

"I'd give you the tape but I don't know if you have a cassette player. Do you?" My finger hovers over the eject button, ready to hand it to her just in case.

She shakes her head no. "Anyway," she says, "we'll be driving around together a bunch. You can make me a Spotify playlist or I'll just listen to it here with you." Her smile lights up her face; I'm seized by a desire to do anything to keep it there.

"We should head inside," she says, snapping a photo of the tracklist and handing it back to me. I insist that she keep it and watch her tuck it into her pocket. I never thought, when I wrote it down that same day I recorded all of my favorite songs, that the scrap piece of paper I'd torn from the back of an old book would ever belong to anyone else, much less Nell.

I unbuckle my seatbelt, reach into the backseat for my camera bag, then jog over to open her door for her. She climbs out and looks up at our destination. I follow her gaze. It's as if I'm seeing it for the first time, too.

Mildred lives at the end of her street, a good block away from the nearest house in a butter yellow cottage with a garden of wildflowers on either side of the path to her front door. She's watering the garden when we arrive, wearing a straw hat and dressed in bright blue. In the years I've come to know her, I noticed that she liked to coordinate her outfits so she would only ever be wearing one color at a time where possible. Today, she's in a pale blue blouse layered over a bright aqua tank and royal blue shorts. She hasn't even noticed we're here.

"Millie," I call out as I reach over the front gate and unlock it. "I hope we haven't kept you waiting!"

"Thomas, my dear boy!" she exclaims. She drops the hose and holds her hands out to me. Obediently, I let her cup my face and plant kisses on either cheek. I step aside to introduce Nell, but Mildred's already locked onto her, cupping Nell's face and going, "And you must be Nell; oh, you're a beauty, aren't you? Roger's told me so much about you."

I watch Nell's expression for any signs of discomfort, ready to step in and run interference to give her space. Instead, she looks relieved; *delighted*, even.

Mildred switches off the water and then leads us into the cottage, apologizing for the mess (there was none) and asking if we'd already eaten. She sits us in her living room where her fat one-eyed tabby, Donut, hops on Nell's lap. Mildred leaves for the kitchen to make us tea and prepare biscuits despite our insistence that no, really, it's alright.

Nell strokes Donut under the chin and I hear Donut purr. Then Nell sneezes.

"I'm allergic," Nell says when I look at her.

"Donut," I say, patting my lap. "Come here, girl."

"No!" Nell exclaims, wrapping her arm around the cat as if to keep me from snatching it away from her.

"Nell. You're allergic."

"So?"

"So you shouldn't be around her."

"It's fine," she says. "I'll take an antihistamine. It's worth it."

I reach for the box of tissues on the coffee table and hand it over. To her credit, she takes one and blows her nose with it. Still, she goes back to petting the darn cat even when her eyes start to get teary and her nose runny.

"Oh, there you are, Donut," Mildred says when she enters the room carrying a tray of tea and cookies. I rise to assist her and set it down on the coffee table before us.

"Nell's allergic to cats," I say.

Nell scowls. "Shut up, Tom."

"Oh, Donut," Mildred says. "Go to your room. Leave the poor girl alone. I swear she has a sense for when someone should be left alone and goes straight for that person. Do you remember when she wouldn't let Roger sleep because she insisted on draping herself on his neck?" Mildred cackles.

I *do* remember; Roger was so groggy from lack of sleep the next morning. He had to lock his door that night because Donut knew how to open it with her front paws, using her body weight to push it down.

"It's alright, really," Nell says, dusting cat fur off her shirt and lap.

"You look like you'd inhaled a jar full of pollen; it's not alright. Let me go get you some antihistamines, darling, and then we can get started. Have some tea."

A faint pink blush dusts Nell's cheeks, almost imperceptible if I didn't know how she normally looked.

"You look fine," I reassure her. She tries to thank me but sneezes halfway.

When Mildred returns and Nell's allergies have subsided, we set the camera up. I wish I could say we were professional about it, but all we really had was a tripod and the brand-new camera I bought.

Nell's fingers are cold and clammy when I take it to remind her which buttons to press and where.

"Are you cold?" I ask. I take her hand and cup both my hands around it then blow into them. She stares at me like I'd spat in her face. I'm about to apologize, but she gives me her other hand and I do it again.

"Thanks," she says quietly.

I double-check everything and then get into my seat next to the camera and right across Mildred, who has settled onto the couch looking ready for the spotlight.

"Ready?" Nell asks. I pull out the sheet of questions for my reference and give her a thumbs up. "Three, two, one..."

Mildred

TOM: Please introduce yourself.

MILDRED: Oh, where do I begin? My name is Mildred Douglas—and that's my maiden name, mind you. I've been divorced twice and the second time around I was like, no more. That's that. Next time I fall in love, we don't need to get the government involved.

What else? I used to be a nurse and I have a daughter, Ingrid, who has blessed me with two grandchildren: a boy and a girl. The loves of my life, really. Nobody else can compare.

TOM: That's wonderful, Millie. Now, when did you first start visiting Second Chance Books?

MILDRED: About thirty-four years ago now. My God, time flies. The shop must be older than both of you, no?

TOM: Yeah. Nell's twenty. I'm twenty-two.

MILDRED: Twenty-two already? My goodness, Thomas; why, I remember when you first showed up, a scrawny seventeen-year-old with the saddest eyes I'd ever seen and—

TOM: [coughs] Millie, how did you find Second Chance Books? I mean to say, how did you come across it?

MILDRED: Why, Roger's wife, Cecilia—whose idea it was to open a secondhand bookstore in the first place—was my greatest and longest friend. I didn't so much as come across it as helped *found* it, I would say. You know I was there when they were brainstorming names? Roger suggested The Last Chapter but I thought it sounded rather ominous. Cecilia, who'd always been the more optimistic of us three, came up with the name: Second Chance Books. She liked the idea of breathing life back into those books, all those stories and ideas that had been worn and loved and subsequently forgotten about. Some of the books are on their seventh chance, but that never mattered to her. Of course, in recent times, Roger stocks newer books—there's a conspiracy theory between us members that he buys them brand new and goes about aging them by tossing them about—

TOM: He doesn't do that.

MILDRED: Because he has you do it?

TOM: No, but it'd be funny, wouldn't it?

MILDRED: I don't believe you.

TOM: You were saying?

MILDRED: Right. [clears throat] I was saying: Cecilia was the heart of the bookstore. She had a magic touch that made every one of her projects an astounding success, and it had been her dream ever since we were kids. She always had her nose in a book, and not just storybooks like we read as kids. No, she was always advanced for her age. She was reading these large tomes, leather bound, and she was every bit as smart as she looked.

I used to hate her for being top of our class, you know. God, I was always second to her: math, science, whatever subject. But when you're young and a girl, you're taught to hate each other, to view each other as competition, and I confused my admiration and love for her brilliantness as hatred for a very long time.

We went our separate ways after graduation, as you do, and it was after my first divorce that I ran into her at the grocery store. She must have sensed my loneliness—my first divorce was absolutely devastating, a complete and total blow to my self-esteem, the loss of my innocence, I would say—and she invited me over for dinner at her home. I was so lonely that I said yes—this girl I hated all my life and I was to have dinner with her and her husband!

That night, over pot roast and several glasses of wine, she told me about how she and Roger had pooled together their savings and bought a building—the very same one you live in now—and were renovating it themselves to turn into a bookstore. She asked whether I might like to help when it opens, get the word out and all of that. She didn't have to, but she did. And you know what? She saved my life. She got me out of that rut I was in, gave me something to do.

So there I was, juggling my job as a nurse and helping with the store on the weekends—bringing books in, printing out flyers, painting the walls or otherwise calling in my brothers to help Roger paint them... it was a fun time, a very fun time.

Roger and Cecilia never did have children; they'd tried but just couldn't get lucky, and back then, all the other procedures were so expensive. So the bookstore was their baby. They would watch over Ingrid for me here and there when she was born, but that was it. Roger still had his job teaching at a local college, but Cecilia gave her all to the bookstore. Night and day, night and day, she was working to make it the best it could be.

But just a few years after the shop opened, the most terrible thing happened. Cecilia was diagnosed with leukemia. Awful. Terrible. I remember collapsing when she told me the news. I was wailing and wailing. But you know what? She was strong. She cried, yes, but she made her peace with it.

They closed the shop for a few months to regain their bearings. And after some time, when they were ready, we proceeded with the grand re-opening and everyone we loved was there: our families, my boyfriend at the time, some friends from school and frequent customers and all of that.

She didn't get so bad until a few months after re-opening the store. She was tired all the time, she wasn't eating much, she would cry to me about how tired she was of the trips to the hospital. For a while, we all thought they might close the store for good this time; it wasn't making nearly enough and Roger wanted to leave work to care for her full-time, but she made both of us swear to not give up on it. No matter what. She used what little strength she had and gripped me by my collars and made me promise. "If Roger gives up," she said, "you have my permission to slap him across the face and drag him back in here." *[laughs]*

He never did give up. He kept his promise to her through and through.

TOM: So you were there when the book club was founded?

MILDRED: Of course! It had been my idea, you know. One of the most difficult things about Cece's diagnosis was the knowledge that she had limited time left. And I knew how much she loved books. She was a voracious reader, as I said, and it killed me to see her grow too weak to keep reading. And she was always telling me, you know, one of the things she was most sad about—other than leaving Roger and I behind, of course—was that there were so many books in the world and so little time. That was how she said it: "So many stories, so many lives I won't get to live."

So I pulled Roger aside one time and asked whether she might like it if we got some of our friends together and read to her. We had our very first meeting that weekend.

But it wasn't enough. If we focused on one book at a time, she would never live as many lives as she could, inhabit all those stories she might have otherwise missed out on. So each of us—Roger, my then-husband, some other friends—started reading separately and then summarizing those books and what we liked about it at each meeting. We'd bring quotes—only the best ones—and we'd have her pick which one was her favorite at the end of the night.

She always chose Roger's, but he had an unfair advantage of knowing every facet of her interests and personality better than any of us. Didn't stop me from trying to outdo him, of course. And I came close to it—once. *The Waves* by Virginia Woolf. I think the copy I'd given her is still with Roger.

NELL: Did she ever write her own stories?

MILDRED: Plenty. But she was always shy, Cecilia. She was content to share them with Roger and I.

I'm sure he still has them somewhere. I know he kept all her journals.

TOM: I've seen it. It's in a box now to make space for my things, but I've seen it.

MILDRED: Plenty of wisdom in those journals. She gave me permission to read through them before she passed.

TOM: I'll get them for you, Nell. I'm sure Roger won't mind. *[clears throat]* So, Millie—given your history of the book club, could you share with us how it's changed over the years and what you liked about it then and now?

MILDRED: Roger has done a fantastic job at keeping book club relatively the same throughout the years, even when people moved on and the roster changed or dwindled over time. We're the only ones left of the original group, you know?

In the earlier days, I'd only been doing it for the social aspect: caring for a friend, meeting up with others. I wasn't a big reader at all, really. But the more I attended, the more fascinated I became about all these stories my friends were reading: *Metamorphosis* by Franz Kafka, Dostoevsky's *White Nights*, even *Hamlet*—which I hated studying in high school because I could never penetrate the language, until Roger tracked down a live recording of a play and told me to listen along as I read. It's my favorite Shakespeare play now, you know? And I do love a good audiobook these days. I get to bake and do my own thing while immersed in a story.

These days, it's still somewhat the same. I enjoy the social aspect of the book club, I enjoy hearing and discussing people's latest reads, but I think—I think for me, and maybe for Roger, my favorite part about it is that it keeps Cecilia's memory alive. Here we are, sitting in my living room, and we would have otherwise been complete and total strangers—you would have passed each other on the street and not known—but because of her love of literature, and subsequently Roger's love for her, we've been brought together. Our lives have been changed, irrevocably, forever transformed, because Cecilia had a dream and had the courage to not only believe it but make it happen.

And in some ways, it took Roger's faith in that dream to keep it going, too.

TOM: Could you share with us a favorite memory from book club?

MILDRED: Of course. This was several years after Cecilia had passed and I was going through my second divorce. I'd been a wreck; it was one misfortune after the other, and I stopped attending book club all together. Roger would call to check up on me—Cecilia had made us promise to take care of each other and in those days the promise felt more like a curse than a blessing as I'd wanted to be left alone—and I would always pick up the phone and hang up without saying anything just to keep it from ringing.

My daughter, Ingrid, had no idea what was going on with me. I wasn't answering her calls either, and I would sleep through alarms and miss my grandchildren's recitals or birthdays and—it was a dark time in my life. It happens.

Then one day, Roger showed up out of the blue and insisted I get dressed and follow him to the store. I put up a good fight; believe me, I did. But there is no standing in the way of Roger when he wanted something; it was as if Cecilia had left that part of her with him after she died.

So I get in his car and we drive to the store, and guess who's there, reading from a comic book? My grandson, Xavier, who has dyslexia and has always had trouble with school. It turns out that Roger had been helping him practice his reading; he preferred comics because the visual aid made it easier to make sense of what was going on.

TOM: So the comics section—

MILDRED: Yes. Roger started stocking comics for Xavier, you're correct.

So, on that day, Xavier's younger sister, Quintana, was sitting front row next to Ingrid and her husband, Sam, and I burst into tears. I hadn't realized how much I missed them, how happy I was to hear their voices.

I had the bad habit, you see, of withdrawing from life whenever I got upset. And I was worried, deep down, that by doing this, I was pushing the people I loved away, and that they'd hate me for it. At my age, yes, I know!

But my grandchildren didn't hate me, and Ingrid and Sam only wanted to make sure I was okay.

Roger did that for me. He tracked my daughter down and asked her to come visit, because he promised Cecilia we'd look out for each other. And when he couldn't do that for me, he took care of my family until I could get back on my feet and go back to being a mother and a grandmother full-time.

I will never forget the look on Xavier's face after he finished reading and the club broke out into applause. Roger had given him the opportunity to take his struggle and turn it into a glorious moment with the right amount of grit and hard work.

Roger saved my life that day. Really. I mean it.

Nell

Guilt is clawing up my throat. After the interview, Mildred shows us photo albums full of pictures from her youth: there's Roger and Cecilia the day they opened the bookstore, Mildred on her first wedding day, and then her second. It was a different time, and you could tell from their eyes that they had their whole lives ahead of them to dream and become and they knew it.

As Tom packs up the tripod and camera, I help Mildred carry the empty teacups and tray back to the kitchen. Anything to lessen my guilt. If I'd known Second Chance Books wasn't just any old bookstore I might have thought twice about signing on the project.

But then again, when are bookstores ever just bookstores?

Then I think of Kate, of the baby, and of our Way Out. *Beggars can't be choosers.* The commission will save my life. I just have to remember that.

"Oh gosh, look at the time," Mildred says. "I completely lost track of it."

"Do you have somewhere to be?" I ask, my guilt compounding. If we made her miss an appointment, I know I'd blame myself for not keeping better track of time.

"No, it's not that," she says. "I'm meeting Ingrid and my grandchildren for dinner tonight, and I meant to bring a few things. Xavier's been craving apple pie so I promised him I'd make him some, but I haven't got enough time to do that *and* get ready. I can't very well go to dinner looking like this, can I?"

I don't see what's wrong with her attire so I don't say anything. Just chuckle nervously.

"Bah," she says, waving a dismissive hand. "I suppose I'll just have to make it up to him another time."

"Why don't we help you make it?" I seem to have developed the habit of speaking before thinking it through. I have never baked anything in my entire life. Were she to leave us in charge, Xavier would never crave apple pie ever again in his life.

Mildred's eyes light up. "Would you?"

Too late to back out now.

"Of course," I say. As if on cue, Tom enters the kitchen with the camera bag slung across his chest.

He looks different somehow. Something about his demeanor around Mildred. He looks almost... confident. Self-assured. A far cry from the nervous, uncertain guy at the beach.

Mildred regards him with squinted eyes and a pursed-lip smile. "I like her," she says, then pats him on the shoulder. "I'll write down the recipe for you, love, and then you two can get started. Everything you need is in the pantry over there but if you have any trouble, just holler, alright?"

When Mildred leaves to get ready, Tom cants his head to the side and furrows his brows at me. I explain our new assignment.

"I thought you'd want to get out of here as soon as possible," he says.

"I thought so, too."

Tom sets his bag down on the counter and I busy myself with washing the teacups.

Mildred returns with a thick wad of paper with hyper-specific instructions scribbled in neat script.

"Thank you again," she says, cupping my face and pressing a kiss to my temple before leaving once more to get ready. When I meet Tom's eyes, he's trying to suppress his laughter and desperately failing.

"What?" I snap.

"Your face is bright red."

I touch my cheek. It's warm. I turn my back to him, embarrassed, and say,

"Go get the flour in the pantry. We have work to do."

I may not have any experience in baking, but I do know how to follow instructions, and once I get into the swing of it—measuring ingredients as precisely as possible, pouring them into a bowl for Tom to mix, who, by the way, *yes, chef's* every instruction I give him—it's easier than I imagined.

We finish the dough and refrigerate it before moving to work on the filling: 2 tablespoons of freshly squeezed lemon juice, 3 pounds of baking apples, 2/3 cup sugar, so on and so forth.

Tom swipes his thumb on my chin and tucks my hair behind my ear. It seems to happen in slow motion, as if we'd been dipped in honey and each movement was just as sweet. Even the shiver that runs up my spine takes its time; I feel it inch higher and higher, and I draw in a deep breath to mask my quiver.

His eyes are glued to the bottom of my face—my chin, probably. But maybe my lips. Possibly my lips.

Bewildered, I step back and look at him. He blinks at me, confused, then his eyes grow and his cheeks turn pink.

"You had flour on your face," he said. "And you kept flipping your hair back, so I thought—"

My cheeks burn again. The twelve-year-old me is internally doing cartwheels and screaming in excitement. I fix my gaze on the bowl in front of me and do my best impression of someone unfazed by his touch.

I can feel him staring at me still. Waiting for an answer. For me to say it's okay or express my discomfort. I don't know how I feel; I appreciate the gesture, I guess, because he's Tom and I've quickly learned that Tom does as Tom wants, but if he keeps touching me—

No. I don't even want to go there. I *can't* go there. Nothing good ever comes out of going there.

"Could you cut up those apples, please?" I ask.

"Yes, chef."

We finish the pie and stick it into the oven to bake. Tom had insisted we slice up the dough to make a lattice top layer, and for ambitious beginners, I have to say: not bad. Not bad at all.

We begin to tidy up; Tom returns all the ingredients to the pantry and hands me used bowls to wash. When he finishes his tasks, he offers to take over for me but I wave him off. He leans back against the counter with his arms crossed over his chest, staring off into space, seemingly lost in thought.

I sneak glances here and there. With the late afternoon sun leaking in through the window above the sink, he's bathed in golden light. His profile is striking: a sharp nose that turns up at the tip, a strong jaw shadowed by freshly-shaven stubble. But it's not his chiseled features that move me. It's his soft dark curls cascading off his head, making me wonder how it might feel to tangle my fingers in them, to scratch lightly at his scalp and see if he likes it. It's his gentle gaze and plump pink lips that look perpetually pouted and—

Okay, no. Twelve-year-old Nell is banished from my mindscape.

I turn down the heat and let the cold water douse my hands. When I glance back at Tom, he's still lost in his own head.

"You okay?" I can't help but ask.

"Huh? Oh. Yeah, I'm fine. You?"

"Good," I say. I rinse a silver mixing bowl and set it aside to dry. "What were you thinking about?"

"Oh." He's quiet for a few seconds. "I was just wondering what you were doing after this. Or what you do at all on weekends."

"I *do* things," I say petulantly. "I have a life, you know."

He straightens up, eyes widening. "No, I know, I—"

I laugh. "I'm just messing with you, Tom." This is more like it. I tease, he's flustered. Not the other way around.

Cheeks flushed, he relaxes against the countertop once more.

"To answer your question," I say, "not much, really. I don't usually leave the house if I don't have to." A truth that would have embarrassed me to admit to anyone else my age, because people my age lead colorful lives, both social and professional. I think I'd be embarrassed to admit it to anyone else, period. I'm sure if I told Roger or Mildred, they'd tell me to go out there, make the most of my youth and all of that.

But not Tom. He says, "Me, too," with a stupid grin that makes me laugh even more.

"I try to catch up on chores," I say, "or my other work."

"You work someplace else?"

Shit.

"Kind of," I quickly say. I remind him of my capstone project, now my go-to excuse it seems, another fact I would have been happy to have him forget had it not been for my clumsiness. Despite my pursuing Creative Writing in college, I still feel sheepish letting people know I write, because I can see myself in their head: a sad, lonely girl with no social life who substitutes fictional characters for real people and makes up stories in her head to fill the void. What void? She doesn't even know. But anyone can see she has no friends.

I used to think my former best friend, Daphne, and I would tackle higher education together. But somehow Mama fucked that one up for me too, and now Daphne—the same friend who shared her love for Studio Ghibli films with me—walks past me at St. Catherine's without a second glance.

"Oh, right," he says, grinning. "The romance novel."

My cheeks burn.

"Are you seeing anyone?" he asks suddenly.

"What?" I blurt out.

"You know. Like, you write romance novels. You consume a lot of rom-coms. You must be good at love."

"We've been over this, Tom. I'm not *good* with love."

"You got me a date with Paulina."

"That hardly means anything."

"You're joking," he says. "I would have never thought to do what you told me to."

"That doesn't mean I'm good with love," I say. "Just that you're worse at it than me."

He cackles. "That's fair."

I rinse my soapy hands and dry it on a kitchen towel.

"So, are you?" he asks.

I freeze. I'm not delusional enough to think he's asking for himself, but still.

"I mean, if it's alright for me to ask. You obviously know I'm not seeing anyone."

Oh, God.

I turn away from him and fuss with the bowls I'd just washed, wiping them down with a towel and setting them back in their proper places.

"No," I say. "And before you ask: I've never been with anyone before either."

"Why not?" he asks. "I mean... Just wondering."

Hands outstretched and standing on my tiptoes to return a bowl into a cupboard, I whip my head to face him and say, "Have you seen me?"

"Why do you think I asked?"

I let his words hang in the air between us. I'm still in the same position, struggling to place the bowl on the highest shelf where it belonged. "Are you being mean?" I ask.

"No?" Tom approaches and nudges me with his hip. He takes the bowl from me and slides it into place with ease. "Have you seen yourself?"

My hand flies up to tug on my bangs. "I try not to."

It's not that I'm horrified by my own embodied existence (maybe a little) but I try not to put too much weight in how I look. Mama was incredibly beautiful, and while most people would have viewed her beauty as a blessing—something to be proud of—I'd seen firsthand the ways it had also been a curse.

The truth is that beauty—if you're not lucky enough to have been born with it, then attaining it first and then maintaining it—costs so much more than just money. It is all-consuming and requires maximum effort to keep up with the ever-changing trends of plump lips, matte skin, thin brows, and dewy skin. Big asses and heroin chic.

But always a flat stomach. Always, always.

Mama never let me play with the other kids wherever we moved because she didn't want me scraping my knees and incurring any scars. When I was a chubbier kid, she used to talk about how she was skinnier at my age. She'd look at me with disappointment in her eyes as if my weight was a moral failure and go, *"You know, when I was your age..."*

Then there was all the other procedures that went into maintaining one's appearance. The thought of picking and pruning on schedule, of watching my weight out of fear of being undesirable.

All of it exhausts me before I can even begin.

Mama thought it was the woman's job to work hard and maintain a man's interest. Her desirability was her power. It was the currency, she believed, with which women used to buy love.

But I didn't care about any of that—if there was someone out there for me (which I severely doubted) they would not be the kind who cared about it, either. I want to run wild and do my own thing, away from the dichotomy of beautiful and ugly, away from the fear of aging, where I could transcend my own physical existence and just be.

Which is why I try not to look in the mirror, except when I brush my teeth at night and in the morning, or to make sure my clothes don't have holes in them before I head out.

"You're kidding," Tom says. "Nell, you're beautiful. Any guy would be lucky to have you."

See?

"Because I'm beautiful?" I ask.

"Well, yes, but—"

"There's more to a person than how they look, you know."

"I know that," Tom says. "But you're beautiful inside, too."

I roll my eyes. "Have you looked?"

"I mean, I think so," he says. "I'd like to, if you think I haven't. Not in a perverted way. You know. We're speaking in metaphors, so like—"

"I get it, Tom." I huff and tug on my bangs.

"You're always doing that," he says.

"Doing what?"

"Pulling on your bangs."

It's infuriating, all these little things he picks up about me. It feels like there's no place on this Earth where I could hide and he wouldn't find me. We could never see each other again after today, and fifteen years from now, we'll run into each other, and he would still know me.

How *aggravating*.

"They're taking so long to grow," I say, crossing my arms to keep myself from tugging them again.

"Why are you in a hurry?"

I open my mouth to speak then clamp it shut. I realize, in that moment, for all my thoughts and opinions on beauty, I still care a whole lot about how I look.

"Nell?"

"Because I look stupid, okay? There. Are you happy?"

He furrows his brows. "You don't look stupid." He chuckles as if I'd said the most absurd thing on earth. "You look like a young Audrey Hepburn."

"I wish."

"Wish granted."

We stare each other down like it's a stand-off.

I'm the first to cave.

"Fine," I say. "I'll buy you lunch tomorrow."

He snorts. "You don't have to. I mean it. All of it. Someone out there will see you and he'll know he's just become the luckiest guy on Earth."

Someone, a voice in my head says. *Not me.*

God, can I shut up already?

I roll my eyes again. "Save the flattery for Paulina. A girl agrees to go on one date with you and suddenly you're all about love. You've got it bad."

His face falls serious. He leans his hip into the edge of the sink, blocking my way. "I think—I think in some ways, it's all anyone want to be about. Love, I mean. Don't you think?"

"You're confusing love for sex," I say.

That's all it boils down to at the end of the day, isn't it? Why Mama was so worried about how she looked, why she stressed every single birthday that she was getting older? "Aging out" is the term she used. I remember.

Then, in a rage, she would say stuff like, "Men don't give a shit about you if they're not even remotely interested in fucking you. You don't exist to any of them if your existence is unattractive to them."

Kind of hard to want love when you hear someone say things like that on a near-monthly basis growing up. And, of course, let's not fucking forget the husband of the year, Henry.

"Isn't that just a part of it?" Tom asks.

"They're not mutually inclusive for everyone," I say.

"Right. But who doesn't want love?" he asks, standing to his full height.

Me, I think. What good has wanting love ever done for the women in my family? There are times, yes, where I still ache. I yearn. But I tell myself this: is it not a sign of insanity to want the very thing you know you can never have?

"Not even just the romantic kind," Tom says. "All forms of it. Platonic. Familial." He pauses to think. "What else?"

I don't know what else. I get my romantic fix through fiction where it's safe to explore anything and everything without incurring any more personal trauma than I probably already have.

"You sound like my mother," I say. "That's not a compliment, by the way."

Tom chuckles and relaxes back against the counter. "You know," he says, "for someone who loves love stories, you're pretty cynical about love."

"I don't *love* love stories," I say—which he and I both know is a lie. "And it's not like I've gotten good examples of it. Have you?"

"No," he says. "I mean, just now, with Roger and Cecilia, so I know it exists. I'll find it one day."

God. "You sound incredibly like my mother."

"And did she find it?"

"No," I say. "She found God, though."

He smiles. "Good for her. Your mom's always been cool. Divine love and all of that."

"Sure," I say. "Now she's just dust in a vase collecting even more dust."

Realization dawns on his face.

"I'm so sorry," he says. "I didn't know. I—"

"I'm back!" Mildred announces as she waltzes into the kitchen, dressed in a fine dress and fluffing her hair up with her palms. "Oh, wow, it smells heavenly." She peers into the oven and then throws us two thumbs up. "You did wonderfully, you two!"

I turn to Tom, who looks like a puppy I'd just kicked across the face. I hate it, but my hardened heart softens. Just a little.

"Shall we head out then?" I ask.

He nods. "I'll take you home."

Tom

It's tense in the car when I drive Nell home. My whole body burns; I drive slowly because my vision has splotches of light and I can hear my own heartbeat thrumming in my ears. I consider pulling over and asking whether she knows how to drive. She lives so far away, I worry I'll faint halfway through the journey and land us in a ditch.

I don't know how that conversation got away from me; maybe hearing Mildred talk about love got to me more than I thought because I started thinking about Paulina and how excited I was for our date and then I started thinking of Nell, what she'd be doing while I was on my date, and how much I wanted her to also go on a date and feel the same excitement I was feeling. If I knew about her mom, I would have never said anything, and now I'm feeling stupid all over again, wishing the ground would open up and swallow me whole.

I was a man possessed. The words just kept flowing from me: *have you seen yourself? You're beautiful.* I don't know where on God's green earth I found the courage to say that to her face, but at the same time, something had stirred in me, something that needed her to acknowledge that simple truth. It wasn't even that I had discovered her beauty myself, more so that I needed her to remember it exists. Sometimes we live with something for so long that we forget it's there. And it wasn't a matter of opinion, was it? She *is* beautiful, inside and out. Even without eyes, anyone could see that.

She's kind and smart and patient—with me, especially. Today's interview proves that. I haven't had a friend my age since I left home. It's nice to be around someone from the same generation as me; there were some things, certain experiences no matter how small—like getting home from school and watching Spongebob reruns on television—that most adults around me would never understand.

And somehow I managed to mess it all up.

The silence in the car is suffocating. Whatever ease we'd found conversing before is gone, and my knuckles are turning white from how tightly I grip the steering wheel. I glance at her every now and then, but she's not looking at me; she's angled her knees towards her door and stares right out the window.

My phone rings. I'm grateful for the interruption.

"Could you put it on loudspeaker, please?" I ask Nell gently. She obliges and sets my phone right back on the dashboard.

"Thomas," Roger's voice crackles through the speakers.

"Hi, Roge," I say. "You're on speaker."

"Are you on your way back?"

"I'm just dropping Nell off. She lives like an hour out, so—"

"Can she hear me? Eleanor, are you there?"

"Hi, Roger."

"There you are." I can hear the smile in his voice. "How'd it go?"

"It went well, I think." There's no trace of the edge in her voice I'd heard earlier. I don't know whether to be relieved or concerned.

"Have you two had dinner?"

"Not yet," I say.

"Well, come meet me at Amici's across the street. I'm craving their bolognese."

I glance over at Nell, prepared to decline on her behalf so she could go home and get some rest.

"Sure," she says, and somehow I know I've been forgiven. Not completely, but enough.

I turn the car and head in the opposite direction, back home towards the bookstore.

Roger is sitting in our usual booth at Amici's, his back to the window with a view of the ocean, perusing the menu even though he could probably recite it in his sleep. They haven't changed their menu since they opened over four decades ago, making it a point to say that on the front page. Giuseppe, whose grandparents founded the restaurant and who now manages it, always says, *"If it ain't broke, don't fix it."*

Amici's is at the far end of High Street, with its striped green and white awning, red brick walls speckled with mirrors and posters, candlelit gingham tables, and chalkboard menus. It's one of the last remaining bastions standing against the encroaching Vanguard Properties developments aside from Second Chance Books, and it's obvious. High Street is a sorry excuse for what it used to be, all SOON TO OPEN! tarpaulins and not much else.

I miss the weekends when everyone who worked in High Street would dine at Amici's at the end of the day. Everyone bought out by Vanguard's moved on, moved some place new. But still we remain.

Sunset is the best time to eat here, Roger once said, and it's obvious why: when we approach, the sky is an oil painting of pink, purple, and orange.

Nell slides into the seat opposite Roger where I normally sit. I hesitate; I've never sat next to Roger during dinner, always across him, and it feels weird to start now. But I don't know whether she wants to sit next to me. I don't want to assume.

She scoots over and stares at me questioningly as if to ask, *Why are you just standing there?*

I slide in next to her. Even with her nearly pressed against the corner, our thighs still touch. My skin burns where it meets hers.

I peek at her. If she was bothered by it or even remotely affected at all, she showed no signs.

Just me, then.

"And how's Mildred doing?" Roger asks by way of greeting. We tell him about the interview and watch his eyes soften at the mention of Cecilia, so I take the chance to ask whether he might still have her journals lying around.

"Of course," Roger says. "She was a prolific writer, but so incredibly shy and private about it. I never show them to anyone unless I think she'd be okay with it. Only Mildred and I have read it, I think, unless you've been snooping around, Thomas."

"No," I say. "Do you think she'd be alright if Nell read it?"

"I don't have to," Nell is quick to interject. "I respect her privacy."

Roger waves her off. "She would have loved you, and I know she'd haunt me if I didn't let you read it. I'll loan you the first one since there's plenty. Finish it and if you want more, I'll show you where I keep the rest."

"You know, Nell's a writer too," I say.

She glares at me. "*Tom.*"

My cheeks flush. Was it supposed to be a secret?

"Are you?" Roger asks nevertheless.

"I write. Here and there," she says.

"What do you write?"

The color of her face deepens from pink to scarlet with every passing second. "Fiction, mainly," she says, "but I'll write anything if it pays enough. Articles for medical websites or copies for start-ups."

I bring up the fanfiction she used to write in our youth. If looks could kill, I'd be dead by now. Even though there are worse ways to die than at the hands of a beautiful girl, I take it as a sign to shut up indefinitely.

She and Roger dive into a conversation about the bookstore and writing. I munch on the free garlic bread to keep myself from talking. It's not my fault I was excited; I'd been surrounded by literature for nearly half of my life now, and this is my first time being around someone who didn't just read it but wrote it, too (Louis being the exception, considering he has yet to finish *anything* he's started).

Giuseppe comes and takes our orders—spaghetti bolognese for Roger, carbonara for Nell (after much consultation with me), and an arugula and prosciutto pizza for me.

Before Giuseppe leaves, he says, "The sharks came by again today." He's adopted Roger and I's term for the employees of Vanguard Properties.

"Did they?" Roger asks. "They've left me alone, surprisingly."

"Sharks?" Nell echoes. I quickly explain it to her.

Giuseppe calls over a waiter to take our orders to the kitchen and pulls up a seat next to Roger. "How on earth did you manage that?"

Roger shrugs. "I haven't heard from them since Hopley Head." Vanguard Properties offered us an all-expense paid trip up north to see how they transformed the sleepy seaside town into a bustling tourist destination. I guess they hoped we'd be convinced of the good they could do to Newbury, but Roger and I only accepted so we could have a nice, free vacation with no intention of ever switching sides.

"Strange that they've stopped coming just as I'm seriously considering taking the bait."

"Roger," I warn.

He shrugs. "I won't be here forever."

"Okay, enough of that," I tell him. I'd stuff garlic bread into his mouth if it would shut him up.

Roger chuckles. To Nell, he says, "He hates when I address my own mortality."

I do. I can't imagine living in a world without Roger. He saved me— literally. I owe him my life.

"Second Chance Books is here to stay, and so are you." My tone is firm and serious.

Roger regards Nell and Giuseppe. "I plan on leaving it in his name."

My jaw drops. News to me. *Great* news, of course; there's no place else I'd rather be in this world than Second Chance Books, but again: what good is this world without Roger in it?

"Really?" Nell asks.

"Well, what good will it do me when I'm dead?"

I narrow my eyes. "Roger."

He throws his hands up in surrender. "Okay, okay, I'm done."

Giuseppe leaves us to assist another table of diners. Conversation dies down as we eat. It's not until Nell excuses herself to freshen up that Roger starts speaking again.

"You were driving her home?" he asks.

"It felt like the right thing to do," I say.

"Good. Good. You'll start picking her up every morning then, so she doesn't have to take the bus."

I gape at him. "That's an hour each way. I'd have to wake up at six—"

"So?"

"So, I like to get enough sleep at night, Roger. And gas—"

"I'll pay for the gas."

I give him a look. The store only ever earns enough to break even; there's a chance, of course, that he's got some wealth tucked away but I know what this is. I see where it's going. After I turned eighteen, Roger has been obsessed with trying to matchmake me with random girls. At this point, I think I've been set up on a date with every single local girl my age, all thanks to Roger. Of course, I never went if I could help it, which also meant every single local girl my age probably hates my guts.

"What?"

"Roge, you can't be serious."

"It's the right thing to do."

I sigh. "I'll pick her up on weekends we're working on the thing for the club anniversary," I say, still not wanting to spoil the surprise. "And drive her home, then. Maybe if she sticks around for book club, too. But every day? Roger, come on."

He throws his hands up and leans back against his seat. "Fine."

"Fine."

Nell returns and Roger doesn't waste time telling her I'll be her chauffeur from now on. *Every day.* He was nice enough to not make me pick her up every morning, but he did insist I drive her home daily.

Traitor.

I swear, sometimes I don't understand that man.

"It's really not necessary," Nell says, chuckling nervously. "I live so far away."

"But it is," Roger says. "Please don't worry about it. It would make us feel better knowing you got home safe, and it'll save you on bus fares." The sneaky old man.

Nell looks at me as if to ask for help. I shrug. If I decline on her behalf, I'll just look like an asshole, and once Roger's made up his mind about something, there's no changing it. Besides, there's worse people to be stuck in a car with for an hour. Roger would never let me hear the end of it if we decline.

"Okay," she finally relents. "Thank you."

Nell

Tom parks outside my house and it occurs to me that I'm not sure what my next move should be.

Do I invite him inside for some tea? No, that's too much. But to leave him out here after he'd driven an hour to bring me home—surely that would be too rude.

Do I hug him? Give him a kiss on the cheek?

I stare out the window at the yellow semi-detached house I call home. I fell in love with it when we first moved, the first house I've ever lived in with a proper front- and backyard. Even though my room was cramped, it was mine. The privacy of my own room was a luxury we previously could never afford, but Kate's marriage to Henry changed that.

Now, as if seeing it through Tom's eyes, the house just looks drab. Devoid of a garden or anything anyone would like about a home.

I feel my insides churn, wondering what he might be thinking. I mean, he grew up in a mansion. If I remember correctly, their living room was the size of our entire first floor.

Tom clears his throat. "Is this the right place?"

I sit up. "Oh, yes. Sorry." I unbuckle my seatbelt and gather my things. To my surprise, he steps out of the car and pulls the door open for me. I must look like a baby deer learning to walk for the first time, or a robot malfunctioning when he walks me up to my front door, because I seem to have forgotten how to move my legs normally.

Tom leans in. In a panic, I press a kiss to his cheek and mumble a quick 'thank you' before launching myself through the front door and slamming it shut behind me.

Kate stands in the entry hall holding a laundry basket against her hip, head canted to the side. "Who was that?"

"Who was what?" I drop my things off in the kitchen, Kate now trailing behind me.

"A guy just walked you up to the front door."

"Oh." My cheeks flush. "Do you remember Tom? Whelan?"

Kate shakes her head. She'd already been working when Mama was a cleaner at the Whelans, so she never got to spend time with them as much as I did.

"Never mind," I say. I don't want to get into my complicated employment situation anyway. "He's my friend."

She smiles at me—actually smiles. Not one of those fake ones that don't reach her eyes. A real one. That's the first time I've seen her look happy in days. For a brief second, it's like I have my sister back again.

"He's cute," she says.

"Please." I roll my eyes, but I can't help but smile, too.

"Just because love never worked out for me or for Mama," she says, "doesn't mean you should close your door on it."

The smile is wiped off my face.

That's rich, I think. The night Kate left home—left me—one of the things she told our mother was that I was being raised to be stupid in love. That a diet of romcoms, fairytales, and Happy Ever Afters would lead me to settle for the first person that looked my way.

That had been Mama's pattern, after all. Why we never had any money.

She would meet a guy, convince herself he was the one, and give him her all. Time, money, attention. She never had enough saved up because she was always funding her boyfriends' vices: alcohol, gambling, cigarettes. It didn't matter if it left her two daughters starving in a cramped apartment with no electricity. Love was the most important thing in the world to her, at least until they broke her heart and she became a woman scorned, forcing us to pack up our bags and move to the next town where she'll meet someone new, and rinse and repeat.

I made a promise to myself that same night to be better than that. Better than Mama. Even after I'd forgiven Kate, I never broke my promise to myself. If love made fools of us all, then I would simply never fall in love.

"We're just friends," I say.

"Friends don't drive an hour each way just to get you home."

"They do if their boss tells them to."

Kate and I stare at each other. She looks as if she might say something but thinks better of it. I know she's got a hundred questions swimming in her head.

"Hungry?" she asks instead.

"I'm good. My boss took us to dinner." She doesn't need to know which boss, exactly.

"That's nice."

The light flickers overhead. I look up just as we're shrouded in darkness. Kate curses under her breath.

"Wha—" I reach for the light switch and flick it up and down.

"They weren't supposed to cut us off until next week."

"Cut us off?"

I blink, willing my eyes to adjust to the darkness. I can't see Kate, only hear her.

"We're behind on payments," she says. "For power." Some things, I guess, are easier said in the dark.

"How behind?"

"Just this month."

"What?" All that money I gave her—where did it go?

She starts explaining—she prioritized food, she had to pay for a doctor's appointment out of pocket, etcetera, etcetera. There's a strain in her voice I haven't heard since she told me Henry left.

My heart rings in my ears.

"Kate," I say, holding my hands out to find her. I squeeze her arms and pull her into a hug. She chokes out a sob. "It's okay. I'm not mad. It's okay, Kate." She's much taller than me, my sister. My mom used to joke that her father was the giant in *Jack and the Beanstalk*. Still, I stroke Kate's hair the way she used to stroke mine. I let her cry.

She pulls away as she draws a breath and swipes at her cheeks. "I'm sorry. Pregnancy hormones." She pinches my cheek. "It's going to be okay. I'll figure this out. I'll call Hen—"

"Like hell you are," I say. She's under enough stress as it is; the last thing she needs is to ask her deadbeat soon-to-be-ex-husband for financial help.

"Nell—"

"No. I'll handle it."

"But—"

"I'll ask my boss for an advance. It'll be fine." Jane probably won't agree to it—she's a woman so staunchly against handouts, but I'll have to try.

My eyes adjust and I see her, my sister, looking so much younger and more put upon than I remember. More broken.

I hate Henry. I hate him with the force of a thousand suns. How can you vow to love someone your whole life, to stay true to them, to care for them in front of all your family and friends just to turn your back on them? At her most vulnerable! She's carrying his child for God's sake! My mother dated the worst of men, but at least they never married her. What's his fucking excuse?

"Nell..." Kate's voice is soft. Scared.

"We're going to be okay, Kate," I tell her. I tell *myself.* "I promise."

If not now, then eventually. *Soon.* Because Us Garcia girls stick together. There's nothing we can't get through.

Tom

My skin buzzes where Nell's lips had touched it. I drive back to Newbury in silence, replaying the scene over and over in my head.

I move in for a hug.

She kisses my cheek.

My stomach flips at the memory. I touch my cheek as if I might find a trace of her there.

My phone rings, jolting me out of my thoughts. I pick up and put it on loudspeaker without looking at the caller ID.

"Hello?"

"Hi, Tommy!" Paulina's high-pitched voice is drenched in sunshine. Just hearing it fills me with warmth. "Just calling to check if we're still on for our date?"

Our date. We're going on a *date*.

I, Thomas Whelan, am going on a date with Paulina Coombs.

Holy shit.

"Hello?"

I clear my throat. "Hi, yes, I'm here," I say, tightening my grip around the steering wheel and sitting up as if she can see me. "Yes, we're on." Why am I talking like a robot? *Be normal, you idiot.*

"Perfect. I'll see you soon, then?"

"Absolutely."

When she hangs up, I stare blankly at the road ahead. My cheek still burns where Nell kissed me. Not even a phone call with Paulina could make me forget.

Fuck.

My excitement was supposed to last longer than a thirty-second phone call. I'm going on a date with Paulina fucking Coombs, so why can't I stop thinking about kissing Nell back?

Armed with the past week's love lessons from Nell and a desperate desire to forget she ever kissed my cheek, I arrive at The Drowsy Poet feeling confident and ready for whatever Paulina throws my way. She's already there at our previous table, waiting for me.

She stands to greet me as I approach. She kisses both my cheeks and pushes her sunglasses up on her head. When we place our orders, I go for a lemonade.

"It's nice to see you again," she says as we settle back into our seats.

Remember: ping-pong.

"I'm so sorry again," I say. "About last time."

"I hope it went over well?"

I blink. "Which?"

"You said there was an emergency. Or your friend, did. Ella?"

"Nell," I correct her. "But yeah—no, our boss was just—he needed some help with deliveries. There was a mix-up and... you don't want to hear about it." We laugh. "How have you been?"

"Good, good!" she exclaims. "I just got back from Nice with my cousins." I'd forgotten that about her. She has family in France, so she was always jet-setting off to the Riviera.

I wait for her to throw the question back but she never does. So I plow ahead. "What have you been up to these days?"

"Not much, really." She tucks her hair behind her ear. "Well, that's a lie. Do you remember Sharon?" Sharon was—or I guess, *is*—Paulina's best friend. They were practically attached at the hip all throughout school. "Well, we're working on starting our own boutique in town. We really got into designing our own jewelry—she went to school for it, but I took up Marketing so I'm essentially our PR person. But we've started looking at properties, 'cause her Aunt Jane says Newbury's going to be the ultimate artist town in all of Cerulea. Even bigger than Cheltham. She showed us their plans and everything. That's actually why I'm here!"

I'd also forgotten how much she could say in just under a minute. "That's—that's great, Polly." The nickname slips from my tongue. Her features soften and she places a hand over mine.

"Listen. I don't know what happened, why you disappeared when you did, but I never got to thank you."

Thank me?

"You were right. About Greg. We went on a trip that summer after graduation, and I found this entire folder of girls' photos on his phone. He was—God, he was a pervert, and you tried to tell me and I didn't listen. I had love goggles on. I should have listened to you."

My heart seizes in my chest. If I hadn't left, if I'd just waited—

"Greg's always been an asshole," I say quietly.

"I tried to warn the other girls, but they wouldn't listen. And I had no proof. The fucker's running around having faced zero consequences, and your stepmother's lawyers are covering for him. No offense."

So my dad's still with my stepmom. Cool.

"He caught me going through his phone and—" Paulina gets this glassy look in her eyes and looks away. "It was a lot. But what got me through it is that you tried to do right by me, and that meant that there were still good people in this world. People who loved me—truly. You were the only boy who ever well and truly loved me, Tom, did you know that?"

My heart's hammering now; my head spins and I drop my gaze to focus on the grain of the wooden table between us to keep myself from fainting.

All I've ever wanted, here five years later. But who even cares about that? Paulina went through hell and back, and now *she's* here. Stronger than ever. If I could go back in time, I'd punch Greg harder. Break his nose. Make him suffer, the fucking asshole.

"I'm sorry," I say after some time.

"It's okay." She smiles at me. "I mean, no, what he did wasn't okay. But what doesn't kill you makes you stronger and all that."

"How come you didn't look for me?" I blurt out. My self-centeredness is not lost on me; it makes me cringe. I can hear Nell criticizing me in my head: *get over yourself, Tom.* But I can't help it. It's one of those questions I think about late at night when I can't sleep.

My father had sent his publicist's assistant to check up on me that first month with Roger. Just once and never again, if only to make sure they didn't have a PR nightmare in their hands, as if I'd ever rat him out to the papers. Then my best friend, Finn, kept calling and calling, saying the band needed me and that he missed me, and once he threatened to come see me but he never did. I don't blame him for giving up on me. Surely if Paulina knew where I'd gone, she would have looked for me?

"I thought you didn't want to be found," she admits. "But I'm so glad, Tommy, you don't even know how glad I am that we've reconnected. I've missed you so much."

My stomach drops.

She knew. She knew and she didn't even try. She squeezes my hand but all I can think about is, if the roles were reversed, I would have looked for her. I would have exhausted every option and given her the chance to tell me to fuck off instead of assuming it's what she wanted.

But she's here now, isn't she? She's been trying. Even when I was dodging her, even when I had to leave our first date so suddenly.

And anyway, if it wasn't for her, I would have never met Roger. I would have never run into Nell again.

I have to give her that. She's given me another chance, and if this is meant to go anywhere—if I *want* this to go anywhere—I have to give her a chance, too.

I manage a smile. "I missed you, too, Polly." I squeeze her hand back. *You don't even know how much.*

Nell

At home on Saturday, I refresh my email over and over, waiting for Jane's reply to my formal request for an advance when Tom calls me. I pick up and he starts talking a mile a minute, telling me all about his date.

"Wait, slow down, slow down," I say, laughing.

"Nell, it was amazing," he says, breathless. "She said she'll come to the next book club meeting and that she wants to meet you properly."

I don't know why, but my heart clenches. No, that's a lie. I know exactly why. No matter how many times I tell myself not to go there, my heart races towards it. My twelve-year-old self has more control over my heart than I do, I guess. A guy like Tom's hard to quit.

"That's—that's great, Tommy," I say. "So you don't need my help anymore."

He chuckles. Somehow, that hurts even more than I expected. It's not like I was hoping he'd grovel and beg me to never leave his side, but still.

"I don't know about that," he says. "But it went really well, Nell. If I need any more help, I'll let you know, yeah?"

"Yeah." I chew on my bottom lip. *Don't be a bitch, Nell. Jealousy's not a good look on you. Be happy for him.* "So she's coming back next week?"

"Uh-huh."

"Cool." *Cool, cool, cool, cool.*

My phone beeps.

Jane.

I've never been more grateful for a reason to stop talking to Tom.

"Hold on a sec," I tell him. I pull my phone from my ear and check the notification.

JANE

> Are you free to call?

"Tom, I have to call you back," I say. "Something came up."

"Is everything oka—"

"Everything's fine, I just have to go. Talk to you later. Bye!" I hang up just as Jane's caller ID appears on screen.

"Eleanor," Jane says. When she calls me by my full name, I know I'm in for bad news.

"Hi, Jane," I say.

"I received your request, but unfortunately—" I let out a breath. I tune her out. She gives me a whole spiel about how she wishes she could help, but unfortunately, her hands are tied. HR says once they start giving people advances, then everyone will start asking for them and it'll fuck up the payroll or whatever. I don't know. I'm not listening.

I force a smile to my lips. "I understand," I tell her. "Thank you for trying."

She asks for an update on Roger, and I tell her I'm still working on it.

"Good, good," she says, "well, don't take too long now."

"I won't."

"I expect you back in the office soon. My niece is a terrible assistant. I've missed three meetings now because of her." She barks out a laugh and I chuckle along to be polite. Finally, she dismisses me and ends our call.

I flop down onto my mattress facedown. I groan into my pillow.

What on earth am I supposed to do now?

I suppose I could ask Roger, but my guilt is bad enough as it is. Still, a voice in my head tells me this is urgent. And anyway, I *do* do the work. I'm out there sorting bookshelves every day. *Do you know how heavy a stack of books can be?*

I roll onto my back and stare up at the ceiling. If Henry didn't leave, this wouldn't be a problem. But even before that, if Mama wasn't the way she was, maybe we would have had more money.

I trace my family's series of bad decisions back until I'm making up stories about an ancestor whose transgressions cursed our entire lineage to be both unlucky in love and finances. Because at this point, how else can you explain our shit luck if not through magic?

It doesn't pay our bills, but it at least gets my mind off the impending doom and the pressure I feel. It helps me forget, for a moment in time, that Tom's date with Paulina didn't just go well.

It went really, *really* well.

Tom

The first thing Nell asks me when she sees me waiting for her by the car is whether Roger's inside. I tell her he's out on another errand.

"Why? Did you need something?"

She shakes her head. "Just wondering."

I pull the passenger side door open for her. I want to tell her, whatever it is, it'll be fine—and I'm sure there's something because she's got that thousand-yard look in her eyes all over again.

Today, we're interviewing Louis at the middle school where he's teaching remedial English classes for the summer.

I turn the stereo down as we near the school.

"Hey, Nell," I say. "You feel comfortable taking the lead this interview, or do you still need me to do it for you?"

Nell pouts at me. I'm struck by this inexplicable feeling—like I want to squish her cheeks and go to war for her at the same time. I clench and unclench my grip around the steering wheel instead.

"Could you?" she asks. "Please?"

"Of course." If she pouted at me again, I'm certain I'd do anything she asked.

Louis is reading a copy of *Letters from a Stoic* by Seneca at his desk when we enter his classroom. His permed curls are pushed back by a pair of sunglasses while his thick-framed reading glasses sit on the bridge of his nose.

"Mr. Park," I say in that customary overly formal greeting of ours.

"Ah, Mr. Whelan." He stands and holds his hand out for me to shake. When I take it, he laughs and pulls me in for a hug, clapping me on the back.

"You've met Nell," I say when he releases me, gesturing towards Nell, who steps forward with this bashful look on her face.

"I haven't," Louis says, shaking her hand. "Not formally, but Roger's told me all about you. Welcome to the family."

Her eyes widen.

"He means the book club," I say.

"Right. Thank you," says Nell.

"We'll set up, then we can get started." I hand my camera bag to Nell so she won't have to talk to Louis unless she wanted to.

I'm helping her get the tripod up when there's a knock on the door.

"*Yoohoo.*" Annabel is standing in the doorway, holding a lunchbox in hand. She's grinning at Louis then blushes when she sees me and Nell. "Oh, hi, Thomas. I didn't know you'd be here today."

"I didn't know *you'd* be here today," I return.

"Ewan had a football tournament so I was in the area. Are you two here for the documentary?"

I nod. Nell stretches out a hand to introduce herself. They exchange pleasantries, and then Annabel hands Louis the lunchbox. "My mom gave me her recipe for the shepherd's pie you like, so I thought I'd make you some today."

"Oh, wow. Thanks so much," Louis says.

Nell and I exchange glances.

Louis turns to us. "Actually, do you guys mind if I step outside for a bit? I actually haven't eaten, so—"

"Go ahead," I say, waving him off. "It's nice seeing you, Annabel."

"You, too, Tommy." We watch as Annabel steps out with Louis trailing behind her. When I look back at Nell, her brows are high up on her face.

"Does she like him?" she asks.

"That's what Roger thinks."

"Who brings someone lunch like that? No, not just lunch. *Homemade lunch.* That's different."

"Friends?" I hazard a guess.

She gives me another look. She doesn't have to make a buzzer sound for me to know I gave the wrong answer.

"Is this another lesson?" I ask.

"I told you," she says. "It's in the notebook I gave you. It's the little things. Those matter infinitely more than grand gestures. Little things you can do every day. You can't whisk someone off to a destination constantly, but you can bring them lunch, you know?"

I remember. I read through it every night, but the only thing I can ever commit to memory is how she loops her O's and L's in script.

"So, like, driving you home?" I blurt out.

We fall quiet. She tightens the screw that holds the camera in place, and then stands up to her full height.

"Yeah. Things like that," she says as our eyes meet. "But obviously with the weight of romance behind it. You and I are just friends."

"Absolutely," I say. *Just friends.* That's all we are. All we'll ever be.

So why the hell am I disappointed?

"Should we bump Annabel up the list and interview her next? Maybe we could get her to spill."

"Okay," I say, averting my gaze to the chalkboard behind Louis's desk. "I'll tell her."

Louis

NELL: *[laughs]* Stop.

TOM: I'm just testing to see if the camera works.

LOUIS: Hi, sorry to keep you waiting. I'm ready now. Where do I sit?

TOM: Just at your desk, please. That's great. Nell?

NELL: We're rolling.

TOM: Perfect. Okay, Louis, could you start us off by telling us a bit about yourself?

LOUIS: Hi. I'm Louis Park. I'm currently teaching third grade English at Newbury Prep, but I'm a novelist first and foremost.

NELL: What is it that you write?

LOUIS: I like to write a lot of speculative fiction, a lot of literary hybrids. Right now, I'm working on a piece that incorporates a cult and a private investigator who loses his best friend to it. I'm nearly done with my third draft, and I expect to be querying soon.

NELL: You don't intend to self-publish?

LOUIS: That's kind of a last-resort option for me. For now, I want to try my hand at getting traditionally published. It's still different, you know.

NELL: Self-publishing is becoming more and more a viable option these days. It's democratized the industry insofar as the kinds of stories that are made available to us and all of that.

LOUIS: No, for sure, for sure. I just don't see myself going down that route. It's much harder to get your name out without a publishing house's backing too. I mean, they've got a whole marketing department dedicated to that.

NELL: Right.

TOM: So, Louis, when did you first start visiting Second Chance Books?

LOUIS: About three years ago now.

TOM: And how did you find it?

LOUIS: Do you mean what I think of it, or literally how I found it?

TOM: Literally, but you can answer both.

LOUIS: Well, I love SCB. Of course. But Roger was my dad's professor in university and they kept in touch. When I moved in the area, my dad suggested I pay him a visit, so I did. I was pretty down on my luck at that time. I was getting rejection letters for the first novel I'd ever written, one after the other. I was thinking of quitting writing altogether, and Roger knew I was a writer because my dad had called ahead to let him know I was coming.

So he asked me, you know, in that voice of his, "Hey, Louis, how's the writing coming along?" And you can't lie to his face. You can try. But he looks you in the eye and the truth just spills out, you know? So I told him how I was feeling. How close I was to giving up.

Hell, I think just an hour before I saw him, I *had* given up.

So I pour my heart out, right? And he gets up and doesn't say anything, and I'm sat there feeling stupid while he disappears in the back of the store. You remember this, Tom. You were there.

I'm thinking of leaving. I want to call my dad and tell him his professor was an asshole. Then Roger comes back and sets this book down in front of me. *The Artist's Way* by Julia Cameron.

"Before you give up," he said to me, "at least give this a try."

I mean, what the hell, right? What have I got to lose?

That book changed my life. It completely changed the game for me. I don't think I'd have gotten this far without it. And obviously I have Roger to thank for that.

TOM: Did you join book club soon after?

LOUIS: I did, yeah. After that first week, which revolves around recovering a sense of safety, I ran back to the store to thank Roger. You guys were in the middle of a meeting. I remember Annabel was onstage with Evelyn on her lap. Ewan was running around somewhere.

TOM: He was on Mildred's lap.

LOUIS: Right, exactly. You were there. You remember. Roger smiled at me from the front and gestured for me to take a seat.

Annabel was reading a passage from Bell Hooks's *All About Love*. I still remember. I bought a copy that same night.

I remember thinking, finally. I'd found my people. I was the odd one out in university; I shifted from an Engineering degree to English literature—an E for an E, my dad used to say—halfway between my junior year when all the friend groups had been established and there was no more space for me.

But everyone was so welcoming at book club. And I liked that we didn't have to read the same books. I've found a lot of great literature because of that, books I otherwise would have never picked up.

Of course, sometimes I question the odd attendee's tastes here and there—remember when someone read that badly written sex scene from that erotica? I mean, at least read Anaïs Nin or Mary Gaitskill. But I digress.

TOM: Could you share with us your favorite memory from book club?

LOUIS: It has to be when I let Roger read a copy of my draft and I was feeling shitty about it. I thought it was a lump of coal, insofar as literature goes. A dud. I was ready to scrap it all together.

"Not yet," he said. Imagine my surprise when, that week, he read one passage aloud to book club. I'll never forget the feeling when I heard Bobby ask: *"What happens next?"*

Nell

I'm a nervous wreck when we return to the bookstore. Roger is doing the crossword puzzle at his usual table.

"Hi, Roger. Can we talk?" I eye Tom. "Privately?"

Roger's face screws up in concern. "Yes, of course." He gestures to the backroom, which he's turned into his own studio flat. He seats me by his desk and grunts as he lowers himself onto his mattress.

"The shop used to be bigger. And then I got old." He chortles. "Tom used to sleep here and come upstairs to do his business. But I couldn't keep climbing the stairs, and, well—young men need more privacy, I feel. So we closed shop a few weeks, had a bathroom and everything constructed down here. Quite useful, actually. Book club members used to have to buy breadsticks from Amici's all the time just to—" He clears his throat. "What did you want to talk to me about?"

There's no way out but through. I suck in a breath. "Is there any way I could get an advance on my salary? I know I'm not due to be paid until, like, next month or so but our power's been cut and my sister's pregnant so she can't get any work. And her husband's not with us anymore, so it's—"

"I'm sorry to hear that."

"What?" I blink.

"Your brother-in-law. Did he pass recently?"

"Oh. No. It's nothing like that. I *wish* he was dead, but no. He just… left." I clear my throat. "So—"

Roger sits up straighter. He clasps his hands together on his lap. "I'm assuming," he says, "because you're asking me for help that you have nobody else to ask. May I ask you a question?"

Anything.

"Where are your parents? In all of this?"

"Dead."

He blinks at my word choice. Most people like to dance around death; they say someone's not with us anymore, someone's passed on, etcetera, etcetera. To call them dead makes other people uncomfortable, but it's the concise truth. It encapsulates the suddenness and the finality of that severance between this life and whatever comes next. If there's anything that comes next.

"Both of them?"

"As far as I'm concerned."

"Meaning?"

"Meaning I never met my dad and I don't intend to. My mom took her own life a few years ago."

My words hang in the thick silence between us, clunky and weighted. My eyes sting. I worry Roger will say no.

"Your sister. How far along is she?"

"Nearly five months now."

His eyes crinkle when he smiles. "Not too long now." Roger stands and retrieves a red leather book and his phone from the shelf. He lumbers towards me and hands me the book. "My wife's journal. Come. I'll have Thomas transfer the money to your account. I'm not too good with my phone. I only got it because Tom insisted I *'move into the 21st century.'*"

Every ounce of tension within me vanishes in an instant. I exhale a breath of relief and follow him out. There, standing at the counter, is no other than Henry, looking just as relieved to see me.

Tom

My first thought when the guy who introduced himself as Henry, Nell's brother in-law, was that he was a prince. He had to be. Everything about him screamed money: his tanned skin, his effortlessly combed back brown hair, his attire. He spoke in a posh accent I only ever heard from people in the capital, or on TV when the King addressed the public.

The only thing that didn't match everything else about him was the frazzled, urgent look in his eyes.

I knew Nell had a sister. That she was pregnant. But Nell never mentioned a brother-in-law. I considered the chance he might be lying until Nell steps out of the backroom with Roger and immediately scowls.

"What are you doing here?"

Immediately, I'm on guard, ready to jump in to intervene and protect Nell from this intruder, no matter the cost.

"I need to talk to you," says Henry.

"Get out!" she yells. I've never seen such rage on her delicate features. It crushes me. I want to take her into my arms, shield her from the world, make sure nothing and no one can make her feel this negatively ever again.

If there was anything I could do to ensure Nell's life would be all smiles and rainbows from here on out, I would have already done it. Instead, I keep my eyes fixed on this Henry guy, fingers twitching to grab him by his collar and chuck him out of the store.

"Nell, please," Henry pleads. "At least tell me how Kate is doing."

"Better, without you." She marches forward and grabs him by the arm before proceeding to try and drag him out of the store. He stiffens, holding his place.

"Nell, please. I messed up. I know I did. But—"

"Get out, get out, get out!"

Nell's voice cracks. I take it like a whiplash to the heart.

"Eleanor." Roger's tone is commanding, but his expression stays gentle. Understanding.

Only then do I see the tears streaming down Nell's cheeks.

I step out from behind the counter. I pry Nell's hands loose from Henry's arm and push her behind me.

Henry towers over me at least five inches, but in the moment I'm not scared. Only determined.

"Go," I tell him. "You're not welcome here."

Henry's mouth opens. His expression hardens. His jaw clenches.

He stalks out of the store without another word.

I turn swiftly to check on Nell. She lets out a shaky breath and swipes at her cheeks with the heels of her palms.

"I'm sorry," she says, chuckling. "I don't know what got into me. I just—"

I shush her. "It's alright," I say. She doesn't have to explain anything. I know everything I need to: that she's hurting, that Henry had been the cause. I brush her hair away from her face and use my thumbs to swipe at her cheeks. He'll never step foot in this store ever again. In my head, I promise that to her.

"Thomas," Roger calls out to me. "Give Eleanor some space. I need your help with something."

I peer into Nell's teary eyes as if to ask for permission. *Ask me to stay*, I implore her in my head. *Let me be here for you.*

"Go," she says, squeezing my hip. Her touch lights a fire on my skin. "I'll be fine."

I comb my fingers through her bangs. Swipe at her cheeks once more. *I can stay. Please ask me to stay.*

She laughs and shoves me off.

"Go, Tom. I'm fine."

Nell

The advance from Roger helps settle our balance with the electric company. There's enough left to cover next month's bills, too. With the power on, the light returns home—both literally and figuratively.

I don't tell Kate about Henry's visit. I only hope he's smart enough not to visit the house when I'm gone, or I'll really get murderous.

In truth, I'd been anxious all week that Henry would dare make a return, but it seems he knows to leave it well enough alone.

I hope so, anyway.

Come Thursday, I'm helping Tom and Roger prepare for book club. I'm too immersed in Cecilia's journal—a mistake, if there ever was one, considering my reason for being here—so Roger allows me to opt out of presenting a passage onstage. Tom, on the other hand, isn't so lucky.

"You've dodged your duties long enough," Roger says. "I'm putting you first."

When the guests start arriving, Mildred and Annabel make a beeline towards me.

"Hi!" Annabel greets in a sing-song voice, pressing a kiss on both my cheeks before handing me over to Mildred, who wraps me in a hug. I never got to meet my lola, but I imagine this is what it must feel like to have one.

Mildred excuses herself to speak with Walter, this smartly dressed bald man with glasses who is inspecting the bottles of wine on the table, leaving me standing there with Annabel.

Annabel hooks her arm with mine and leads me to the front row, where I diligently take a seat next to her.

"I hear Tommy's playing today," Annabel says. She wiggles her brows at me. "Is he dedicating it to you?"

I nearly choke on my own spit. "What? No, it's not like that. He's seeing someone," I say. A little thrill ran through me earlier when Tom told me Paulina couldn't make it tonight. And then I felt stupid and pathetic for feeling that way, so I told him I was sorry and started avoiding him the rest of the night. I glance around the room and find him tuning his guitar in the corner. When our eyes meet, he smiles.

Darn that stupid, handsome smile.

Annabel's voice cuts through my train of thought. "Is he? Really?" She leans in conspiratorially. "And it's not you?"

"W–why would it be me?" I stammer. I avert my gaze to the shelves behind her, unable to meet her eyes.

"I don't know. You're the first girl he's shown an interest in as long as we've known him. Louis and I thought…" she trails off. "Well, I suppose we thought wrong. Are you presenting today?"

Shown an interest in? I'm desperate to ask what she means, but instead I shake my head. "Are you?"

She nods her head eagerly. "I've just finished reading *The Little Prince* with my twins. They didn't really get it but it moved me to tears. Such a great book." She fishes her copy out of her purse and shows me all the pages she'd bookmarked, with certain passages underlined several times in red ink.

Our conversation is cut short by Roger coming onstage.

"Another full house tonight," he says by way of greeting. "Thank you all for coming. I see some new faces, so let's take a moment to welcome everyone." Annabel claps her hands, so I follow suit.

"Tonight is a special night, because I've finally convinced my boy to play a song for us," says Roger.

"Get on with it!" Mildred yells from somewhere in the back of the room. The crowd breaks into poorly stifled laughter.

"Alright, alright. Thomas, get on up here." Roger beckons for Tom, who sheepishly steps on stage and grimaces at the spotlight in his eyes. Roger sets the mic on the stand, and I brace myself. This could either go really well, or really terribly.

"Uh, hi." The feedback from the microphone makes us all cringe. "Sorry. I—"

Annabel hoots. "Go Tom!"

He smiles sheepishly at her. His pale face has turned pink.

Our eyes meet again. I give him a small nod of encouragement.

He takes a deep breath. All the while, I'm thinking, *please don't sing "Wonderwall". Please* do not *sing "Wonderwall".*

"This is—uh—'These Streets'. Paolo Nutini. Good song."

Someone whistles from the back of the room. I glance back and see Louis grinning from ear-to-ear.

Tom begins to strum the guitar gently. I'm holding my breath. I remember liking his voice, but then again, I was twelve, going on thirteen. What if I'm remembering him as better than he was?

If his voice sounds like nails on a chalkboard, am I prepared to get up there and make a fool of myself so he doesn't have to do it alone?

All my worrying is for naught, because once Tom sings, my racing mind is stunned to silence. Contrary to his nervous demeanor, his singing voice is rich, smoky. More mature than I remember, and better, too. Even with his eyes closed, he is confident and self-assured. As if it was more natural for him to be singing than speaking. As if this was precisely what he was put on earth to do.

He sings with conviction, as if he'd written the lyrics himself. The rest of the world falls away, and it's only him, his guitar, and the warm spotlight on his face.

I have never seen him more at home.

When he finishes, the room is still. You could have heard a pin drop.

Then we erupt into cheers.

"I had no idea he could sing like that!" Annabel says to me, gripping my arm before clapping furiously. I clap with her until my palms are red and sore. Tom grins. His eyes find mine. I have to fight the urge to run up the stage and give him a big hug.

Fresh off the high of a well-received performance, Tom and I continue our lessons on love the rest of the week. A voice in my head tells me to hold still, just wait—eventually the other shoe will drop. But I ignore it; if it's not meant to last—nothing ever is—then I should still at least enjoy the good times while it's here. I need the memory of this to get me through whatever bullshit might come next.

During our lunch break, Tom flips through our shared notebook of romantic ideas. We're sitting on the floor in the back—or I am, and he's laying on his back while we share lumpia that Kate had made for me this morning.

"You think I should buy her flowers?" he asks.

"For your third date," I say. "The first two are too soon to tell, you know?"

"Okay," he says, then sets the notebook down. "Are you ever going to let me read your writing?"

"No."

"Why not?"

"Because." Because when I write, I am my most honest self. My most vulnerable. And if he makes fun of what I write, I'll never recover. I'll be too embarrassed to ever look him in the eye again. "I don't want you thinking the stories I write are my fantasies."

"So what if they are?"

"Then I don't want you thinking I write as a substitute for real life experiences."

"Do you?"

I keep my mouth shut. He takes my silence as an affirmative.

"Is that why you read romance novels?" Tom asks. I open my mouth to speak but find I don't know what to say. I guess? Maybe? *No.* I just like to read.

"I don't know," he says after some time. "I enjoy our lessons, but I still want the real thing."

I tell him about mirror neurons—how, when we read, our brains react as if we're experiencing what's happening on the page ourselves.

"Don't you want the real thing?" he asks. "For yourself, not through the lens of some fictional character, which in my opinion makes you even more far removed from the experience."

When did he get so opinionated?

"It's not in my cards," I say.

"What do you mean?"

"We've talked about this, Tom. What do you want me to say?"

"I don't know," he says. "The truth?"

I glare at him. "I *am* telling you the truth."

"Not all of it," he says. "I want to know everything there is to know about you." His eyes burn holes into mine. If I was the heroine of a romance novel, this is where I'd make my move. I'd grab him by the collar and kiss him and tell him, *there*. There's your truth.

Instead, I sigh. I tell him about Mama and her boyfriends and his stepmother's pearls. About the night Kate left. About how every single time I've witnessed someone I love fall in love, it ends in tragedy.

"I don't want that for myself," I say. "I'm content being alone."

"No man's an island," he offers. "And by your logic, that means if Paulina and I end up together—"

My heart seizes in my chest. "You're assuming I love you," I tell him, though the words come out less confident and teasing, more nervous and guilty.

He smirks. "Don't you?"

I toss the notebook at him. He dodges it and bursts out laughing.

"You're so annoying," I say, turning away so he won't see my burning cheeks.

"I'm sorry about my dad," he says. "He's a proper dickhead. But I still think you should give love a chance."

"It's going that well, huh?" I taunt. "You and Paulina?"

He shrugs. I hate how smug he's being. I hate that I find him even more handsome like this.

"Fine," I tell him. "Sit up."

"What?"

"Sit up and look at me and tell me who's going to love me."

Tom blinks at me.

"Sit up!"

"Alright, alright!" He sits up, dusting crumbs off his chest, and fixes his gaze on me.

"Now answer my question."

"Who's going to love you?" he asks.

"Yes. Romantically, so don't say you or Roger or Mildred, either."

He bites his lip.

"See? You can't even think of anyone."

"I don't know a lot of people!" he cries out, exasperated. "But I know lots of people would love you, Nelly, whether I know them or not. We've talked about this before, too."

Nelly. The nickname goes straight to my stomach.

I huff and turn away. "I'm not interested in lots of people."

"Then who are you interested in?"

There's a little voice in my head whispering the answer, but I picture myself clamping my hand over it. *We're not going there,* I tell myself. *Love makes fools of us all.*

"It doesn't matter," I finally say, crossing my arms.

"Sure it does. You're my friend. I care about you and what you think, what you have to say. So of course it matters. Of course it does." He's looking at me seriously, brows raised, eyes soft and encouraging.

Not going there. Not going there.

"Give me a name," he says. "No matter how outlandish or unlikely."

"Gee, thanks for the vote of approval, Tom."

"Stop stalling."

I rack my brain for a name, literally any name to get him to shut up. It's crazy that girls get a reputation for being obsessed with love when Tom here is proof that boys are just as obsessed with it, if not more so.

"Hugh Dancy," I say. "But specifically in *Ella Enchanted.* Very princely."

Tom furrows his brows. "Who?"

"Actor," I say, then shake my head. Mama used to say Tom would grow up to look just like Hugh Dancy as Prince Charmont. But why am I even entertaining this still? "It doesn't matter. I can't afford to pursue relationships right now. I have other stuff going on. More important than kissing and all that other stuff."

"What's more important than kissing?"

I quirk a brow at him only to realize, when I see the smirk on his face, that he's teasing me.

"You're the one who said love isn't always about sex," he says. "Is it? For you?"

"No," I say. "I don't know. Never had it."

We're silent. After a beat, he says, "Me neither."

"You neither, what?"

His cheeks are even pinker than his plump lips. "I've never had sex."

I burst out laughing, incredulous. "You? Never? Not even once." He shakes his head. "Not even a handy." He shakes his head again. "Never? Seriously?"

"Why are you so surprised?" he asks.

I stare at him, unsure how to answer. I mean, he's handsome. I thought for sure guys this handsome had that part easy, no matter how stupid with love they were.

"Nell," he says, "I needed your help asking a girl to grab coffee with me. What makes you think I'm in any way, shape, or form, pulling long enough to bed someone?"

I can't help it; I'm full-on cackling now. "That's so embarrassing," I tease, even though I don't mean it. The truth is that I'm relieved; what if I gave him advice and he was like, *no, actually, Nell—*

"Wow," he says, even though he's starting to laugh himself, too.

"Aren't you embarrassed?" I continue teasing him. "You're a virgin."

"Well, so are you," he says. "What, are you going to race me now? See who loses theirs first? I have a date this Saturday. I'm like, one step ahead of you."

I laugh harder.

"Stop laughing!" he cries out. "I want my first time to be special, okay? I want it to mean something."

I have tears in my eyes from laughing so hard. I can't find it in me to stop laughing long enough to say: me too, Tom. Me too.

Based on Cecilia's journals, she and Roger had a fairytale romance. All the planets aligned to get them together, from their mothers being schoolgirls together to them attending the same schools. They were always in each other's orbits. I can't imagine not loving someone who's been in your life the whole time. All those run-ins and missed opportunities were a mere spiral they were on until they caught up at the bottom, the final point, and fell in love.

Love, I learned, is the result of proximity—forced or otherwise—and a series of actions that build on one another. Showing up for each other when no one else does, in ways no one else could. No matter the trope—whether enemies to lovers or workplace romances, the two leads get to the bottom, to the heart of the other person, and find that it beats in sync with their own.

And then they can't let go.

Then, of course, there's the obvious biological function, the catharsis of pent-up tension, the bodily language of love which was sex. Tom and I left it largely alone; we figured, whichever one of us gets there first, we'd know what to do.

Separately, of course. I was pretty shocked when he said he's never been with anyone before, and then even more shocked when he was surprised that I was a virgin, too.

We're laying on the hardwood floor between two shelves during our break again, our new routine, listening to Neutral Milk Hotel's "In the Aeroplane Over the Sea" and getting cracker crumbs all over our chests.

"Do you believe in soulmates?" he asks.

"I didn't believe in love just a few days ago, Thomas," I say. "I'm still not sure I do."

He sits up and gapes at me. "Seriously? Even after we watched all those movies? You watched all those people declare their love for one another and thought, *nah*, this can't be real."

"It's fiction," I say.

"Roger and Cecilia's love wasn't fiction. You are literally laying in the proof of their love, and you tell me it wasn't real?"

"Okay, then the exception."

Tom lays back down with an exasperated sigh. "And you call me hopeless."

My phone beeps with an e-mail from Jane. I excuse myself to read it.

From: jane.waldron@vanguardproperties.com

To: eleanor.garcia@stcatherinesuni.edu

Subject: Progress?

Hi, Nell.

Any updates on your progress with Mr. Fitzgerald?

From: eleanor.garcia@stcatherinesuni.edu

To: jane.waldron@vanguardproperties.com

Subject: Re: Progress?

Hi, Jane!

Sorry for the delay in updates. As per my last e-mail, I informed you that Roger intends to leave the bookstore to my co-worker, Thomas Whelan, in the untimely event of Roger's demise. Seeing as that appears to be unlikely by the end of summer, our alternative is to bump up the offer to sweeten the deal of my pitch.

That said, Roger doesn't seem to be interested in the financial benefit of selling the store. He seems primarily concerned with his own mortality and what that will entail for Tom, who he seems to have taken in as his own son. If Tom is taken care of, I suspect there's nothing Roger won't agree to, hence my suggestion. The good news is Tom trusts me, although Tom is even more against selling the bookstore than Roger.

Might I suggest we send another agent to broach the subject more directly so I have an excuse to bring it up with them? It's difficult to discuss organically without giving myself away, so I feel that a 'trigger' would help our case immensely.

Let me know what you think!

Regards,
Nell

I return to Tom and set my phone on the table facedown, feeling like the world's worst friend. I have this urge to grab him by the shoulders and come clean. To ask him to help me so it wouldn't be so bad.

Or maybe I could leave. Run away again as Mama and I had several years ago, and never show my face to him ever again.

If he found out the truth, he would never forgive me. I know it.

"Who was that?" he asks.

"Just… school stuff," I mumble. "Reminding me of the upcoming school year and stuff."

He nods and presses play.

Tom

I take Paulina to Old Buoy, the seafood restaurant made to look like a shack across from Newbury beach. Like Amici's, it's another local institution, so much so that the owner—a big, burly man named Frank who looks like if Gandalf dressed only in tropical-printed button shirts and spent most of his days fishing—agreed to transfer to the boardwalk when Vanguard Properties finishes developing it rather than closing altogether.

The seashells hanging over the door clatter when Paulina and I enter. The wooden boards that make up the wall are a faded blue, and posters of ocean-themed illustrations are framed on them. Frank stands behind the counter in the corner of the room, reading *Moby Dick* for probably the hundredth time. He's always either doing that or smoking a cigar out front.

"Are you sure you want to eat here?" Paulina asks quietly as we walk up to the counter. "It's… *empty.*"

I bristle at the tone of her voice. I love this place. It might not be as snazzy or trendy as the newer restaurants in town—people line up for those in droves—but Old Buoy serves the best seafood on this side of the country. They do comfort food like no other.

"Their fish and chips are to die for," I tell her. "Trust me."

She wears a look of uncertainty, but to her credit, she gamely peruses the menu hanging behind Frank's head.

"Hey-o, Frankie-o," I greet, patting the bell on the counter to get his attention. He sighs and sets his book aside. He's a gruff guy, but I know he's soft on the inside. Get him drunk and he's the life of the party. He just doesn't do too well in the afternoon.

"What can I get ya, Tom?" he asks.

"I'll have the fish and chips, if you please," I tell him.

"And for the lady?"

Paulina regards him with a kind smile. "How's your clam chowder?"

I brace myself. Questioning the quality of Frank's menu is a no-no. I asked him about their lobster mac and cheese once, and he yelled at me, asking me if I thought he'd serve trash in his restaurant (again: gruff guy, but a real softie on the inside, I swear).

To my surprise, Frank grins. His teeth are yellowed from smoking cigars, and there's one missing in the top row.

"It's the best of the best," he says to her.

"Then I *have* to have it," she replies.

"What the lady wants, the lady gets." He rings us up and barks the order to his kitchen staff while I lead Paulina to a booth by the front.

"I can't believe it," I tell her. "How did you do that?"

She tilts her head to the side, the perfect picture of innocence. "Do what?"

"Dazzle him. Frank's notoriously hard to please." Not that I can blame him for being dazzled by her. When she looks at you and gives you her attention, she makes you feel special. It's why I liked her all those years ago.

Paulina laughs. "I just smile and make my voice sound as sweet as possible."

"And here I thought it was natural." It's a joke, but when Paulina doesn't reply, I worry I've said the wrong thing.

If Nell were here, she would tell me. She'd whack me upside the head and feed me a line to change the subject with.

I wonder, rather suddenly, whether Frank would take to Nell as quickly as he'd taken to Paulina.

I can't help but smile when I realize he would. Nell's hard not to like, even when she thinks otherwise.

"I went back to Henwick the other day," Paulina says, rousing me out of

125

my reverie at the mention of our hometown. "It was my little brother's birthday."

Paulina has caught me up to most of everything since I left: her parents got divorced and her dad started a new family with his much younger girlfriend (much to her mother's chagrin) but at least Paulina got a younger brother out of it, which she's always wanted.

"Oh, how old is he now?"

She holds out her palm and beams. "Four!"

"Wow," I say, because how else am I supposed to react to someone's younger brother turning four? I pinch the inside of my elbow on behalf of Nell. I can hear her voice in my head tell me I'm being an idiot.

Paulina is undeterred by my lack of social prowess. "You'll never believe who I ran into, either." She pauses for effect, then leans over the table and says, "Finn! Remember? Your best friend?"

My heart nearly drops out of my ass. How could I forget? He was like a brother to me.

Is he mad at me, I wonder? Does he hate me now? I bet he does. I dropped off the face of the earth. I'd hate me, too.

"H–How's he doing?" I stammer.

"Alright, I think. I told him we were seeing each other, and he said that was nice. I invited him to come round. It'd be nice, don't you think? To get together again?"

"Yeah," I mumble. "Sure." My heart hammers in my chest. Black splotches cloud my vision. No matter how rapidly I blink, they won't go away.

Never mind that Paulina just said we were seeing each other. I can't focus on anything else but the panic rising in my chest. If it were Nell sitting in front of me, I wouldn't have to hide this. I could just tell her how I'm feeling, and she'd sit next to me and hold my hand until the terrors subside.

Paulina's voice cuts through the ringing in my ears. "He's working in Hetford now, so it was such a nice coincidence that we were in town at the same time. His sister's getting married next year and—"

Frank sets down two paper cups and a pitcher of water on our table. With shaky hands, I pour myself a drink. The cold water slides down my throat, helping somewhat.

Paulina doesn't seem to notice I'm in a crisis. She carries on talking, about something now or another, but I'm not listening.

I stand, quickly excusing myself and then going to the restroom. Paulina must think I've got a bad stomach at this point, but it's fine, it's fine. I just need some space to get my head on straight.

I fumble for my phone in my back pocket and take it out. There are no notifications, no texts from Nell to anchor myself to.

I want to call her, to ask her for advice, but she's probably busy. Anyway, if I do that, I'll probably be letting her down. All those lessons and I'm still ill-equipped to go on dates. She'll drop me, for sure.

I open my photo library and scroll instead for the clips we took when we were testing my new camera. I transferred them to my phone to check the quality, and boy am I thankful. I press play and Nell's face fills the screen; her laughter echoes in the bathroom.

I'm telling her to stop making faces, but she keeps throwing up peace signs and sticking her tongue out.

"Nell, I'm serious. Sit still," my voice comes from behind the camera.

Nell sits but strikes a pose. *"Like this?"*

Her voice soothes me.

I hear myself sigh in the video. *"Okay, can you just—Tell me something about yourself. I'm trying to see if the audio quality's any good."*

Finally, she sits upright and stares into the camera. My heart slows to a steady rhythm.

"I'm Eleanor Garcia, but you can call me Nell. I like books and cats, even though I'm allergic to them. And… my best friend is Thomas Whelan, who is a dork and currently behind the camera."

"You're just saying that."

"No, I'm serious."

"I'm actually your best friend?"

"No, you're a dork."

I laugh. In the video and in real life.

I can always count on Nell to make me feel better.

Always.

After Old Buoy, Paulina takes me for a stroll along one of the newer streets. She links her arm in mine, showing me this store and that, and the whole time I'm sweating, thinking, *how do you walk normally again?*

Turns out I can't balance having a girl on my arm and walking at the same time.

"Don't take this the wrong way," Paulina says, "but next time, I'm picking where we're eating."

"You didn't like Old Buoy?" I ask.

"It's alright," she says. "I prefer the restaurants in this area."

This area feels like it's in an entirely different town altogether. I don't recognize a single thing about this new Newbury, with the shiny storefronts and expensive cars parked along the curb.

It unsettles me to think we're only a few blocks away from Second Chance Books. How can something like this, so devoid of personality and color, exist so close to home?

I want the old Newbury back. I want the shabby storefronts and the locals who've left. I want a girl who likes Old Buoy as much as I do.

I swallow down that last thought.

You're being unfair, Nell's voice in my head says. *What if she just doesn't like seafood? That's not enough to cast judgement on her. Who knows? Maybe you'll like the restaurant she picks, even if it's new.*

"Are you ever going to properly introduce me to your boss?" Paulina asks.

"What do you mean?" I ask. "He knows you already. You gave him your number to give to me."

Paulina laughs. "You're so adorable, Tommy," she says before pressing a kiss to my cheek. It's wet and sticky on my skin. I have a strong urge to wipe it against my shoulder.

"I think he's at the store right now," I tell her. "Do you want to go meet him? Again?"

She nods her head vigorously. I lead her down the street and the few blocks it takes to get to Second Chance Books.

There, Roger is reading *When Breath Becomes Air* by Paul Kalanithi. He looks up when we enter and smiles warmly, though his smile is interrupted by a hacking cough.

I pull away from Paulina to move towards him. "Are you okay?"

He waves me off. "Just swallowed my own spit. Ignore me. Hello again, Paulina. Did you two have a nice time?"

I barely have to do the introductions because Paulina steps forward and does all the talking. She sits across from Roger, leaving me to sit between them.

Their conversation flies from one topic to the other, and Roger laughs louder than I've heard him laugh in a while when Paulina tells her version of the night I left.

"I genuinely thought he was on drugs," she says. "I was so worried about him. If I'd known he was completely sober—"

"I mean, I told you," I interject, unable to hide the slight irritation in my voice. "You wouldn't believe me."

Roger pats my lap. He turns the subject to books and invites Paulina to the next club meeting. She promises to be there just as her phone rings.

"Oh, gosh," she says, rising suddenly. "I'm so sorry but I have to go. It was so nice meeting you properly, Roger."

My brows furrow. I cleared the whole day for her. Where was she going now? "Do you want me to drive you?"

Paulina waves me off. "My friend is picking me up." As if not wanting me to be jealous, she adds, "She's a girl."

"Right." I meet Roger's gaze and clear my throat. "I'll walk you outside."

When I return to the bookstore, Roger's staring at me inquisitively.

"What?" I ask.

He purses his lips and shakes his head. "Nothing."

"Yeah, right," I snort. "What did you think of her?"

Roger shrugs. "She's alright."

"Just alright?"

"I can think of someone else who'd be better for you."

This time, it's my turn to stare at him.

He throws his hands up in the air in exasperation. "I'm too old to beat around the bush. You've given it a go. Why don't you ask Nell out on a date, see how it goes?"

I'm surprised by how quickly I answer. "She doesn't like me like that."

"Like hell, she doesn't."

"What do you mean, *'like hell, she doesn't?'* Don't make it weird. Nell and I are friends. That's it."

Roger huffs.

"Roger!" I cry. "Did she say something? What do you know?" This man is about to have me analyzing every single interaction I have with Nell, and I can't afford that. I've made that mistake once—and sure, I've just gone on a date with the girl I made that mistake to, but Nell is too special, far too precious to lose over a wrong assumption.

"I don't know anything," Roger says as he slowly rises from his seat. I reach forward to assist him but he waves me off. "It's not like I was married for years and years."

Nell

Another weekend spent refreshing my email over and over, waiting for Jane's reply while taking care of my sister and being filled with the anxiety of someone being hunted for sport. Tom's on a date with Paulina, and I'm sure it's going well. I bet he's taking her to his room and singing her a song and then she'll lean over and kiss him and then—

My phone beeps. My hand flies towards it before I've even registered my hope that it'll be Tom texting me another SOS, giving me an excuse to break him out of there.

Why would I even want that?

I'm happy for him. Paulina is the perfect girl for him. She's beautiful, and pretty, and she's known him forever, and I might not know her, but I know Tom, and I know he wouldn't like anyone who wasn't at least nice.

Instead of Tom, my bank is informing me of a transfer totaling a month's worth of salary working at the bookstore. I sit up, confused. Surely there's been a mistake?

I can't accept this. This is too much.

Maybe Roger forgot to stop auto-payments?

Yes, of course. That must be it. I'll go there and I tell him, and if Tom and

Paulina happen to be there… Well, that's just a happy coincidence, isn't it?

"Eleanor!" Roger beams when I enter the store. "I wasn't expecting to see you today."

"Roger," I say. There are no signs of Tom and Paulina around. I swallow my disappointment—I shouldn't even *be* disappointed—and focus on Roger.

He holds up a hand and grunts as he sits down. Then he gestures for me to continue. "I think there's been a mistake." I tell him about the money and he chuckles.

"That's not a mistake, Eleanor," he says. "That's your salary."

"But you already gave me an advance."

He shakes his head. "Not an advance. A gift."

What? But—

"You needed help. I was in a position to help you." He lifts one shoulder. "It's that simple."

I gape at him. No one has ever given me that much money before—not without expecting anything in return.

As if on cue, Tom emerges from the door behind the counter, freshly showered.

Fuck.

They've done it. I'm sure they have. I bet they told each other they loved each other and—

Tom smiles at me encouragingly. I snap my eyes away from him and back to Roger.

I can't help it. I ask, "Why?"

"Why not? I've lived a long life. I've saved up enough over the years. I'm old. That money won't be of use to me for long."

"*Roger.*" Tom's tone is curt, chastising.

"What? It's true!" Roger laughs. "It's my money. If I want to give it to you, Eleanor, you can't tell me I can't."

My lip quivers. I feel a surge of fondness wash over me. I lurch and throw my arms around him in a tight hug.

Roger laughs and pats my back. "Love is given, dear Eleanor, remember? Not earned."

I squeeze him tighter. He is too good for this world.

Which makes what I'm doing all the more difficult.

I push all thoughts of Tom and Paulina away to realign my focus on convincing Roger to sell, and helping Tom with the interviews so I don't blow my cover.

On Thursday, we visit Annabel in her apartment to conduct the interview. She lives on the third floor of one of the newly built brick flats near High Street, and we circle the street a few times in search of the right one because there were rows of them, all identical. When we find it, there are the stairs to take, and the long sunlit corridor to pass in search of her unit.

There's a pep in Tom's step that's no doubt because of Paulina. I keep my distance—if not for me, then for my twelve-year-old self.

We ring the bell and wait outside the door for Annabel to let us in. I tell Tom I'm ready to take over. Annabel's a single mother to twins; there were things I wanted to ask that I could maybe share with Kate.

She still cries every night, my sister; for different reasons now that all our bills have been settled. Is it Henry? The pregnancy hormones? A combination of the two? I catch her staring at her reflection in the mirror sometimes, usually when I'm on my way out; she smooths her hand down her bump, and then her face crumples as she starts to cry.

Once, late at night, she asked me whether I thought she'd turn out like Mama. Before I could answer, she laughed and told me *never mind, good night, go to bed.*

"Hi!" Annabel greets us cheerfully when she opens the door. I'm struck all over again by how beautiful she is: dark braided hair, big brown eyes, and the sweetest smile. She's dressed in a white blouse and dark jeans, a simple outfit by any means, but she looks almost fresh out of the runway.

"Come in, come in! I'm so sorry about the mess. I haven't had time to clean in between work and getting the kids ready for their summer programs. Ewan's in football, you know, and Evelyn's taking ballet." She trips on a toy firetruck but catches herself in time. "Ewan! I told you to tidy up after yourself, darling, please!"

The mess she pertains to is an explosion of toys littered about the living room. Dolls and stuffed toys and miniature cars on neon tracks. Ewan comes racing out from his bedroom to collect his belongings, scarcely saying a word to either of us.

"I'm really so sorry," Annabel says.

"It's no problem at all, Annie," Tom says, offering her a reassuring smile. Annabel visibly relaxes, as if those were the exact words she'd been dying to hear this whole time.

"Would it be alright if we filmed in the kitchen?" she asks. "It's the only place I get any semblance of peace and quiet these days."

"Of course," Tom says. Annabel leads the way. As Tom begins to set up, I take my chance and step towards her.

"Motherhood is tough," I say. "Not that I'd know."

"Count your blessings," she says. "It's a thankless job. Even though it's oh-so-rewarding all the same, if I could go back in time with the guarantee that I'd end up with the same two lovable buggers I have now, I'd tell myself to hold off a little longer. Your twenties are for getting drunk with your girl friends and not changing diapers and getting puked on."

"I hope you're getting enough rest?"

"Not nearly enough," she admits. "But Louis comes over sometimes. Takes the twins out to the park so I can sleep in."

Oh, they definitely like each other.

I don't know the best way to segue into my question, so I just go for it. "My sister's expecting soon. But, like—it's complicated." She cants her head to the side. I take that as invitation to expound. "Her husband—"

"Let me guess," Annabel cuts me off. "Cheated?"

"No, actually. Just left, but… is it that common?"

"You'd be surprised."

"I was hoping maybe—"

Annabel turns away from me and towards the counter, where she tears a piece of paper from a memo pad and scribbles on it with a pen. "Say no more," she says. "Us girls have to stick together." She hands me the paper, her number now scribbled on it, and flashes me a smile. *A sign.* Mama's sent us an angel. "Give this to your sister and tell her to call me, okay? If she has any questions or needs advice, I'm here."

I stare at the numbers, dumbfounded.

Just like that?

"It really takes a village," Annabel says to me as if sensing my confusion. "I don't think I'd have survived without all the help I'd received in those early days. My ex-husband was a cheat, so I know all about it."

I'm reminded of what Roger said: that love is freely given, not earned.

"Okay, guys," Tom exhales. The camera stands proudly on the tripod next to him. "Ready?"

Annabel grins at me. "Ready."

Annabel

NELL: Hi, Annabel. Could you introduce yourself to our viewers, please?

ANNABEL: Do I look at the camera?

TOM: You could, but Mildred and Louis spoke directly to me, so—

ANNABEL: No, right, that looks more professional. Okay. *[clears throat]* Hi, I'm Annabel Murray. I'm twenty-eight now, and I'm the proud mother of two kids—one boy, one girl.

NELL: And when did you first start visiting Second Chance Books?

ANNABEL: Two years ago!

NELL: How did you find out about it?

ANNABEL: Well, I work as a receptionist for a dentist's office nearby. At that time, I was only applying for the job and I'd gotten the hours mixed up. Wait, no, I hadn't; they just moved my interview to after lunch due to an emergency procedure, and it was Saturday so all the places were full—as you can imagine. Evelyn gets a bit cranky when she's overstimulated, so I was looking for a quiet place for us to go when we came across it. Tom was dozing off behind the counter, I remember, and Ewan thought that we'd wandered into Santa Claus' home when he saw Roger reading a book.

I'd frozen in place because, I mean, when you're the mother of two kids, you become hyper aware of other adults who might not want your kids around when they're enjoying their leisure time, especially not kids like Ewan who are so rambunctious when they want to be. But Roger smiled at me and said hello, welcome, and I remember—gosh, I'll never forget the look on his face when Ewan asked if he was Santa Claus.

Do you remember what he said, Tom? He said, "No, but I could be." And he let my kids pick out any book they wanted—I was afraid they'd pick up something raunchy or traumatic but turns out there was a section for kids' books—and he gave it to them as a gift.

When my interview came, the twins didn't want to leave, so he promised me they could keep reading there and he'd keep them safe. I was nervous, of course, but I felt that I could trust him. If it had gone any other way, this would be a completely different interview, but thank God, am I right?

NELL: No, for sure. And how soon after that did you join the book club?

ANNABEL: A year after, I think, so just last year. Around that time. My marriage was falling apart and I needed an excuse to get out of the house, a safe place to spend time with my kids as my ex and I sorted it all out.

I say 'sorted' but it was more like we hashed it out, we fought. Sometimes I'd go to book club meetings with red eyes and Roger would let my kids run around and sit me in the backroom so I could have a private space to cry.

Then Mildred caught on, and Mildred's had two divorces, so she was like, an expert at these things. I'm allowed to say that; she says it herself. *[laughs]* So she starts visiting me in the back and talking to me and coaxing me out of my shell, and then she introduced me to Louis, who met my kids first funnily enough, and we've been friends ever since.

NELL: What would you say you like the most about book club?

ANNABEL: Wow. Huh. Let me think.

Well, it's like family, isn't it? It's this warm, welcoming place where everyone pitches in to help one another. There's so much love to go around—love for books, love for each other.

You know some of the members attended Evelyn's recital last year? You were there, Tom. Remember?

TOM: Yeah. She did the little spin thing.

ANNABEL: A pirouette! Yeah!

NELL: Does she have another one later this year?

ANNABEL: Yes! You should come! Bring your sister! I mean, if the baby's not born yet, or if she has time after.

NELL: I'll tell her.

So, Annabel, our final question: do you have a favorite memory from book club, and could you share it with us, please?

ANNABEL: Well, it's not so much an event as a moment in time where I distinctly felt that I was home there. I'd found it, my place, my people.

I'd spent all my girlhood searching for that feeling of safety and belonging, and I looked for it in all the wrong places, the wrong people. It wasn't until Louis got up on that stage and read *The Orange* by Wendy Cope that I found it.

And for the first time in my life, I loved and felt loved and didn't doubt it. I had no doubts at all.

Nell

God is punishing me. He knows that I know what I'm doing is terrible, and that's why there's been a barrage of my introductions to the sweetest, kindest people I've ever met.

Can't the people of Second Chance Books all just be assholes? That would make my job so much easier.

Tom's leg is bouncing as he drives us back to the bookstore. He must be excited to see Paulina, who's coming later tonight.

We prepare wordlessly for book club. I go out to buy more cheese and wine from the deli. Attendees come alone, then in pairs, then in groups. I'm arranging the cheese board when I hear Tom greet Paulina. I watch as he pulls her into his arms. Her eyes close, her perfect face tucking into the crook of his neck.

Must be nice.

Try as I might to fight it, to be a modern girl of the twenty-first century who would make any feminist proud, the mean green monster of my envy rears its ugly head. Paulina hasn't even done anything wrong. She just exists, and for some reason, her mere existence is a reminder of all the ways in which I fall short.

I will never be the kind of girl someone will look at and pine over for as long as Tom's pined over Paulina. If I wore half the things she did, I would look like a child playing dress up in her mother's closet. She looks like she walked straight off the runway, beautiful in every way. Perfect, even.

I look in the mirror and it's like my skin doesn't even fit right over my bones.

I just have to accept that Paulina is privy to the secrets of femininity that I will never have access to. *Ever.*

But there's room for both of us, right?

"Hello, darling." Mildred's cold hands cup my cheeks. She's dressed in bright red today: a red polka dot blouse, a swishy maroon maxi skirt, and burgundy velvet loafers. She looks like a pomegranate or an apple in the best way.

I startle. "Mildred! Are you cold? Would you like some cheese?"

She laughs and waves me off. "I was just coming to say hi."

I stuff my hands into my pockets. "Hi."

She glances over her shoulder. I follow her gaze to where Paulina and Tom are laughing by the door.

"Who is that?" she asks.

"Paulina," I say. "Tom's... I don't know. Future girlfriend, I think."

"I thought that was you?"

I nearly choke on my own spit. "What? No." I force a laugh, as if she'd said something hilarious. "We're just—no." I bite my lip. "What gave you the impression, though?"

Mildred gives me a look. "I'm old enough to recognize the signs. It's not new to me anymore."

Signs?

She gestures her head towards where Louis and Annabel are chatting. Snippets of their conversation float towards us, something about his work and her twins. "You see the way they look at each other?"

"Yeah," I breathe. Like the other hung the moon in the sky, just for them. There's a reverence in his eyes he reserves only for when he's looking at her. She glows when she's in his presence.

But Tom and I don't look at each other like that. *Do we?*

Mildred pats me on the cheek and returns to her seat.

The book club goes by without a hitch—for the most part. I jot down the interesting books people mention: Jorge Luis Borges's *The Library of Babel*, *Walden* by Henry David Thoreau, *Piranesi* by Susanna Clarke, and *Beartown* by Fredrik Backman. Then Mildred calls me up onstage. She invites everyone to give me a warm welcome and a round of applause.

My eyes bulge open. I twist backward to make sure there hasn't been a mistake. Maybe there's another Nell Garcia somewhere in this room?

My eyes meet Tom's, and he hoots and hollers. Paulina laughs next to him and claps. Annabel leans forward and pushes me off my seat. Dumbstruck, I find my way to the stage. Mildred hands me the wireless microphone. The bluetooth speaker Tom had dragged out from Roger's room crackles next to me.

Okay, Nell. You can do this. All you have to do is read a passage from something you read and explain why you like it.

Except I hadn't prepared anything. I hadn't even volunteered. I open and close my mouth. In the back, I see Paulina cover her face and lean into Tom. Jealousy pricks me in my racing heart.

In the front row, Roger throws me two thumbs up.

"Hi," I say, if only to buy myself more time. I could go into the shelves and pick out a copy of Daphne du Maurier's Rebecca, but that would take too much time. I don't even know if we have a copy, and I left mine at home.

So I recite the only poem I've ever memorized, the first poem I ever "got": E.E Cummings' *[i carry your heart with me(i carry it in]*.

I go slowly so I don't stumble through my words. I fix my gaze on the bell hanging over the door, right above Tom's head, so I don't have to meet anyone's eyes. My body quivers from nerves, and with it, my voice. When I finish, the room is silent. Expectant.

"I—uh—found that poem right after my mom died," I start. "I couldn't sleep, so I'd go to the living room where my sister's in-laws kept all their books." We were living with Henry's parents at that time, right before their wedding. I tell the crowd how I found a collection of poetry, this thick tome with verse still impenetrable by my novice mind until I reached E.E. Cummings' poem tucked in the middle and everything clicked. I read it over and over until I memorized it and could recite it to myself in bed. It was a small comfort in a time of great stress. The first time literature had *literally* saved my life.

I press my lips together. "It's even more interesting to see on paper. E.E. Cummings"—at this, I hear someone snicker. My eyes snap to the source of the sound and find Paulina's hand clamped over her mouth. I draw in a breath and proceed. "He was really playful with his punctuation. Didn't use capital letters and all of that. A better writer would be able to give a more in-depth analysis of why, or what it means. But I just like it. And I think sometimes liking things are enough."

I stand there for a second longer before holding the mic out to Mildred. She reclaims her spot on stage and the crowd politely applauds me at her instruction. Annabel pats me on the shoulder, and Roger tells me I did a good job.

I blink back the inexplicable tears that have formed in my eyes.

Paulina lingers as we pack up for the night. I feel her even when I don't see her, like a fly buzzing nearby. She disappears behind the shelves, at which point Tom approaches me.

"I like the poem you read," he says. "Probably because you read it."

Please don't. I'm exhausted. It's one thing to have to interact with strangers, and another to get up on stage to read to a room full of them. I just want to crawl under the covers and sleep forever.

"Hey, listen," Tom says, placing a hand to stop me from stacking the used paper cups to be tossed with the rest of the trash. "Paulina asked me to drive her home. You can wait for me here and I'll come back for you. I'll give you my keys so you can rest upstairs."

I clench my jaw. "Don't bother."

He blinks, taken aback.

"Sorry, I just mean—go. Don't worry about me." I force a smile to my lips. "I'll be fine."

"But—"

"Go."

Tom gives me a look: *Are you sure?*

I nod. Paulina emerges from the shelves and I give her a wave. She waves back.

Tom pats me on the arm. "Thanks, Nell."

"Sure."

I watch as they exit the store and into the night. Paulina hooks her arm around Tom's, and I get this feeling in my chest. Like there it is: the other shoe, dropping, dropping, *fallen.*

Tom

The road to Paulina's apartment is newly paved, smoother than anywhere else in town. She lives in one of the newer, pricier apartments in Newbury, even newer than Annabel's, a couple minutes out from High Street and closer to the beach. There's a lot more shops open here, none of them local, all of them higher end with products that cost premium prices, and the streets are brightly lit by high-powered streetlamps. Driving here feels like driving in an entirely different town altogether. You used to be able to see the beach from here, a damned good view at that, but now it's blocked by her building, as if only the residents of her apartment were entitled to that beauty.

She switches the radio off when the car sputters to life and turns the air-conditioning way up. "It's so humid out," she says by way of explanation. I can't shake the feeling that it should be Nell in the passenger seat, not her.

After Roger suggested I date Nell, I haven't been able to get it out my mind. Holding her hand, going on dates with her. I know it's wrong, and I know I shouldn't, but she's the last thing I think of when I go to bed, and the first when I wake in the morning.

It's just a little thought experiment anyhow. I'm certain there are no romantic feelings there from either side.

Still. I'm itching to get this ride over with so I can spend an hour singing along to the radio with Nell while I drive her home.

"Did you have fun?" I ask, slowing at a stoplight. Paulina nods her head vigorously.

"So much," she says. "I'm thinking of getting up there next time. I mean, surely I can't do worse than your co-worker." At this, she guffaws. My brows furrow.

"Nell?"

"Yeah? That's her name, right? The one who cried immediately after she got off-stage? My God, I felt so sorry for her. I mean, why even sign up—"

"I don't think she did. Sign up, I mean." I tighten my grip on the steering wheel and fix my gaze on the road ahead. The light turns green. The car rolls forward, and I fight the urge to stamp on the gas to get her home as quickly as possible. *Since when was Paulina such a mean girl?*

"I think Nell did great," I say after some time.

"Oh, sure, of course," she says. "I didn't mean that she was terrible. Just seemed a little unprepared compared to the others, that's all."

We arrive at her building. She stalls, so I unbuckle my seatbelt, get out the car, and open her door for her. I walk her to her front door, where she stalls yet again. I can tell she wants me to kiss her. I want her to go home and leave me alone already.

"Well," I say, gesturing to her door. "Good night."

Paulina bites her lip. She bats her lashes at me. I will myself to feel as I once had, but no dice. I can't get the music started in my head, no ancient song, no melody—not like when I'm with Nell.

"I'll see you soon?" Paulina asks, fumbling with the keypad next to the glass door.

"Sure," I say. I hold my breath when she presses a kiss to my cheek, close enough to the corner of my lips that if I'd turned, we'd have been kissing. I offer her a small smile. I wait until she disappears into the lobby before returning to the car and driving home.

At the bookstore, Roger is inspecting the shelves nearest to the counter.

"Where's Nell?" I ask.

"Gone home," Roger says simply.

Oh. "I told her to wait for me."

Roger simply shrugs.

My disappointment is telling. I shouldn't have driven Paulina home. I should have kept my promise to Nell.

I should have realized sooner that what I felt for her was more than just platonic.

I meet Nell at the Cerulea National Museum in Hetford, a two-hour drive from Newbury. It's one of the oldest buildings in Cerulea, with a grand façade adorned with intricate carvings and columns reminiscent of Greek architecture. It stands tall and proud, a testament to Cerulea's rich history.

I used to spend my breaks between college lectures exploring the exhibits, given I refused to dorm in the city and couldn't just drive back and forth between Newbury and Hetford so easily.

I've always felt like walking between exhibits is like jumping through time or watching Cerulea in fast-forward. You see portraits from the days of Cerulean nobility in one room, and then you see modern exhibits with thought-provoking and interactive art in another. There's a feeling of reverence in the air all throughout.

I was pleasantly surprised when Nell asked to meet there instead of the bookstore, but who am I to say no?

"Hey, Tom," she greets when I walk up the stone steps to the front of the neoclassical building where Bobby worked as a security guard. She's wearing loose dungarees over an oversized white shirt. I'm struck by her beauty, the kind that's slow to sink in, a wrecking ball in a pool of honey, but stays with you for the rest of your life. Changes you forever. Fills you and makes you fall in love.

Something shifts in me. I don't know what. But there's something. Whatever it is, I know I can't keep going the way I have. I look at her and I hear the music; everything sings. And when you fancy yourself a musician like I do, you'd be stupid not to face it at one point or another.

I follow her inside. I pay for our tickets because Bobby, our next interviewee, isn't getting out of night shift until nine, and it was only eight.

"How'd it go last night?" she asks.

"With Paulina? It was okay." *I wish I'd driven you home instead.*

Nell clears her throat. "Did you kiss her?" Her smile is stiff but when we meet eyes, she wiggles her brows.

"No," I say pointedly.

"Tom!" she cries out, exasperated. A staff member glares at us and I smile apologetically before dragging Nell into the next room, displaying abstract art from Cerulean artists.

"What?"

"That was your shot. She asked you to drive her home. Did you walk her up to her front door at least?"

"The front door of her building, yeah."

Nell blows out a breath. Strands of her short hair fly away from her face.

"Did I have to go all the way up to her apartment door?"

"Yes, *duh.*"

Seriously? But I didn't want to. "Isn't that overkill?"

"How else is she going to invite you inside?"

I just shrug and say, "Maybe next time."

"So there is a next time? You secured that, at least?"

I give her a look.

"I've held up my end of the deal," she says to me. "It's your turn."

Oh. For a second, I thought maybe she was just invested in me. Or not me—my love life. "Well, what do you want to hear?"

She shrugs. "I don't know. How are you feeling? Are there sparks?"

"Sure," I say.

"So when you see her next—"

"I'll kiss her and then tell you how it went."

"Well, not specifically in that order."

I laugh. "Why not?"

"Because you should only kiss someone if they consent. And if the situation calls for it. And if you want to. *Obviously.*"

"Obviously," I echo.

A little voice in my head asks: *is the situation calling for it now?*

I can't stop thinking about it. About tucking her hair behind her ear and cupping her cheek. Pushing the straps of her dungarees off her shoulder.

Hearing what kind of sounds she'd make if I—

"Oh, look!" She runs towards the museum's latest exhibit, cutting my train of thought. It's displayed in a vast white room, a dark line slashing through the walls marked by years that trace Cerulean history. There are displays of old pots and pans dug up by archaeologists, a diary some two hundred years old, and some clothes depicting the average style of a Cerulean resident in the 1700s.

My fingers itch to take a photo. I pull the camera out of the bag and hold it to my eye. I wait for Nell to wander into frame and—*click*. She glances back at me questioningly. I shrug.

We wander down the aisle. There are photo albums you can flip through, displaying vintage photos of people and places that no longer exist.

It reminds me of that trip Roger and I took to his hometown. We took a photo that sits framed in my room now, of the two of us standing next to this field near his childhood home.

The first settlers of Cerulea had lived there. I remember, looking at the empty patch of grass where a great hall once stood, being seized by the desire to record this: my being alive, Roger's. I wanted not just to learn about the lives that were lived there, the happiness that was had whether shared or alone, but to document my own so that one day, some schmuck a hundred years from now will have an answer when they look at the rubble of where I lived and loved.

I told Roger this, my fascination with the quiet parts of history—what becomes of their happiness when everyone who remembers it is gone?—and its intersection with this new desire to record it. That's why Roger gave me my first camera when we got home, and why I took History in uni. After that, I filmed everything: the way slanted sunshine sinks into the room through the spaces between buildings, the look of concerted effort on Mildred's face as she tried to decide between two books before ultimately buying both as she always does. Roger's laugh, which came so frequently I eventually stopped recording because it sounded as familiar as my own breathing.

But so far, my collection of photographs and short clips have been just that: a collection of random, almost disparate things in my day-to-day life. Things that, as you're living, seem of little to no importance.

But looking at this album, I realize I'm not taking them for me. I'll print out the best ones and keep them in an album. And one day I'll drop it off at an antique store and spend the rest of my life wondering how far in the world it's traveled. If it survives, which I hope it does. Then soon enough I'll be dead and no one will remember and a historian or a researcher will happen up on it and it will have clues to how a guy like me lived in a time like this. Like when those scientists put those songs and that letter in that spaceship in case it makes contact with alien life. *Hi, hello, how do you do?*

I hope, selfishly, that they'll see the outtakes I took of Nell and know for sure that she was loved. If not by many, then by me.

The thought startles me. I watch Nell inspect the other displays and am overcome by fondness for her.

Of course I love her. Nothing else makes sense until I accept that.

I take another photo of Nell. I don't want to just remember her in this moment, quiet, like this. I want the rest of the world to remember her, too.

I might not have achieved much—I certainly don't think I'll be remembered for anything—but how many emperors have died in obscurity? I'm not interested in the exception, and I know—I imagine this part of me stretching out into the future, finding a home in somebody new. They'll wonder the same thing, too. And because of Roger, because of the very first camera he gave me, enabling me to pursue this hobby, they'll have an answer. I'll make sure of it.

We wait for Bobby in the courtyard where food stalls offer a wide array of drinks and snacks. Nell had purchased some churros, and because you can't eat inside the museum, we sit side-by-side on a bench while she eats.

"Didn't you say you took up History in uni?" she asks.

"Uh-huh." I wipe chocolate from the side of her mouth with my thumb. Before I've thought about it, I've sucked it off my finger.

If Nell notices, she doesn't say anything.

"What was it like?" she asks instead.

Lonely, for the most part. I kept to myself, afraid to make any friends, still traumatized from what I'd done and why I'd done it. I was constantly worried about running into someone from home, of the questions they might have, and of my answers reaching my family.

"It was alright," I tell her. "Not for me."

"How come you didn't take up music?"

I shrug. "It's always been my dad's thing." For a time, I couldn't pick up a single instrument without feeling like it would alert him to my presence. And anyway, I'm pretty sure my former bandmates hate me now, for ditching when I had.

"So? He doesn't own it," she says.

I snort. "Why don't you tell him that?"

She holds her churros out to me. I politely decline.

"Did you ever feel lonely?" she asks. "In school?" I look over at her and she's staring out at the distance.

I nod. "Even outside of it."

"Really?"

"Yeah. Like, I mean, I know I have Roger and the club members now, but at that time, I was new to it all and so I didn't really... fit in. You know?"

She nods. And to my surprise, I feel seen. I believe her. I know she's not just nodding to be polite or to keep the conversation going. It's not fucking ping-pong. It's real.

"You never told me how you wound up here," she says quietly. So I tell her. About Greg. About Paulina. About running, and the bus ride, and passing out on the street. I tell her all of it, not holding back.

"Well, of course she rejected you," she says with an incredulous laugh. "I would have too if it turned out a guy who I thought was my friend was only my friend because he liked me."

My jaw drops. Still, I can't help myself. I start laughing, too. "She was my friend first. I didn't like her until later on in high school."

"Still."

I shake my head, but I can't lie: what she said makes me rethink my perspective on what happened, at least when it comes to Paulina.

Nell lifts a churro to her mouth, chews, swallows, then says, "You're lucky she even wants anything to do with you now."

If anyone else had said that to me, I would have been irked. Not even Roger could have gotten away with it. But somehow, hearing it from Nell, all I feel is gratitude. That she's comfortable enough to be honest with me. That she's not softening the blow, so to speak.

"Believe me," I say. "I know."

She doesn't stop there, though. She says, "You've watched too many rom-coms if you ever thought showing up to a girl's window late at night and confessing your love to her out of the blue, after telling her that her boyfriend's been spreading her nudes no less, would result in a happy ending."

Okay, maybe I'm starting to get annoyed.

"You're lucky she didn't punch you square in the nose," she continues.

"Okay, okay," I say. "I get it. I was an idiot."

Nell grins. "But you know better now."

"I know better now," I echo. "Because of you."

She blinks and then looks away. "Exactly," she says. "Because of me."

"What do you think of her?" I ask. "Paulina, I mean. And be honest."

She gazes out at the courtyard and considers my question thoughtfully. Finally, she offers me another smile and says, "I like her."

I don't know why that surprises me. "You do?"

She nods. "Uh-huh. You guys look cute together."

"Really?"

Before she can respond, Bobby's voice comes from behind.

"Hey, Tommy boy." I stand, and there's Bobby, still in his uniform, grinning at me. "You ready to go?"

I glance over at Nell. She finishes the last of her churro and dumps the paper tray in the nearby bin. "Let's go."

Bobby

NELL: Tom?

TOM: Ready!

NELL: Okay, Bobby. Please introduce yourself!

BOBBY: My name's Robert Barnaby, but everyone calls me Bobby. I work the night shift as a security guard at the Cerulea National Museum and I'm the proud owner of two rescue cats named Biscuit and Gravy.

NELL: And how long ago now did you start visiting Second Chance Books?

BOBBY: Regularly? Going on six years this year, just right before Tommy boy here arrived.

NELL: How'd you find out about it?

BOBBY: My father was Roger's friend and colleague from back when Roger used to teach first-year English Literature at St. Catherine's. I grew up visiting the store.

NELL: I didn't know he taught at St. Cathy's. So you've always been a part of the book club?

BOBBY: Well, yes and no. My parents used to bring my sisters and I to meetings, but I was always a rowdy kid so I could never sit still. And then, you know, we grew up, we went our separate ways...

I didn't actually join the book club until I got out of rehab. It's—it's a funny story, actually. I don't mind talking about it.

My last year of school, I got involved with a bunch of... well, I try not to hold grudges, but they weren't the best people, you know? Shady is what I used to call them, but let's just put it this way: they were the questionable sort. Not the kind that would make your mother happy to see you gallivanting around with, you know?

So I started using. Nothing too hard and serious. At first, it was just for fun. A way to make a fun night even better. There was lots of pressure from my parents to get into a good school—if not St. Catherine's, then someplace similar. All my sisters got into good universities. My sister, Tilly—Matilda—she was going into law. I wasn't sure who I wanted to be, much less what I wanted to do.

And you know how it goes. The story's different but always the same. They warn you in school, you know. It's a slippery slope. You build your tolerance and then you start to use more and more and—

Those were some dark times. I was a shell of a man. Everyone has their own reasons for getting into it, their own experiences. This one's mine.

I was doing anything—everything—just to get my fix. I'd steal from my parents. From my sisters. When Roger found me, I tried to steal from him, too.

Everyone had given up on me at that point. My family had cut off all contact, and I don't blame them. If you'd seen me then...

But Roger never gave up on me. He'd take me to Amici's. Buy me dinner. Get me talking. At first, I was just going along because, I mean, free food, right? And if I don't have to spend on food, that's more money for drugs. But then I started looking forward to it.

He really got to me. And one day, he asked me what my plans were after dinner. As if he didn't know my routine at that point. As if an addict like me could be doing anything different with their time.

And I broke down. Because for the longest time, I'd resigned myself to—you know, my addiction. That's just who I was. I thought it was a fixed thing.

But Roger didn't think that of me. Even when everyone did. He still thought I was capable of being someone else, doing something more. And it made me realize how sick and tired I was of my life. How jealous I was of other people who seemed to have it together, you know?

That night, he checked me into a facility. Paid the whole cost. And it wasn't easy. A few times, you know, I'd get out, relapse, and go back in. But he never gave up on me. He'd send me books to read while I was in there, and he'd come see me whenever he could. And by the time I started to get better, my parents had passed. It's—I try not to kick myself for the time lost.

But I'm better now. My sisters and I meet every Sunday. I'm present in my nieces' and nephews' lives. And now—a sober six years later—here I am.

Attending book club was a natural progression from our meetings back inside. It's, you know, accountability. But it also gives me something to do. Something to look forward to. And it's nice, you know? To be part of a community that wants what's best for you. A community that has your back.

I don't ever want to let them down. I've done that before and—it's not worth it. The high is never worth it. But you know what is? *[laughs]* You're going to call me a sap.

NELL: We won't. Promise.

BOBBY: Well... alright, if you promise.

It's love. Love's always worth it. No high can even come close to the joy I feel to love and knowing I'm loved in return. You can call me cheesy, but it's true. I wouldn't be here today if not for love. Roger's and everyone else's.

Nell

I can't stop thinking about Bobby after our interview. What book club means to him. What the store means to him. And what I'm doing, if I'm successful— I'd be taking that away from him. All for money.

Sure, I'm driven by necessity—but so is he. Who's to say my needs are more important than his? Than anyone's? The commission I'll earn from the bookstore's sale will be life-saving, but Second Chance Books has also saved Bobby's life. And Tom's. If it closes down, I'm taking away its ability to save countless others.

I push the thought away to take care of Kate, and again when Annabel comes over for dinner.

Kate's gone all out. She cooks all of her best dishes: kare-kare, lumpiang togue, tortang talong—and garlic rice, of course.

"Do you remember Daphne?" Kate asks while she has me fry the rice for her. I grumble in response. Other than Tom, Daphne was my only friend. How could I ever forget her?

Kate chuckles. "She was obsessed with garlic rice, do you remember? Every time I make it, I think of her. Even now."

I don't feel like talking about my former best friend, but this is the happiest I've seen Kate in days, so I don't say anything.

"I wonder how she's doing," Kate says.

"Good, I'm sure," I say, unable to hide the bitterness in my voice. "I mean, she's rich." That girl has never wanted for anything a day in her life. The worst of her problems is probably something like wearing last season's clothing or whatever.

I know that's mean of me to say, and I know after what Mama did she has good reason to not want to talk to anymore, but still. It's not like I asked Mama to sleep with her dad. I was just as surprised as she was to find out.

I'm grateful the subject turns to Annabel and I can forget about Daphne again.

When Annabel arrives, she and Kate hit it off almost immediately. I barely have to do any talking.

She brought books with her, Annabel, baby books that she says had all the information she could have ever needed when she was pregnant. I stack them on the desk in Kate's room for our later perusal. She invites us to the upcoming art market in Cheltham where her sister's jewelry store is hosting a booth.

"How are the twins doing?" I ask.

"They're sleeping over at Uncle Louis' tonight."

"Is that your boyfriend?" Kate, oblivious, asks. The corners of Annabel's mouth turn up as she bites her lip.

"Oh my God," I say. "Is he?"

"Not yet! He'll ask me soon, I hope."

We all squeal, the three of us, as if love had never done us any wrong.

"And you and Tom?" Annabel asks.

"Your friend?" Kate asks.

I realize that I still haven't explained to her my complicated employment. "Yes," I answer quickly. "I mean—no. We're just friends."

Annabel snickers. "It doesn't seem that way."

Kate widens her eyes at me. "Is there something you're not telling me?"

"No! God, no!" I exclaim. I laugh nervously. "Tom and I are just friends."

Annabel rolls her eyes. "That's what Louis and I always say."

I'd almost forgotten what I'd asked Jane to do until Eliza, a junior agent, shows up at Second Chance Books later that week. I would have appreciated a heads-up.

My heart hammers in my chest but she doesn't acknowledge me beyond a polite smile. She knows not to give me away.

Roger invites her to sit at one of the tables. She's brought a briefcase full of documents: brochures, plans, calculations for how much the land is worth. I pretend to organize a shelf nearby so I can eavesdrop.

"It was too good to be true." Tom's voice startles me and I drop the stack of books I was holding. Roger and Eliza pause to look at us, and I mumble a quick apology.

"What was?" I ask.

"The clear waters."

"Stop speaking in code."

He sighs. "The sharks are back."

My skin prickles. *They never left.*

"I know," I say, opting to play it cool. "I've been standing here trying to eavesdrop."

Tom folds his arm over the shelf and leans against it. "Roger will say no. He always does." I can't tell whether he believes it or is trying to convince himself he does.

"It's so bullshit," he says. "They've gotten their grubby little hands all over the country. Can't they leave this town alone?" He pulls a book out from the shelf and shoves it back in gruffly. "You know, Newbury was fine before they came here. We weren't a tourist destination, but we had everything we needed."

I set the books I'm holding aside to start placing them back on their proper shelves. "You know," I start. "If they never started developing Newbury, Paulina would have never moved here. Neither would have Annabel. Remember? From our—"

"Yeah," he cuts me off, breathless. "Yeah. I guess."

We fall quiet. We listen in on Eliza trying to sell Roger on VP's ideas.

"It's still not worth it," Tom says. "If it came down to it, I'd choose this place over Paulina."

That shouldn't thrill me, but it does.

"I'd choose this place over anything," he carries on. "You can offer me all the money in the world but I still wouldn't change my mind."

"Surely you don't mean that," I say. "You can take the money and open up a new store. You can do whatever you want."

He shrugs. "Sure, but it wouldn't be the same. I like how things are now. You, me, Roger. This store. Don't you?"

I do.

"I guess," I say. "But I don't know. The only thing constant in life is change, right? Just because things change doesn't mean we have to give up the things we love. I'm sure there's a way this place can be transformed... you know, if Roger sells it."

I eye him cautiously.

"Would you sell?" he asks. "If it was up to you?"

If he'd asked me a month ago, I would have said yes. But now, confronted by this question, I'm not so sure.

"I don't know," I say.

Tom huffs. "I like my life here. I like how predictable it is.

"I like waking up each morning knowing what to expect: the bookstore exactly as we left it the night before, Roger already dressed in his work clothes but still dawdling about in his slippers. Thursday book club meetings. Depending on the day of the week, the same customers, each time, every time, without fail. And you. I like seeing you at the start of every day, waiting to be let in."

Our eyes meet. My body burns like I'd been placed under the sun and he'd taken a magnifying glass to my soul.

It dawns on me then. What I'd be giving up if Roger agrees to the sale.

I'd be losing the best thing in my life that money can't buy. And I know— I know for a fact that if Tom finds out I had a role in it, he'll never forgive me. He'll never talk to me again.

"Thank you for your time," I hear Eliza say just before the bell tinkles above the door, signaling her departure. Roger appears next to us and sighs.

"They suggested we transfer the book club to the library." *My pitch.* I'm about to ask what he thinks of the idea when Roger shakes his head. "Tom, to the counter, please. I have somewhere to be, but I'll be back in an hour." His eyes meet mine. He looks exhausted and paler than I remember. "Eleanor."

I straighten, heart thumping in my chest. "Yes?"

He shakes his head again. "No reason. Just saying hi." He pats me on the arm and turns to leave.

Tom

Ever since the day at the museum, I can't seem to stop thinking of Nell. Every time I see her, my spirit lifts. It soars. It flutters wildly in my chest like a caged bird, desperate to be set free. But then I think of Paulina. Of how well things are going, and how long I've wanted things to happen between us. It seems foolish to back off now, just when my dreams are coming true.

I make up an excuse to tell Paulina about being incredibly busy the next few weeks, just so I wouldn't have to see her. It's a coward's move and I know it, but I need some time to get my head on straight. It wouldn't be right to keep stringing her along when I'm not certain about how I feel anymore.

Nell and I are having lunch in-store when her phone buzzes.

"Shit."

"What's wrong?" I ask.

"I forgot I told Kate I'd go with her to the market today."

"What market?"

"The Artist's Market in Cheltham. Annabel's sister has a booth and we promised to visit." She pauses, then adds, "Maybe I can get you something to give Paulina?"

Roger tosses me the car keys. "Go."

I open my mouth to protest. He needs our help setting up for the book club meeting later that evening.

"Go," he insists, "but be back before seven, and with something prepared. Both of you. And do bring your sister along for book club, Eleanor. I'd love to meet her."

In Cheltham, the warm sun hangs over the cobblestone street, making everything golden. We drive past the canopy of tents arranged in neat rows, each housing an eclectic collection of food and art, all made by locals.

I park along the curb, a little ways away because of how many people have come to town to shop and look around as we have. The smell of fresh baked goods wafts in the air, strengthening the closer we walk towards market. I catch snippets of various conversations as we pass people by.

We meet Kate by a booth where someone's selling sorbets. When Nell introduces us, Kate pulls me into a side hug and asks whether she can get me anything.

"I'm good, thank you." I'm too stunned by the Garcia sisters' striking resemblance, which I'd completely forgotten about: the dark hair, though Kate's is longer and billowy; the button nose, the bright brown eyes that tilt upwards, full lips and full cheeks. They look like their mother as I remember her. Beautiful.

We follow her to Annabel's sister's booth, where Annabel's assisting in the selling of handmade jewelry including this thing called *Forever*: non-tarnishing permanent bracelets welded together instead of a clasp.

I catch Nell staring at one and ask her whether she wants one.

"Are you offering me *Forever*, Thomas?" Her tone is playful, her one eye squinted.

My cheeks burn. "If you want it."

"No, you should get one for Paulina," she says, all traces of teasing me wiped from her face. Her tone is flat, even. "You two can match."

But I'd rather match with you.

I don't say anything. Just watch her pick a bracelet out for herself and dream up a scenario in which I'm brave enough to tell her what I want—*who* I want.

She picks out a delicate silver chain, which Annabel's sister, introduced to us as Abigail, wraps around Nell's wrist to measure the right size.

"Hi, Tommy," Annabel greets. She has a knowing look on her face that unsettles me, like she knows something I don't.

"Hi, Annie. Where's the twins?"

"Around here somewhere. They're with Louis. Are you also getting a *Forever* bracelet?"

I hold out my wrist to her. Nell can't say no when she's distracted. "Yes, please."

When it comes time to pay, I pay for us both. Nell tries to protest, but Annabel backs me up.

"Just say thank you," she says, so Nell turns to me sheepishly and thanks me.

"You're welcome," I say, grinning.

We wander the market when Kate, Annabel, and Abigail start chatting amongst themselves.

It's set up the same as it's always been every other time I've come here, but it's as if I'm seeing the place with new eyes.

There, the crocheted bags and handmade jewelry—staples now at this sort of event. Across it, a booth selling fruits and homemade jam. Two tables away, an artist is drawing live caricatures of paying customers. Behind him, a painter sells her impressionist landscapes displayed on wooden easels, right next to a local store exhibiting their traditional Cerulean tapestry.

Roger has always said that this is the place where Cheltham's soul comes alive. I never understood what he meant until I looked over and saw the excitement on Nell's face. She's thrilled to be here.

So am I.

I just wish Nell would stop pointing at things and telling me I should get it for Paulina. I'd much rather spend my money on her, so I buy Nell a strawberry sorbet and raspberry for me.

"When you said your sister was pregnant," I say, "I didn't realize how much."

She scoops sorbet into her mouth. "I told you the baby's coming soon."

"I know. But it's still crazy to see. Would you ever want to be a mother?"

She makes a face. "God, I don't know. I haven't thought about it. Do you want to be a father?"

"With the right person, I guess." We stroll aimlessly, wandering from this booth to that. Pop music blares from the stereos littered about. The summer sun is warm on our skin.

"What are you planning on reading tonight?" I ask.

"I don't know yet."

"You should read something you wrote."

She makes a face at me again.

"What?" I ask.

"I'd rather die."

"You've never let me read a single word. Not since you were thirteen. I let you hear me sing."

"So?"

"So it's my turn. I want to see what all the fuss is about."

"There's no fuss."

"I'm fussing. I want to be able to say I was one of the first people to read your work when you become a bestselling author."

Her cheeks redden. She scoops more sorbet into her mouth.

"I've been reading Richard Siken's poetry," she tells me. A deflection, I know, but I'm so desperate for any information she'll give me about herself that I take it. "I really like the 24th stanza in *you are jeff*."

"That's what the poem is called? *you are jeff*?"

She nods. "It's from this collection of poetry called *Crush*, which explores various aspects of being gay, desire, and queer life. But what I love about it is, without stripping it of its queer context, it's able to resonate deeply and widely, regardless if you match the specific lenses through which it was written in. I think that's a mark of a great poet." Nell turns to me and smiles.

"I love when you talk books to me," I say. She thinks I'm joking, so she laughs.

We circle back to Abigail's booth where Annabel is waving us over. Kate's sitting behind the counter while Abigail fans her face.

Nell surges forward. "What's wrong? Is everything okay?"

"She's fine," Annabel says. "I think it's just the heat."

I pull my keys from my pocket. "Come on. I'll take you two home."

"But—"

"I'll tell Roger it was an emergency."

Nell is doom-scrolling on her phone in the passenger seat as I drive them home. The air-conditioner's on at full blast, and Kate is still fanning herself in the back.

I glance over at Nell's screen. Some medical website listing symptoms for God knows what. I stretch my hand out and cover her screen.

"Tom—"

I shake my head. "She's fine, Nelly," I whisper. I take her hand in mine. I give it a squeeze. She chews on her bottom lip but doesn't pull away.

After I drop them off at their place, I drive back to the bookstore and make it in record time.

Paulina's already there, waiting for me. She kisses my cheek and shows me the book she's brought to read aloud: Eve Babitz's *Slow Days, Fast Company*.

"Where's Nell?" Roger asks. I explain the incident with Kate. He nods, understanding, and orders me to buy more wine because Walter brought some friends.

As I fall in line at the store, I look up the poem Nell intended to read tonight: paragraph 24 of Richard Siken's *you are jeff*:

*You're in a car with a beautiful boy, and he won't
tell you that he loves you, but he loves you. And you
feel like you've done something terrible, like robbed
a liquor store, or swallowed pills, or shoveled yourself
a grave in the dirt, and you're tired. You're in a car
with a beautiful boy, and you're trying not to tell
him that you love him, and you're trying to choke
down the feeling, and you're trembling, but he
reaches over and he touches you, like a prayer for
which no words exist, and you feel your heart taking
root in your body, like you've discovered something
you don't even have a name for.*

And there it is again: the caged bird, desperate to fly.

Nell

What was I thinking, telling him about Richard Siken's poetry? I might as well buy a megaphone and declare my love for him in front of everyone at the book club. A love which I'm certain is just my twelve-year-old self being nostalgic.

When he texts me that night to check up on Kate, I send him a single thumbs up emoji: detached, apathetic, the complete opposite of how I was feeling.

I remind myself of the score: he loves Paulina, not me.

I focus on brainstorming for my capstone project for want of something else to do. I review my notes. I sketch out rough scenes for the book. And then I realize, after a day and a half, and a couple thousand words in, that I'd been basing the male love interest on Tom and force myself to take a break.

I go for a walk.

No good. When I see the sunset, all I can think of is how much I want to call him up and ask whether he's seen it.

I put on a podcast.

Still no good. The volume doesn't go up high enough to drown out his voice in my head, calling me Nelly.

When I return home, I see a familiar face waiting for me. I rub my eyes just to make sure I wasn't hallucinating but she's there. She's really there.

I march right towards the girl crying on our stoop and stop only when I nearly ram into her.

Daphne. My oldest friend, my only friend. I haven't seen her since her mother caught Mama sleeping with her father. At that time, Mama was her nanny, and just as she had with the Whelans, she used to bring me along to their mansion to study and play. We were fifteen. I thought her dad was just a generous man, that he'd enrolled me into the same school as Daphne because he liked that we were such close friends, and because we were the only two Asian girls within the vicinity so it was good to have each other. That bubble quickly burst less than a year later.

We saw each other again in freshman year of college and I thought maybe we could pick up where we left off—stupidly, I think now—but her eyes glazed over me like I didn't even exist. I stopped trying shortly after that, and when we passed each other on campus, it didn't even hurt anymore. I noticed her every time, but it didn't hurt, and that was more than I could ask for.

I'd hear about her, here and there, mostly from classmates having loud conversations while waiting for class to start, or in line at the cafeteria. She threw all the best parties and was dating the captain of the football team. She was the school's It girl on steroids.

And now she's here. Outside my house. Crying.

"What are you doing here?" I demand.

"Nell—"

"What the hell are you doing here, Daph?"

"I didn't know who else to turn to, I—"

"You can't be here," I tell her.

"I have nowhere else to go."

"So you came here? Are you out of your mind?"

"No? Yes? I don't know, Nell!" Her frantic tone matches mine. She chokes out a sob and then adds, "I just—I needed a friend and I didn't know who else to call."

What about those girls in freshman year? All those other people she surrounded herself with when she passed by me and didn't so much as look my way and acknowledge that I exist? Where are they now?

"You can't be here," I say again. I take her by the shoulders and spin us around, marching her towards the sidewalk.

"Nell!" Kate bellows. I stop and turn to see my sister standing in the doorway, hands on her hips.

"Are you seeing this?" I tell her.

"Yes. I asked her to come in but she wanted to wait out here. For you."

Oh, my day just keeps getting better, doesn't it?

I sit across Daphne at the dining table, glaring as she stuffs her face full of Kate's egg tarts. Kate pours her a cup of chamomile tea. Jane's blowing up my phone asking for updates, but I tell myself to just reply later.

"You still haven't told us why you're here," I say.

"Nell." Kate's tone is chastising.

"If she's going to eat our food, we deserve to know why she's turned up out of the blue all of a sudden."

Daphne opens her mouth, clamps it back shut to swallow, and then starts to sob again. Kate coos and smooths her hand over Daphne's dark hair. "When you're ready, love," she says. "No rush. You can stay here as long as you like."

"Yeah, and maybe you can cover our bills for us."

Kate glares at me. "*Eleanor.*"

I hold my hands up in surrender. Still, I add: "She's rich, though. I'm sure Mommy and Daddy won't mind."

"In case you've forgotten," Kate says to me, "our mom wasn't so very nice to her family, was she?" So she doesn't remember the Whelans, but she remembers the Lee-Aldridges.

"You're joking," I snap. "It's not like David tripped and fell into Mom's temptress cu—"

"*Nell!*"

I clamp my mouth shut.

"My boyfriend was cheating on me," Daphne manages in between hiccups, "with my best friend."

Jesus. "Fuck men," I say. Kate glances at me reproachfully but I know she agrees.

"I didn't even catch them," Daphne carries on. "They came clean because they were in love. *In love!* Can you believe that? I gave him everything—four years of my life—just for him to throw it down the drain. And that's not even the worst part."

It's not?

"The worst part is everyone in our circle sided with them when I got angry. Like they've all had time to process the information and now I was the big, ugly monster standing in the way of their Happily Ever After!"

Kate hands Daphne a box of tissues. Daphne blows her nose.

"I can't tell my mom because she loves Jacob, and she's close friends with Violet's family, and it's just a cluster-fuck of fucking bullshit!"

Wow. I don't think I've ever heard her cuss that much ever. She was as ladylike as they came, crowned the Diamond of the debutante season when she turned 18 and all of that. I didn't even think she could cuss.

"Can I sleep over tonight?" she asks. "Jacob keeps trying to visit me at home, wanting to talk, and I just—I just need to get away for a little bit."

"Of course," Kate says. "You can sleep in Nell's room."

"What?" I blurt out, but Kate continues, undeterred.

"It's not going to be as nice as your room, I'm sure, but she's got a mattress and it's better than the couch."

"What about me?" I ask.

"Next to me or the couch. Your choice."

"You could sleep next to me, Nell," Daphne offers. "Like when we were kids."

I make a face. "I'll take the couch, thanks."

'Tonight' turns into one more night turns into three. Before I know it, it's Friday, and Daphne still hasn't shown any signs of leaving.

Kate doesn't seem to mind. I come home every day to them watching reality TV on the couch, and she's even started teaching Daphne how to cook more than just scrambled eggs and bacon.

Tom had taken the hint and left me largely alone at work, except once to ask if everything was alright at home. I reassured him I was okay and we kept it at that.

When I get home that Friday, though, they're not on the couch. Kate's napping, Daphne tells me, and she's bored out of her mind.

"You could go home," I offer as I pull the fridge door open and peer inside.

"Are you kidding me? The maid called and said Jacob and Violet filled the foyer with white roses and a note that says 'We miss you, we're sorry.' My mom's blowing up my phone with texts saying I should just be happy for them. Home is the last place I want to be right now."

Tell me about it.

I take out leftover menudo from the night before and reheat it with some rice. Daphne pulls herself up to sit on the counter and swings her legs.

"Who's that guy who's always dropping you off?" she asks. "Is he your boyfriend?"

"No." I watch my plate spin circles in the microwave.

"He should be," she says.

"You tell me your boyfriend cheated on you with your best friend and you think I'm chomping at the bit to make a guy my boyfriend?"

She shrugs. "Is he nice?"

"He's already seeing someone else," I tell her. "In case you were getting any ideas."

"I'm not a snake," she snaps. "I would never do that to you, or any other girl. Especially not after this."

"Good," I say. The microwave beeps and I take out my food, carry it to the dining table, and hope she gets the sign and leaves me alone.

Instead, she trails after me.

"Your sister makes really good food," she says. "So did your mom. I'm so sorry to hear about her, by the way."

I shove a spoonful of rice into my mouth so I don't have to say anything.

"I always liked her, you know. I used to wish she was my mom instead of my own. If my dad had the balls to leave my mom, maybe we could have been sisters. That would have been nice."

I resist the urge to stab my forehead with my fork.

Daphne frowns and touches my hand with hers. I jolt upright and pull my hand away.

"Ooh, you know what we should do?" she says suddenly, sitting up and clapping her hands together. "We should go out. You, me, maybe your co-worker, and if he has another cute friend—"

"No."

"Yes."

"Absolutely not. Tom and I have a strictly professional relationship—"

She snatches my phone from the table and holds it to my face to unlock it. "So his name's Tom?" She's so quick, I hardly have time to react. When I stand to try and grab my phone, she dodges me and runs out of the kitchen.

I give chase.

"Daph, give me my phone back!"

Daphne laughs.

"Daphne, I swear to God—"

"Tom Whelan, is that him?" She taps the screen and holds the phone to her ear. "Ooh, it's ringing!"

I'm going to kill her.

"Hello?" she says into the phone. "Is this Tom Whelan?"

"Daph!" I whisper-yell.

"Yes, hi, this is Daphne. I'm Nell's friend! She asked me to call you because she has something to say. I'll put you on speaker now, hold on."

She taps the screen once more.

"Go on, Nell," she says to me encouragingly, holding the phone out with a mischievous smile.

I forgot that about her. She never takes no for an answer.

I heave a sigh. "Hi, Tom," I say.

"Nelly," he says. "Is everything okay?"

"Fine, yeah. I was just wondering..." Daphne rolls her wrists, gesturing for me to go on. "Did you want to go out tonight?"

Tom

Who, exactly, does Nell expect me to bring tonight?

Roger?

Paulina?

No, I can't do that. If I can't even talk to the girl I like about another girl, then making them hang out is strictly off-limits.

I tap my fingers on the counter, waiting for Roger to finish saying goodbye to the sharks who'd dropped by again to ask whether he might reconsider selling the lot. When Roger shuts the door behind them, I pounce.

"Roger," I say. "Who can I ask to go out with me, Nell, and her friend tonight? Do you think Louis might be down?"

Roger laughs.

"Stop laughing," I demand. "This is your fault." I haven't properly gone out in ages. I don't even know what I'd do when we're out. Something tells me high school parties are vastly different from night clubs you go to in your twenties.

"How is this my fault?" I follow him to the tables where he grunts as he sits down as if the short walk from the door had exhausted him.

"You hired her," I say. "You set me up."

Instead of denying it, Roger says, "I did, didn't I?"

The worst part is I don't even want to wipe that smug smile off his face; I'm grateful for it. But that doesn't answer my question. "I can't invite Paulina. I have no one to ask."

"So you like her? Nell?" he asks.

I give him a look.

"Use your words, Thomas."

"Obviously I like her, Roge." I can't stop thinking about her. I close my eyes and I see her there. I hear her laugh, blending with that ancient song.

Satisfied, Roger pats his belly. "What about that friend of yours? Finn?"

"Finn?" I echo.

I thought you didn't want to be found, Paulina's voice echoes in my head.

"I haven't spoken to Finn in ages," I say. Finn moved into town a few months after Nell left. We were instant best friends, bonding over our love for the same bands and music.

"Well," Roger says, planting his hands on his thighs and smoothing it down to his knees. "First of all: if you like Nell, you better be working on breaking it off with Paulina. You're being incredibly cruel to her. I won't let you get away with it.

"And secondly, with regards to Finn: every reunion starts with a simple hello. If you can get that out, you'll be talking before you know it."

I stare at the number on my screen, my thumb hovering the call button. I speed-run through all the excuses and consolations I could come up with, like he might have changed his number so at least I can tell Roger I tried. Or he might pick up, hear my voice, and then block my number altogether.

No matter what I come up with, it culminates with me telling Roger I at least tried, and then asking again whether Louis might be a viable option instead.

I call.

My heart races in my chest as the line rings. He could still hang up on me, I tell myself. It'll be fine.

"Hello?"

"Hi, Finn. This is—"

"Thomas fucking Whelan, you absolute bellend. Holy shit!" Finn laughs on the other line. "I never thought I'd hear from you again. What the fuck. How have you been?"

Whatever pressure had built up in my chest instantly deflates. I can breathe again. My eyes sting and I blink back the tears from how relieved I am to hear that he doesn't hate me.

"I've been good, yeah," I manage, hand cupping around the base of my neck as I let out a breath.

"You fucked off the face of the earth! I looked everywhere for you. They wouldn't let me file a missing person report because your dad said you left on your own accord, but Jesus, where have you been, Thomas?"

I looked everywhere for you.

I fall back against the seat and hold my head in my hand.

Roger was right. *Again.* I was a stupid fucking idiot.

"Just—around," I say.

"Holy shit. I can't believe it."

Me neither. "Hey, listen," I say. "Are you free tonight?"

"Yeah, why?"

"How do you feel about going out for drinks with some friends of mine? Just two."

"Two drinks or two friends?"

"Two friends." I don't know if anyone's putting a limit on drinks tonight.

"Are they girls?"

I let out a breath. He hasn't changed one bit. "Yeah, Finn. They're girls."

"Aaaalright, my man. Just tell me where to go and I'll be there ASAP."

"Wait, Finn," I say.

"Yeah, Tommy?" His voice is distant, like he's already set his phone down and put me on speaker so he could start getting ready.

"One of the girls—"

"It's not Paulina, is it? She said you were dating?"

"Kind of. I don't know."

"Oh, shit!"

"Yeah, no, but it's not that. One of the girls—her name's Nell—"

"Say no more, Tom. She's all yours."

"That's not what I meant," I start to say. But what did I mean, anyway? And why did it feel good to hear him say she's mine?

Nell

Daphne took one look at my closet and deduced that she would not find anything appropriate for tonight's events. Everything I took out was either too bland, too frumpy, or too outdated. It takes one phone call and her driver's picking us up to take us to the city to buy new clothes.

"You really don't have to do this," I tell her. In fact, I don't want her to. I don't even want to be here. Kate forced me to go along. I would have been happy wearing something I already owned.

If Daphne thinks buying me clothes is going to make up for ditching me when I was struggling just as much over the news that Mama was having an affair with her dad, she thought wrong.

Daphne shrugs. "I want to."

I chew on my bottom lip and look out the window. Daphne reminds me a lot of Paulina in the sense that she knows something about being a girl that I don't. It can't just be the fact that she can afford better clothes and better food. There's something about the way she and Paulina carry themselves that no matter how many hours I meditate on affirmations, I will never be able to emulate. They have the kind of confidence you can only be born with.

Her driver drops us off at downtown Hetford, where boutiques line the street boasting of clothes I can't even dream of affording. I follow Daphne into one such store, content to just look around, help her indulge in some retail therapy, and then go back home to wear a hand-me-down from Kate that she's tailored to fit me better.

Daphne, however, has other plans. She gasps and holds up a sparkly silver dress, and just from one glance, I already know it's two things: way too short and way too expensive.

"You would look incredible in this," Daphne says.

I check the price tag. 567 Cerulean crowns. "No, I won't." I walk off towards the couch, Daphne's heeled boots clicking after me.

"At least try it on," she says.

"I'll look like a disco ball in that thing."

"A pretty disco ball," Daphne insists.

I scowl at her.

She sighs and plops down next to me. "Is it because you really don't like the dress, or is it just me you don't like?"

"Can it be both?"

Daphne chuckles. "That's fair. I'll find you something else, then."

"Don't bother," I tell her.

"Why not?"

I consider whether to tell her the truth or not. She doesn't deserve my vulnerability, but at the same time, wouldn't it be nice? To get something off my chest and not care what the other person will say?

"I mean, aside from the fact that it's probably going to be more than I can afford?" I relent. "I don't know. I wouldn't feel comfortable in it. I just know I wouldn't."

"Because?"

"Because," I say, wringing my hands. "I'm not the kind of girl who looks good when I get dressed up. I'm not like you." *Or Paulina.*

Paulina would know exactly what to wear in this situation. She'd have Tom eating out of the palm of her hand.

"And before you say anything," I add, "I know it sounds pathetic. It sounds so much more pathetic aloud than in my head."

Daphne frowns. She reaches out a hand to touch my wrist, and I'm surprised when I don't jerk it back away from her.

"It's not pathetic," she says. "I know how you feel."

"You do?" That's impossible. Daphne's beautiful. She's probably even more perfect than Paulina, if it was at all possible to be better than perfect.

Daphne laughs. "Of course I do, silly. Isn't that just what it is to be a girl? We never feel like we're enough. We're always looking at each other seeing all the ways in which we fall short and hating ourselves for it. But screw that. Tonight, we're not going to care about where we fall in the tier list of who's hot and who's not. Tonight, we're going to dress up in clothes that *we* like and have so much fun, we won't even remember our own names."

My rigid heart softens ever so slightly.

"I still can't afford anything from this store," I say sheepishly.

"Don't worry." She winks at me. "My parents are paying."

My cheeks flush at the memory of my rudeness during her first day with us.

With renewed energy, I follow Daphne around the store, catching all the clothes she wants me to try on with my arms.

"Is your mom still trying to convince you to just be happy for the traitors?" I ask. Daphne's spirits seem to lighten a little when she hears the collective noun I've chosen for Jacob and Violet.

"Yep. I hope your boyfriend brings someone hot. I need a rebound—stat."

"He's not my boyfriend," I clarify. "And don't you want a break from dating? I mean, you just got out of a long-term relationship. Maybe you should use the time to heal and focus on yourself."

She makes a face at me. "Okay, first of all: Kate says he drives you home every day. That's your boyfriend. You just haven't labeled it yet. And second of all: exactly. I'm free. I can do whatever I want, or whoever I want."

Just then, my phone beeps.

From:	jane.waldron@vanguardproperties.com
To:	eleanor.garcia@stcatherinesuni.edu
Subject:	UPDATE????

> Eleanor.
>
> You haven't responded to any of my texts or calls. It's been over six weeks and Roger still refuses to sell. I have half a mind to pull you out unless you can convince him to sell this week. I've been very lenient with you, but enough is enough.

Shit.

My heart sinks to my stomach.

No, no, no. She can't pull me out. Not now. Not yet.

> From: eleanor.garcia@stcatherinesuni.edu
>
> To: jane.waldron@vanguardproperties.com
>
> Subject: Re: UPDATE????
>
> Jane,
>
> I'm so sorry I haven't been able to reply. I've been focused on convincing Roger and Tom that selling the store is in their best interest. You can't pull me out now, not when I've earned their trust and they've just started to listen to me.

> We're making good progress, Jane. I can get you an answer by the end of this week.
>
> I promise.

Jane can probably see through my lies, but I don't care. I need more time.

Kate helps us get ready to go out when we return from the shops. I try not to let my nerves show as Kate fluffs up Daphne's curls and helps her put on a chunky white gold chain necklace.

Daphne had chosen a tight cream dress with a halter top that criss-crossed at the front and wrapped around her neck. The dress was cotton, but the bust had silk chiffon ruching details and had a low cut back. She accentuated her look with thick hoop earrings that matched her necklace and a plum lip, also recently purchased at the beauty store next to the boutique where we'd chosen our clothes.

As for shoes, Daphne insisted on a pair of strappy cream heels that could double as a weapon from how sharp they were. When I asked whether her feet would hurt, she simply shrugged and said one had to suffer sometimes in order to look good. Though I didn't agree with the sentiment, she looked—as one had come to expect from Daphne—marvelous. Truly a sight to behold. If Jacob could see her now, he would certainly regret his decision.

I, on the other hand, got away with a black slip dress with a balconette lace-trimmed bust and an A-line mini skirt. It was the most modest thing Daphne would let me buy; we might have spent a good fifteen minutes or so going back and forth over how much tits was too much. And though she insisted that "short of going topless, there was no such thing as too much", she eventually acquiesced to my perspective. You can see my arms and legs and a bit of my chest—that's it. I'm not trying to give everyone else a free show.

I let Daphne do my eyeliner and stain my lips cherry pink. For shoes, I insisted on comfort over style and wore black leather loafers and white socks. To my surprise, Daphne didn't say anything about my choice of footwear; only smiled and said it was very me.

I opt to take it as a compliment.

When we leave, I reach for my jacket but Daphne slaps it out of my hand. "Trust me," she says. "You don't want to bring this."

It feels selfish to be going out in the middle of a crisis, but it's my duty to pretend nothing is wrong so I can follow through on my promise.

I'm shivering on the bus ride over to Second Chance Books where we agreed to meet Tom and his friend. It's 10 p.m. and I can't help but feel like by the time we get anywhere, things would have begun winding down, but Daphne insists all the best places are only getting started at this hour.

"I really wish I hadn't listened to you," I say, blowing warm air into my cupped hands and rubbing them against my arms.

"Nell," Daphne says, sounding just the slightest bit annoyed. "If you brought a jacket, why on Earth would your boyfriend lend you his?"

I gape at her. "That's why?"

"If you don't want to listen to me, then listen to him," Daphne says matter-of-factly. "No guy loans a girl his jacket if he isn't the least bit interested in her."

"Sounds like you've just been hanging around a bunch of assholes."

That makes her laugh. "True, but still. Aren't you curious?"

"About what?"

"Whether he likes you."

"You keep calling him my boyfriend. I'm pretty sure *you're* sure of the answer to your own question."

"Yes, but you won't listen to me," she says. "So? Don't you want to know— in no uncertain terms? Actions speak louder than words, after all."

"He likes Paulina," I insist.

"Paulina shmaulina. But he's not out with her tonight, is he?"

I give her a look. "Not to rub salt on your wounds, but you just got cheated on. Shouldn't you be all about girl code and not snaking men from other women?"

"Has he made things official?"

"No."

"Has he asked her out again?"

"Not yet."

"So they've only been on one date?"

"Well, more than once, but—"

"And did it go well? Sparks flying and everything?"

"Well, that's what he said, but—"

"And he hasn't made it official?" Daphne clicks her tongue. "Then as far as I'm concerned, he's still in the market. I was with Jacob four years when he started sleeping with Violet. It's not the same."

"No, but—"

Daphne shoots me a warning look. "One dance," she says. "Give him one dance. Grind on him, even. Trust me when I say you'll have him on his knees, begging for you."

"I'm not a snake," I tell her.

"It's not snaking!" she yells. "Live a little!"

As we step up to Second Chance Books, warmth blooms in the pit of my stomach and spreads throughout my body. There's Tom, leaning lazily against the counter in a leather jacket over a white shirt and a dark blue button-down, with dotted accents and left unbuttoned. He's laughing at something Roger said, and then stands straight up when we meet eyes.

I'm not a snake, I'm not a snake, I'm not a—

I'm frozen in place until Daphne shoves me towards the door.

"Hi," I say, more to the room than anyone in particular.

"Oh, Eleanor, you look beautiful!" Roger exclaims, pure joy in his eyes.

"You must let me take your picture, all of you, before you leave. Mildred will want to see this."

"Roger," Tom warns.

"I have housed you and fed you all five years, my boy; I'm allowed to want a photo of you with your friends. You must be—" Roger extends both his hands towards Daphne, who offers a dainty hand and laughs when Roger takes it.

"Daphne," she says. "Nell and I have known each other since we were kids."

"Beautiful name for a beautiful girl," Roger says.

"Can you repeat that to my ex-boyfriend, please?"

Roger erupts in vivacious laughter. "Absolutely. Now, let me get my camera..." He's muttering to himself as he disappears into the backroom.

"Um, this is Finn," Tom says, gesturing towards his friend.

Finn towers over all of us, light brown hair falling in curls down to the back of his neck. He has the lightest blue eyes I've ever seen, and I'm struck by how princely he looked. Surely there was something in the water in Henwick where he and Tom grew up. There's just no way two of the most handsome men I've ever seen could come from the same place.

I shake his hand but he's not looking at me; his eyes are fixed on Daphne, whose expression is unreadable despite the smile on her face.

She looks, I realize, like a predator who's just spotted its prey.

I let my eyes slide over to Tom's face. He presses his lips together in a small smile.

"It's cold," I hear myself say.

"Here," he says, shrugging off his leather jacket. "Wear this."

Tom

I didn't think it was possible for Nell to look any more beautiful until she walked in the bookstore dressed up for tonight. It's like I'd taken a sucker punch from a sledgehammer, all breathless and woozy just from the sight of her.

She's wearing my leather jacket when we head out for the newly opened bar in Newbury, and while I probably should be worrying about running into Paulina here, instead I can't stop staring at Nell.

I bite back the urge to say my jacket looks better on her than it ever has on me. That she should keep it and maybe wear it all the time so I can see her in something of mine. It's not like I can wrap myself around her whenever I get the urge (which happens so much more frequently these days, more than I care to admit), so it'll have to do.

I shove my hands into my pockets and walk by her side in silence as our two friends chatter noisily up front.

This side of Newbury looks different at night. Where Second Chance Books is, the streetlamps are barely ever working so we've gotten used to relying on the pale moonlight.

Here, closer to the newer developments, everything is illuminated. Strings of round warm bulbs hang over the road between streetlamps, giving the area a festive glow.

"So, are you like my replacement or something?" Finn asks Nell.

I glower at him. I'd forgotten about his penchant of embarrassing me in front of girls.

"Meaning?" Nell asks.

"You know. Tom's new best friend."

Nell glances up at me then smiles. "I don't think anyone could ever replace you, Finn."

"Good answer," he says. To me, he adds, "I like her."

And despite myself, I think, *who doesn't?*

The party's in full swing when we arrive. Neon lights swing around the room as the bass thumps in our chests. The floor trembles from all the dancing bodies. Finn and Daphne are already halfway to the bar, holding each other's hands up in the air as they sway along to the beat. We follow, but when somebody pushes past us, Nell clings to my arm and gets a horrified look on her face.

"You okay?" I ask.

"Loud," she says. "So much louder than I expected. And too many people. Way too many people."

I withdraw my arm from hers and take her hand. "Come on," I say, leading her back where he came from. I scan the crowd for Finn and spot him throwing back shots with Daphne. *They'll be alright,* I think to myself. He's a good guy, and if anything happens, they'll know to call us.

We're nearly to the door when I'm dragged back inside. I turn, panicked, wanting to make sure Nell is alright, only to see Daphne clutching her arm tightly and refusing to let go.

"Daph—"

"Where do you think you're going?" Daphne asks. Finn appears behind her carrying two golden shots. He hands one to me, then to Nell.

"No ditching!" Daphne yells.

Nell and I exchange looks.

"One drink," I whisper in Nell's ear. "Then we'll leave."

One drink turns into one dance into one more. A song with a thumping bassline blends into another. The lights are a spectacle, but nothing like the view before me: Nell jumping up and down, her hands in the air, screaming along to the lyrics. Her gaze turns to me and darkens, turns mischievous. She points her finger and mimes reeling me in. With a laugh, I sway towards her. When I'm close enough, I place a tentative hand on her hip. She spins around, her back pressed against my chest, and starts grinding against me.

Fuck.

My brain turns to static. I'm all spark and instinct. She reaches a hand and cups the nape of my neck. I tilt my head forward. I breathe her in. I place another hand on her hip and squeeze. I'm filled with so much want, so much desire, that I have half a mind to spin her around and kiss her.

My eyes flick up. I catch sight of a familiar face. *Is that—*

No. No, it can't be.

I freeze in place, my gaze trained on the person on the other side of the room. I squint to try and make out their features, but with the flashing lights, I'm afforded only a second of clarity before he's sunken into the shadows all over again.

My heartbeat is thunderous. My hands and feet feel cold and numb, but even still, I can feel them tremble. I feel two warm hands settle on each of my cheek. My head is turned, and my eyes meet Nell's.

"Tom?" Concern is etched on every square inch of her face.

"G—Greg," I stammer. My hand flies to my chest. "I can't breathe."

Nell's head whips around, searching for any signs of my stepbrother. "He's here?"

"I—I think—Nell, I can't—I—"

"Okay, okay." She presses her forehead against mine and makes a big show of breathing in and out. "Breathe with me, Tommy. In, out. In, out."

I take shaky breaths along with her even ones. The back of my neck prickles, but I don't dare scan the crowd for the guy who might or might not be my stepbrother.

When I've calmed down enough, Nell pulls me away from the dance floor. "Do you want to get out of here?" she asks. I can't think of anything I wanted more.

Nell glances around. I can tell she's looking for Daphne.

"Over there," I say. Finn's so tall he practically towers over everyone on the dance floor, so they're not so hard to spot. Our friends are wrapped in an embrace, dancing along to the beat.

Nell takes my hand. "They'll be fine," she says, and then leads me out.

The music fades into a distant thrumming as Nell and I spill out onto the street. She wraps my jacket tighter around her body until it looks like it's the only thing she's got on. I stare straight at the lamp post and don't blink to burn the image out of my mind.

Stop thinking of her like that. You're being a perv, Tom.

"I just need a minute," I say. "Then we can go back in."

"We don't have to," she says. "We can just stay out here. Or find some place to sit if you're tired. Are you okay?"

I swallow hard and nod. "I just thought—"

She squeezes my hand. I want to beg her to never to let me go. Instead, I just manage a soft smile.

"We can always drink elsewhere," she says. "Or not drink at all. There's—"

I scan our immediate surroundings. A 24-hour laundromat, a greasy diner, and a neon sign advertising a karaoke bar.

"Have you had dinner?" she asks.

I shake my head.

Nell squeezes my hand again and leads me across the street towards the diner.

Nell lets out a breath when we settle into a booth facing one another. A sigh that says *now that's more like it.* I want to tuck her hair behind her ears and kiss her. Instead, I place an order for a full American breakfast: eggs, bacon, and toast.

"And would you like a drink with that?" asks the waitress.

"Could we get the two-for-one beers, please?" Nell speaks up on my behalf.

"Of course," the waitress says before taking our menus and leaving.

"Two-for-one beers?" I ask Nell.

"I just have a feeling we won't want to be completely sober when our friends emerge from the club a few hours from now."

We pass the time talking, the way we always do. She says whether or not it was my brother I saw, she was happy to get me away from there. "Fuck Greg," she says, which I echo. Fuck Greg a thousand times over.

She tells me all about Daphne, their history, why she's turned up out of the blue all of a sudden, and I tell her about Finn. How I thought all this time he hated me, when really I was just being an idiot.

We talk about our favorite books and our favorite movies, the first time either of us had ever been drunk—at her sister's wedding for her, in Finn's basement for me—and all that jazz. I feel the last remnants of whatever walls we had between us crumble down. Then she asks me whether I've asked Paulina out again and I tell her the truth—or half of it, anyway. A simple *no, not yet, but I will soon.* How soon, I haven't decided.

She shrugs off my jacket and sets it aside. I try not to stare at her skin, soft and tanned and—

"What's taking you so long?"

I blink. "What do you mean?"

"You like her. Why haven't you asked her out again?"

Because I like you, a voice in my head says.

I shrug. "Is there really a rush?"

"*Yes?* You have to strike while the iron is hot. You've waited all this time. What if she starts thinking you're not interested? Then you'll have to start over from scratch."

She won't meet my gaze.

"You're really invested in my love life, aren't you?" I ask.

Her cheeks flush. "I need it for my work."

Right. Of course. I picture her building her walls back up, brick by brick.

I heave a sigh and pull my phone out of my pocket. "Alright, then," I say. Anything to make her happy. "What should I say?"

She sits up. "You're going to ask her out? Right now?"

"Isn't that what you wanted?"

"It's not what I wanted," she says, then adds quickly: "I mean, I'm just encouraging you to go after what you want. You know?"

"Of course." I wait for her to say something else. "So?"

"So… ask her when she's free. Wait, no—say you had fun. Or is it too late for that?" I don't know if I've ever seen her this flustered, this uncertain. She's usually so sure of herself and her ideas.

"I'll just ask her if she's free next Saturday, yeah? We'll go with that." I type out a quick text to Paulina and hit send before I can think it through. I pocket my phone and don't bring it out even when I feel it vibrate with Paulina's immediate response.

"Happy?" I ask.

"Why are you asking me that?" Nell says. "It's your love life."

"I thought my success was your success?" I'm only teasing her now, echoing her words back at her to see what kind of reaction I'd get. I can't help but be disappointed when, instead of blushing, she nods.

"Right. Of course," she says. "You should have probably waited until tomorrow, though. Texting her at this hour makes it seem like a booty call."

Fuck.

The waitress returns with our beers and I take a larger gulp than I probably should.

I mean, okay—really, what was I expecting? For Nell to save me the risk of rejection and say, no, Tom, I'm not happy because that was a test and you failed; you were supposed to say you liked me back, because I like you so much and want to be with you forever and ever?

Get real.

And now Paulina probably thinks I'm thinking of her at this hour, which is never platonic. And I can say that because I've fallen asleep thinking about Nell every night this week—but not like that. Just thinking of her. Her smile, her voice, the way she makes me feel.

I just keep giving the right ideas to the wrong people, huh?

"Where do you plan on taking her?" Nell asks.

"I haven't decided yet. Maybe I'll let her pick where she wants to go." Last time I chose, she didn't exactly like the place.

"And you'll tell me all about it, right? So I can take notes and incorporate it into my writing somehow?"

Don't talk to the girl you like about another girl. But I'm worried that if I don't, she'll see right through me and stop talking to me altogether. That was the deal, after all; she helps me with Paulina, I help her with her capstone project. We might spend hours talking about love and romance, but the Venn diagram of our love lives never intersect.

"Of course," I say. "All the gory details."

She laughs and makes a grossed-out face at me. "I don't know about all of that. Just how you feel, or how she makes you feel."

"Hard," I joke.

Nell balls up some tissue paper and throws it at me. "You're disgusting."

But she's laughing, and that's enough for me.

Nell

My phone rings two hours into our stay at the diner. I worry that it's Jane, but it's only Daphne. She's yelling over the music, asking us where we've gone—if we're being naughty in the bathroom, specifically, is what she asks. I tell her we're at the diner, and Tom and I watch as she drags Finn out of the bar and crosses the street, eyes wild and looking so incredibly inebriated.

They shovel food down their throats and talk loudly about all the fun they had inside. From what I gathered, it was a lot of dancing, screaming along to the music, and drinking way more than any sane person should.

Tom and I have to help them stay upright on our walk home. But Finn and Daphne had other plans; they drag us to the karaoke bar, where—the beer from the diner having settled, and I, feeling buzzed—we drink some more. More drinks than I can count, but still not as much as Finn and Daphne had downed.

Finn and Daphne insist on duetting "Don't Go Breaking My Heart" by Elton John and Kiki Dee. Finn mumbles his parts until he gets to the chorus, at which point he becomes a master showman, making everyone in the bar hoot and holler.

There was no way I was getting Daphne on the bus alone, and though

Tom offered to drive us home, Daphne didn't want the night to end yet, so we go to a convenience store to sober up.

Finn goes outside for a smoke. Tom accompanies him. I sit by the table in the back and Daphne slides into the booth next to me. She's got a goofy grin on her face that makes me laugh.

"What?"

"What?" she echoes.

"You look like you're having a great time."

"I am. Thanks to you." She wraps her arms around my neck and sighs contentedly. "I wish we'd done this sooner."

I bristle. "You're the one who ignored me in school."

I feel Daphne's shoulders slump next to me. Her breathing slows. She squeezes me again. "I know. I'm sorry."

I push her off me to get a look at her. To see if she means it, or if she's just saying that.

"Are you mad at me?" Daphne asks. "I mean, still?"

I clench my jaw. I could have used a friend all those years. And I can stay angry—I feel as though I have every right to—but I think again of what Roger said: that love is given, not earned. I could give her love. I can. Because whatever we put out into the world comes back to us tenfold, and I could use every ounce of love I can get. Lord knows I need it, and I'm tired of pretending I don't.

"I don't know," I say. "I'm hurt. But not angry."

Daphne takes my hand and squeezes it. "I'm so sorry, Nelly. I was so caught up in making my mom happy that I pushed you away. After what happened with our parents—"

I grimace. "We don't have to talk about it."

"No, I know," she says. "But please. Just this once."

I gulp, then nod. Daphne draws in a breath. "I already told you that I would have loved it if we became sisters. It's no secret I wasn't the biggest fan of my parents' relationships."

"I didn't know that."

"Now you do. I've never met two people more mismatched. But I also used to want so desperately to be like my mother. Or at least win her approval. But—" She shakes her head. "I should have just been myself. From the start. Did I tell you she got so mad at me when I shifted out of Fashion

Design into Animation?"

My eyes bulge. "You did *what?*"

She laughs, the pride evident in her voice. "Yeah. Last year. It's put me behind on coursework, but I'm so much happier. I think maybe that's why Jacob cheated on me. Why my mom's siding with him. I'm not who they want me to be anymore. I've gone off-script."

"I'm so proud of you," I say, and I mean it. When we were kids, Daphne always loved to draw. Whenever we'd watch a Disney movie, she always paid special attention to the art. She used to draw in the margins of my schoolbooks: her as Aurora, me as Belle. In our world, we were princesses.

I miss the innocence of our girlhood. I hate that we ever had to grow up.

"Well, don't be too proud yet," she says. "We've yet to see if I made the right choice or not."

"Any choice where you listen to your heart is the right choice."

"Yeah, well..." she trails off. Her eyes wander out the window, where Tom and Finn are laughing. "He draws too, you know."

"Who? Finn?"

Daphne nods. "I'm probably better though."

I laugh. Hook my arm around her. "I missed you, Daph." It feels good to say it. To bare the truth of my heart.

She smiles and kisses my cheek. "I missed you more."

When we get to Tom's, Daphne passes out on Tom's bed next to an already knocked-out Finn.

It's my first time upstairs, and the flat is more sparsely decorated than I imagined. It's more a studio than anything, with an open floor plan and everything. The walls are a dull green with dark wood paneling. Tom's keyboard is under the window, next to his guitar. There's a shelf by the door filled with books and some framed photos of Roger and Tom.

"Where was this?" I ask.

"Roger's hometown," he says. He hands me a glass of water and sits on the couch. I follow and sit next to him, much closer than I intended. The sides of our thighs press into each other, but neither of us makes a move to create some distance.

He's warm. I want to curl up against him and sleep for days. Carrying a loudly singing and dancing Daphne was more exhausting than I predicted it would be. Instead, I stand and move towards the keyboard. I sit in front of it, and he switches it on for me.

"Do you still remember?"

I press a key in affirmative. It rings out a little too loudly, making us laugh, so he turns the volume down.

"Ready?" he asks. I nod.

We begin to play "Heart and Soul" in between fits of laughter. I can feel myself falling deeper and deeper, but I tell myself it's just the alcohol. Tomorrow, I'll sober up and be myself again. It'll be fine. Everything will be okay.

We finish and clap for each other.

"Listen to this," he says. He begins playing a gentle melody, smiling at me every now and then when he catches me looking. He is so beautiful it hurts. I want to reach out and kiss him. I want to make all the hurt and pain and fear in his heart go away.

"Did you write that?" I ask. He nods.

"Did I ever tell you the first song I ever wrote was for you?"

Fuck. I shake my head.

He chuckles. "Yeah. That one. When you left, I was so gutted. You, like, broke my heart, Nelly. I thought it was going to be us forever."

I avert my gaze towards his keys. He's just drunk. He doesn't know what he's saying.

I stand abruptly and return to the couch. He follows suit.

"They had fun," I say, gesturing towards our passed-out friends on his bed.

"So did we," he says. "Didn't we?"

I curse Daphne in my head for falling asleep here. There's nowhere to run, nowhere to hide from the truth that's getting harder and harder to deny.

I scoot closer to the armrest and tuck my legs under me. I allow myself this one last night of peace, because tomorrow, I have to talk to Roger. I have to convince him to sell.

Tom stands and collects a blanket from a closet that he then drapes over me.

"Get some rest," he whispers.

"What about you?" I ask.

"I'll sleep on the floor," he says. He takes two fingers and uses them to close my eyelids, making me laugh.

"You're such an idiot," I say, but stretch my legs and snuggle under the covers.

"I know," he says. "I know."

I wake to the sun in my eyes and the rest of my friends still deep in their slumber. Tom's curled up on the floor next to the couch, so I place my blanket over him to keep him warm.

I step over him to check on Daphne and find her spooning Finn. I snort.

In Tom's closet, I find an oversized sweater and throw it over my dress. He won't mind, I'm sure. With the sun up, I feel incredibly exposed and underdressed. I can't go out in the day looking like I did last night; I have to get decent.

With only a single item on my agenda today, I head downstairs. Sunlight pours into the store from the windows, as if drenched in honey. At this hour, the store is even more quiet than usual. I go through the shelves, admiring my own organizational work as I try to find something to read and pass the time with.

My head swims with last night's events. The alcohol, the dancing, me grinding on Tom and feeling his arms around me, his chest against my back.

My stomach flips at the memory.

He likes Paulina, not you, I remind myself. *Grinding on him was definitely breaking the girl code.*

I never thought I'd be the annoying girl-space-friend of a guy who was seeing someone, but there I was, rolling my hips against Tom like he was mine, setting feminism back a hundred thousand years. Who knows how the situation might have progressed if he hadn't stopped and thought he saw his brother? I might have turned around, wrapped my arms around his neck, and tasted the tequila on his lips, maybe.

Maybe.

I cringe inwardly and blame the gazillion shots we threw back like they were water.

"The early bird gets the worm, Nell?'" Roger's voice startles me, and I whirl to find him holding a mug, his bathrobe over his pajamas.

"Oh. Good morning," I say. "I didn't know you were up already."

He nods and lifts his mug to his lips. He gestures towards the tables and I follow him to have a seat.

"Coffee?" he asks.

"I'm good, thank you."

We sit in silence, me racking my brain for how to best broach the subject of the sale, Roger looking content to just sit there and enjoy his morning.

He beats me to the punch.

"How was your night?"

"Good," I say. But it was more than that. It was the most fun I've had in forever. It was the kind of fun I imagined myself having my freshman year of university, the way the movies always portrayed them: all drunken parties and kissing boys and making friendships for life. Minus the kissing, of course.

"Good," Roger echoes. "I'm glad you kids had fun." He sets his mug down and fixes his gaze on the door. I sit there and watch the distant look in his eyes.

"Is everything alright, Roger?" I ask. I can't bring myself to bring up Vanguard Properties just yet.

"What?" He comes to. "Oh, yes, of course. How's the writing coming along, then?"

"It's..." I flatten my palm and tilt it from side to side. I've got a few ideas, but I'm hoping by the time the new semester rolls around, I'll have something more concrete.

"And are you having fun?" Roger asks.

I furrow my brows at him.

"What's the point in writing if you're not having fun?" he asks. "What's the point of anything?"

"I don't know," I say. And anyway, writing novels feels a lot like what I imagine giving birth to feel like: painful and excruciating and every other synonym you can find in the dictionary.

"That doesn't mean you can't have fun with it," Roger says.

The phone rings. He excuses himself and goes to pick it up. I sit with my hands on my lap before I head towards the nearest shelf to inspect its contents: general fiction spanning decades, with yellowed pages and some copies far older than I am.

Roger returns before I get to pick out my next read. Diligently, I reclaim my seat across him.

I want to just come out with it already. To tell him the truth and watch as disappointment floods his eyes. But Roger looks like he has something to say, so I wait patiently. I try not to stare.

Finally, he says, "I don't have a lot of time left."

I think that maybe he has an appointment, maybe this nice little conversation we have going is coming to an end. But he's got this look on his face that tells me he means something else entirely.

"Cancer," he says, finally meeting my gaze. "I haven't told Thomas."

I'm out of shoes to drop. This time, the ground beneath my feet falls away.

"I've known for a while. I put up a good fight, but the doctor tells me I've got a few months left. I'm in the home stretch. I'm taking care of things so Tom won't be destitute when I'm gone."

I open my mouth and close it just as quickly. I don't know what to say.

It makes sense all of a sudden, why he was always leaving the shop and so eager to take over shifts for me and Thomas. He was probably visiting the doctor, or making the necessary arrangements.

My friendship with Tom, I realized, is just one of them.

He smiles at me. "I've made my peace with it," he says, patting my hand on the table. "So don't worry about me. But—" He draws in a breath. I hold mine.

"Do you like him?" he asks. "Tom?"

My heart seizes in my chest. "He's a good friend," I say.

"That's not what I asked."

No, it isn't. But I can't bring myself to say it. If I let go and let the truth spill out, I'll drown. It's as if speaking it aloud makes it real. God said let there be light, and also, let Nell have feelings for someone she shouldn't. Someone already spoken for.

"He has Paulina," I say.

"That still doesn't answer my question."

I press my lips tightly shut. I can't lie to a dying man, so I won't say anything at all.

"If we sell the bookstore," he says after some time, "it should be enough to keep you and Thomas comfortable for a few years. For life, if you're smart."

"Me?"

"Yes, you. Did you think I'd forget you? I've put in a good word for you at Clover Press. An old friend of mine, an old customer, really, had just been named director and I'm told they're looking for new editorial assistants. The pay is good—better than what I'm paying you now—and if Thomas agrees to sell the store, the sum I plan to leave you should help pay for your final year of university."

I blink hard. I swallow the lump in my throat. It's not enough. The tears come hot and fast, and I drop my gaze to my lap, wipe my tears with my eyes and try to find something worthwhile to say.

I don't have to. Roger takes my hand in his and squeezes. I've known him a short while, and already I can't imagine living in a world without him.

I've never met my grandfather, but when Roger pulls me into a comforting embrace, I imagine this is what it would feel like.

"Please don't sell," I blubber into his shoulder. "I don't want money. I want—"

"Everything will be alright," he whispers, rubbing my back. "I know you have a lot on your plate. I hope this helps lift some of the weight off your shoulders."

I sob harder.

I'll take the weight. I'll take all of it if it means he'll stay. What will happen to us when he goes? What happens to the club? He can't sell the store. This is his home. This is *Tom's* home.

Then it occurs to me: this will destroy Tom. There's nobody on this earth he loves more than Roger. He doesn't have to say it for me to know.

I pull away, frantic. "Tom—"

"You leave that to me," he says. "But Nell, promise me one thing."

Anything.

"Promise me you'll stick around for him. Whether as friends or something else entirely. Don't be a stranger."

I squeeze him tightly, clench my eyes shut and let his steady heartbeat console me. Nothing else matters. He's still here. We still have time left.

"I promise."

"Good," he says. I can hear the smile in his voice. "Life's too short not to act on love, dear Eleanor. Feelings may come to pass but love always endures. Love is always worth the risk."

Tom

I've got a splitting headache. Nell's looking at me funny when I head downstairs that morning and find her talking to Roger. In her defense, I probably looked at her funny first.

She's wearing my sweater. I always thought I'd have to see someone naked to feel like this, but she's wearing even more layers than last night and it only makes me want to kiss her even more.

"Good morning," Roger greets cheerfully. "What are your plans for the day?"

"I figured I was going to drive Nell and Daphne home?"

"Stay and have breakfast first," Roger says.

I start to decline on Nell's behalf, thinking she must want to get home after a long night out, but instead she nods.

"The deli nearby has the most amazing selection of cold cuts and cheese," she says. "I had some during my break last week." I notice her eyes are red-rimmed, like she'd just been crying, but there's no way for me to ask if she's alright without Roger being dragged into the conversation.

Roger purses his lips and lifts his brows. "Well, there you have it."

"I'll go and get some," she says, standing to her full height. "Maybe pick up some bread from the bakery, too."

Roger digs into his pocket for his wallet, but Nell waves him off. "On me," she says, but he won't let her and they go back and forth a little before she finally concedes.

"Did you want me to go with you?" I ask.

"No," she says. "Stay here."

Roger tuts. "Go," he says to me. He doesn't have to tell me twice.

Nell's quiet on our walk to the deli. I chalk it up to exhaustion from the night before. I ask her if she's alright, what she and Roger had been talking about and if she'd been crying over something, and she laughs and tells me it's her allergies. When we return, Finn and Daphne are already awake, each nursing a mug of coffee and a cup of water care of Roger, looking like poster children for hangovers and why you should only drink in moderation.

I try to initiate conversation, but both of them groan.

"Shut up, Tom," Finn says, clenching his eyes shut. "Too loud."

This makes Roger laugh.

We eat our breakfast in silence. Afterwards, Finn goes to shower, and then it's my turn, and when I emerge, feeling refreshed, I find Nell, Daphne, and Finn lounging on the couch, with Daphne's arms around Nell's, her head of curls on Nell's shoulder.

"Did you want allergy medicine?" I ask Nell before we depart to bring her and Daphne home.

"No, thank you," she says, but she doesn't meet my eyes. She climbs into the backseat with Daphne, where they resume their position from the couch. Finn climbs into the passenger seat, complaining about his headache.

I'm the only person awake when the car slows to a stop outside Nell's home. I gently shake Finn, who turns over in his seat and waves me off, so I reach in the backseat to wake Nell.

"We're here," I whisper.

Daphne reacts the same way as Finn, so we park the car under the tree next to the house and leave them there to sleep a little longer while we go for a walk along the meadow opposite Nell's home.

The overgrown grass sways idly along with the wind. Wildflowers bloom, a burst of colors against the greenery. I've never seen anything look so peaceful yet so full of life. I stick out a hand and let my fingertips graze the grass. Nell's watching, but she's got that look on her face as if she's not entirely here.

"Has Paulina replied yet?" she asks.

I'd completely forgotten about that. I know the answer is yes, and it makes me want to throw my phone into the field. Why can't she just forget about Paulina? *Focus on me.* On us, here, together on this bright and sunny day in a meadow filled with wildflowers. My only hope now is that Paulina says no, sorry, I don't want to see you again. Not now, not ever.

"You're scared, aren't you?" Nell asks.

"Me? Scared?" I snort. "No, yeah, definitely. So scared."

She laughs and holds her palm out. "Give me your phone."

"What? Why?"

"So I can read it for you. If she says no, I'll break it to you easy."

If she says no, I'm going to do cartwheels and buy fireworks to set off.

I hand Nell my phone unlocked. She gasps.

"What?" I ask. "What is it?" Please tell me she said no. Please, please, *please* tell me she said no.

"Guess who's going on another date with Paulina this coming weekend?" *Of course.*

I let out a breath. "What'd she say?"

"'Hi, Tommy.'" She wriggles her eyebrows at me. "'*I was wondering when I'd hear from you again. I'm free this Saturday for brunch. Is that okay with you?*' And then three X's. Three!" Nell looks so happy for me but I can't bring myself to match her energy.

"But we're interviewing Walter this Saturday," I say. Walter's the final person on our list.

"We can always move it to a later hour," she says. "And if your date goes on longer than expected, I can take over."

I furrow my brows.

"I managed all those other interviews just fine," Nell says, "and I know how to work the camera."

It dawns on me that if she liked me, she wouldn't be this adamant about getting me to go on this date. I suck in my cheeks and bite the insides of them as I think.

"No," I say.

"No?"

"I'll ask Paulina to reschedule or keep the date to an hour, two hours max."

"But—"

"It'll be fine," I tell her. "Gotta keep her wanting more, right?"

I feel like a complete and total asshole saying that. Nell bites her lip and looks away. I know she's thinking the same thing.

We return to the parked car and find Finn stretched out and awake, lazily leaning against the passenger side door and chatting with Daphne, whose arms are folded over the rolled-down windows.

"There they are," Finn says. "Had a nice little quick—"

Daphne whacks him on the chest. "You guys alright?"

"We were just waiting for you two to wake up," Nell says.

"We're up now," Daphne replies.

Finn rubs his stomach. "Is there any place we can eat here?"

"There's a Chinese takeout place about five minutes away from here. Parking's a bit dodgy," Nell says, "so we can walk it if you're up for it."

Daphne raises her hand. "Can I take a shower first?"

"That would probably be best," Finn teases. "Stinky."

She rolls her eyes and climbs out of the car. Nell tells us boys to wait here and follows Daphne inside the house.

"You alright?" I ask Finn, leaning against the car next to him.

"She's the girl of my dreams, man."

"Who? Daphne?" In school, Finn had a new girl of his dreams every two months. It's nice to know some things never change.

"You say that all the time," I tell him.

"No, I mean it this time." He holds out his hand and begins to count:

"She's smart, she's funny, she can drink me under the table, she's fucking beautiful, and—"

"*And* she just got cheated on and is probably completely emotionally unavailable, unless you want to be her rebound."

"I'll be her anything," Finn says. "Whatever she needs me to be. I'm her guy."

I start to roll my eyes, then realize I feel much the same way about Nell.

Finn nudges me. "Any progress on the Nell front?" While we were waiting for the girls to arrive last night, I caught him up on everything. He can be an idiot sometimes, but I trusted Finn to keep my secrets—even when drunk.

I tell him about my date with Paulina. How much of an asshole I feel now that I realize I've been playing along with this just to have an excuse to keep Nell talking to me. How little I actually want to see Paulina after the last time.

Finn folds his arms over his chest. "Then it's a simple solution, isn't it? Just tell Paulina the truth."

"Are you out of your mind?"

"She rejected you. She can't get mad at you for moving on. And anyway, an eye for an eye, no?"

"An eye for an eye makes the whole world blind, Finn."

"Isn't that what love is, anyway?" He sighs and turns over to me. "Look, man. The only way out of your misery is if you're honest. With yourself, with Nell, and with Paulina. Otherwise you'll just keep digging yourself into an even deeper grave."

"That's morbid."

"That's the truth. You shouldn't string someone along just because you can't make up your mind."

His words hang in the air between us. Suddenly, I'm overwhelmed by the urge to hug him, my best friend, the only person who went looking for me when I disappeared.

"I'm sorry I didn't reach out sooner," I tell him. "And that I disappeared on you guys."

"You should be," he says, then grins. "But if you pay for my lunch, I'll consider you forgiven."

I reach over and ruffle his light brown hair. "Deal."

Nell

Daphne and Finn return to their respective homes that same Sunday. Work proceeds as normal, but every time I look at Roger, my eyes sting and I have to look away to keep myself from crying.

Book club is even worse. I don't know who else knows—Mildred, probably—but I'm too scared to ask in case I'm wrong.

I know, at least, that I can't keep working for Jane and Vanguard Properties. I send her my resignation letter and tell her I don't expect to get paid. She doesn't reply, but I know what she's thinking: *of course you're not getting paid. You just wasted everybody's time!*

Well, I don't care what she thinks. I've found something worth more than anything money can buy. I won't ever regret choosing to do the right thing.

Roger still hasn't told Tom. I don't know when he plans on telling him or why he told me first, but I try to make good on my promise. I look after Tom: I invite him for dinner when he drives me home so he can meet Kate and know he'll always have a family with us when Roger's time comes.

I pack extra lunch for us to share. I go all in with our lessons on love so that he can be happy with Paulina, and he won't have to wonder whether Roger would have approved of their relationship since Roger will still be around to give them his blessing. If we play our cards right, Tom will get his Happy Ever After before summer ends.

I will myself to believe in romantic love for Tom's sake. I try not to be so cynical whenever we talk about it. I pull Roger into our discussions, who lights up every time he gets to talking about Cecilia and their love story.

We talk about the 1 Corinthians 13. Despite the Sundays I spent attending mass with my mother and Kate growing up, I was never particularly religious. Still, it seemed to me a good standard to keep when picking one's partner. I was ready to read it out to Paulina if I had to, if she couldn't make up her mind: Tom is patient, Tom is kind. He does not envy, boast, and isn't proud. He always protects, always trusts, always hopes, always perseveres.

And it's that last bit I'm counting on. When the inevitable comes, I need him to be strong. It hurts me now to even think about it, to imagine a world where Tom doesn't have Roger. But even if it fails—even if Paulina decides a second time that he isn't the one for her (and she'd be stupid to, I'm sorry to say)—I made a promise to Roger to take care of Tom. I might not be able to give him the kind of love he wanted from Paulina, and I might not be the girl of his dreams, but I can be his friend.

I can love him in my own way, and hope that it's enough.

Tom

Nell had gone out to buy us lunch from the deli when my father appears. Roger's gone out on another one of his random trips, so I'm the only one there. I freeze when I see him.

He enters the store like he owns it, sucks out all the air from the room the way he always does, and doesn't say a thing to me. Just sweeps his eyes across the room and exhales a short breath, as if amused.

I hate how much we look like each other. I feel like I'm looking at a picture of myself from the future. Same nose, same mouth, same head shape. His hair's grown thin, but I know from old pictures that he once had the same head of curls, only lighter. The dark hair I got from my mom.

"Can I help you?" It takes every ounce of strength in me to get the words out.

"When Yvonne told me one of her friends' daughters found you working at a secondhand bookstore, I knew it was time to come see it for myself." He drags his fingers across the shelves and inspects them, rubs the dust between his fingers and then wipes it on his pants. *Get out,* I want to scream. *Get out, get out, get out.*

"Your publicist didn't tell you that?" I snap.

He opens his mouth to speak, but Nell's arrival cuts him off.

"Oh, hello," she greets cheerfully, then throws me a questioning look.

My dad outstretches his hand towards Nell, and asks, "And you are?" He doesn't remember her. At all. I clench my fists in anger.

Instead of shaking his hand, she turns away from him and sets the bags of food down on the counter. "We're closed," she says, not even looking his way. "Unless you have business here—say, apologizing to your son—then I'm afraid I must ask you to leave."

My cheeks flame.

"Excuse me?" my father asks.

Nell turns, a smile on her face. "You're excused." To me, she says, "So I got prosciutto, salami, some ham—"

The door opens and shuts. My dad disappears into the street. My jaw hangs open as I stare at where he stood, just moments ago, a little older than I remember him but still very much alive.

"Are you okay?" Nell asks.

"I can't believe you just did that."

Her eyes widen. "I'm sorry. Was that too much?"

"No, no, not at all."

She exhales a breath of relief. "Okay, good. Because fuck that guy. But if he'd come to apologize, then I'd feel really shitty for making him leave before he even could." She takes the food out of the bags and sets it on the counter in front of me. "Do you want bread or cheese?"

A kiss, a voice in my head says. I push the thought away.

"What the hell," she says, handing me a slice of baguette and cheese. "Have both."

Paulina's already waiting for me at the Amici's when I arrive. She's chosen a table out front and stands to greet me as I approach. She kisses both my cheeks and pushes her sunglasses up on her head.

My leg shakes as we place our orders. I'm trying so hard to be here, to be present, but Finn's voice echoes in my head. *The only way out of your misery is if you're honest.* It doesn't help that Nell got in my head about that Bible verse. Paulina's kind, but I don't know about patient. When I change love to her name, it doesn't ring quite as true as when I replace it with Nell's.

"Thomas?" Paulina's voice snaps me back to the present. "Are you okay?"

"Huh? Yes. Sorry. What—what were you saying?"

"I asked if you guys have started prepping for the sale."

I blink at her. "Sale? What sale?"

"The bookstore," Paulina says. "Sharon's aunt said they're building an apartment complex where you guys are this fall. I thought you knew?"

It's like the ground gives out under me. "Roger's not selling the store."

"No?" Paulina scrunches her nose. "Well, I suppose I must have heard wrong."

I try to steady my breaths. "Sharks—I mean, some guys have been coming around again trying to convince Roger to sell, but we're not selling. You probably got it mixed up."

"Probably," Paulina says. There's a tense silence between us. I rack my head for something to say, but there's only one thing I want to ask.

"Did you tell my dad about where I am?"

Her brows furrow. "No?"

"He came 'round to the shop a few days ago. He said Yvonne heard from someone—"

She rolls her eyes. "My mom's such a blabbermouth, I swear. I'm so sorry, did he give you a hard time?"

He tried to. But Nell saved the day.

Nell.

"Paulina," I say. "I have to be honest with you."

She sits up, alert.

"Do you remember the girl I work with? Nell?"

"Yeah?"

I draw in a deep breath. I haven't been fair to her, that much I know. *I hope you're right, Finn,* I think to myself.

I tell her the truth: about Nell helping me win her over, and how all that did was make me fall in love with Nell. How I only asked her out last week because Nell asked me to—*kind of*—and I didn't want to lose that bond we had over love and romance. How sorry I am, most of all, that I let it get this far and used her for my own gain.

Paulina sits there, listening. I half-expect her to slap me in the face, throw her drink at me, or just get up and leave. She deserves to. Instead, she laughs. She laughs and she laughs and I'm so nervous I start laughing with her.

"Why are you laughing?" I ask.

"Because you're an idiot," she says.

"Me?" I can't even deny it. I *am* an idiot.

"Tommy, you'll always be special to me. You're the only boy who ever cared enough to stand up for me, and for that, we'll always be friends. But if you like this girl as much as you say you do, then you're wasting your time. *Go.* Tell her. And then tell me what she says. If she needs more convincing, I'll whip out a PowerPoint."

My jaw drops.

"Go!" she exclaims, shooing me.

She doesn't have to tell me twice.

Nell

It turns out that avoiding heartbreak is a great motivator for doing your schoolwork ahead of time. I'm going through my capstone pitch when Kate yells my name from the front door.

"Just give me a minute!" I call back. But just as I stand from the table to head to the front door, I see Tom standing in front of me, a look of pure adrenaline on his face.

Oh, no.

My first instinct is that Roger's told him. But there are no tears in his eyes. He doesn't seem angry, either.

"Can we talk?" he asks.

I follow him out of the house, back to the meadow where we walked that day with Daphne and Finn sleeping in his car.

"Is everything alright?" I ask. "How'd your date go?"

"That's kind of what I wanted to talk to you about," he says. I wait for him to continue, but he doesn't say anything. Just keeps his gaze fixed on the ground as we walk.

"Well?"

"Just hold on a second," he says. "I'm trying to work up the courage."

The courage? To do what?

Then it hits me. What else would he need courage for?

"Tom, *no.*"

He meets my gaze, a look of confusion in his eyes that turns into resolve. This can't be happening.

"Yes," he says.

"No, Tom. Paulina—"

"I told her the truth. She knows how I feel."

"But haven't you—"

"*What?*" He steps back, laughs. "We've never done anything."

"But—" I feel stupid, suddenly, for ever assuming anything about their relationship. I feel like a child, so immature in my views on love and sex.

"Nell," he says, reaching for my hand. I jerk back, worried that if he touches me, I'll unravel. The truth will come out and there will be no going back.

"I promise you," Tom continues, his gentle eyes peering into mine. There's so much love and reassurance pouring out of him, it's almost palpable. Like I can reach out and touch it, cradle it close to my heart. I want to reciprocate, to give it all back to him but can't.

A voice in my head taunts me, tells me that if I was someone else— someone more like Paulina—this wouldn't be a problem. If I were like her, I'd jump straight into this relationship with Tom, and then it'll be our Happy Ever After.

Paulina.

I hate that even in this moment, with just Tom and I talking, she's there, haunting the margins of our story.

Tom reaches out to tuck my hair behind my ear. I dodge his touch again.

"It's not a problem," he insists.

But it is. After everything I've done, I don't deserve him. He should be with someone better, someone more like Paulina. And love never works out for us Garcia girls. If I let this happen, then sooner rather than later, I'm going to lose him, too.

No. I won't allow it.

"Thomas, we're just friends," I say.

"Are we, though?" he asks. "Nell, I love you. Whatever love I thought I felt for Paulina doesn't even come close to how I feel for you. You're my first thought when I wake up in the morning and the last thing I think of before I go to sleep. Nothing about my life made sense until I met you, and I don't want to have to keep pretending that that's not true. I won't do it, Nell. I can't keep lying to myself like that. To *you*."

Tears spring from my eyes. *Shut up, shut up, shut up.*

"Roger—"

"Knows," he finishes for me. "He was the first person I told."

Everything I wanted to hear and more, spilling out his mouth. But I never accounted for my unworthiness. "What? *When?*"

"Before I came here." He laughs, delighted. "He said he's always known. Even before I did."

Anger surges within me. Roger knew. He *knew* and that was why he told me he was dying. He knew he wouldn't have a lot of time left and wanted to make sure Tom wouldn't be alone. He was betting on my guilt to push me into a relationship with Tom, not caring what it would mean for me—if it would hurt me down the line. I was just a pawn in an old man's efforts to comfort himself in his final days, and the money? The potential job at Clover Press? Consolation prizes to assuage his own guilt. "Whether as friends or something else entirely" my ass.

"Nell," Tom says, placing a gentle hand on my arm. I draw back. His touch singes my skin.

"No, Thomas," I say. "We're just friends."

"But—"

"Haven't you learned your lesson?" I snap. "How many times are you going to keep confusing a girl's friendship for romance?" My words are sharp glass in my throat; it hurts just as much to say them.

Tom steps back, hurt in his eyes. "Nell," he says. "You don't mean that."

"No, I do," I say. I can't stop. The words pour out of me like venom, like acid. He can't love me. Loving me is a surefire way to end up disappointed, and I want more for him. I want him—still, even now—to be happy. To find the love that I don't believe exists. Not for me, not for anyone in my family. And if making him hate me will ensure that, then so be it.

"How stupid do you have to be to make that same mistake twice? After everything. All those lessons, all those conversations." I scoff. "You are so devoid of social interaction with girls your age that you think the slightest bit of attention from them equates to their love for you."

Tom's face screws up. I expect him to say something, to fight back. But instead he sniffs, wipes the tears from his face and turns away.

Regret strikes me immediately.

I watch him get in his car and drive. I try to convince myself this is a good thing. Friends fight, but the fact that he and Paulina made amends means we can get back in touch when he stops being confused and thinking he likes me—no, *loves* me—and go back to being friends.

Still, a part of me worries this is the last time we'll see each other.

I return to the house feeling empty.

"Nell?" Kate stands in the hallway, a look of concern etched on her face. For the first time in forever, I let her hold me as I cry.

Tom

Paulina was wrong. I should have never gone to see Nell. I should have left it well enough alone.

I can't remember the last time I felt this broken. This jaded and angry with the world. This *hurt.* I thought I knew what love was, thought I'd felt it for Paulina, and then I met Nell again. In the same way that whatever I felt for Paulina doesn't even come close to my love for Nell—and I say whatever because I'm certain that there was no way I could have ever loved Paulina—the hurt I felt the night I left home is but a scrape to the pain I feel now.

She was right. How could I have been so stupid? I should have been content just being her friend. Why on Earth would I go and ruin it by wanting to be more?

I park the car on the side of the road and sob. I'm hurt and angry and so mad at her for what she said, for how cruel she'd been when I let myself be vulnerable. But more than that, I'm frustrated. With Nell, for being so stubborn and not wanting to give love—to give *us* a chance. With myself, for even feeling that way.

When I return to the bookstore, I try to keep my face as neutral as possible. But Roger sees right through me. I don't know how he does that; it's like he can read my mind.

"Tell me what's wrong," he says, but I can't. I just sob all over again.

He heads to the door and turns the OPEN sign to CLOSED.

"Come here, my boy," he says, and holds his arms open to me. There, I collapse. I let the tears fall, let humiliation wash over me and know it's safe to feel this way.

"I don't want to lose her," I choke out. My brain racks up excuses: it was a miscalculation, an honest mistake. But even if it was, how on earth do we go back to being friends? Can we, still, when every time she laughs it's like the sun turns up a little brighter, and all I can think about is wanting to kiss her, to taste her laughter, sweet like honey in my mouth?

"You won't," he says. But Roger's just a man. He can't know that. He didn't see the look on her face that told me I already have.

Nell

I tell Kate everything. About Jane and Second Chance Books. I call in sick for work that week. I tell Roger to dock my pay. He tries to check up on me, but I'm too angry—too tired to talk.

I wish I never agreed to work there.

I wish I found it sooner.

I wish Tom would have just kept his feelings to himself.

I wish I'd been brave enough to admit I reciprocated it.

This war wages on inside of me, and the worst part is my instinct is to call him, to ask him what he thinks and have him help me settle it.

But I can't. I made myself clear, and in the process, ensured that we would never be anything ever again.

Not lovers. Not friends.

Nothing.

I haven't been to the columbarium in years. Kate had been more diligent than me, perhaps to make up for her leaving all those years ago. Because I carried no guilt, only anger, it was easier to let time pass and Mama's memory to fade.

But I don't know where else to go. Today, when I looked in the mirror, I saw Mama's face looking back at me. All her hopes and dreams—for me and for herself—reflected in the light of my eyes, the shape of my nose. I became keenly aware of the fact that you can run as far as your legs will take you, for years and years and years, only to end up right back where you started.

I buy flowers. White roses were her favorite.

I see her name on the niche, golden serif on a dark slab of polished marble. Her life, diminished to a small dash between the years of her birth and death. Henry had paid for her niche before he and Kate even married. She said it was how she knew he was the one. He never met Mama, and yet it mattered to him that she would have a final resting place. Somewhere for us to go and visit her, so we wouldn't have to keep her on a shelf next to our things.

I miss her. I hate her and I miss her and I love her so, so much. And I am so angry—*so* angry that she'd left me. Left *us* to fend for ourselves. That she'd placed her self-worth in the reckless hands of idiot men who couldn't have known her brilliance because they were caught up in delusions of their own.

Mama. Oh, my Mama. For all your faults and your fears, I still wish you were here. I wish you'd held on for me. I wish you had sought help. I wish you could hold me now, like you used to, and tell me everything's going to be alright. That us Garcia girls stick together, and that means we'll get through anything—*everything.*

Tell me you were wrong, Mama. That love exists. That Happy Ever Afters aren't just a possibility, but they're guaranteed.

When I was sixteen, you dated that guy—Paul, you remember? He was a hobbyist astronomer and he lived on top of a hill a fifteen-minute bike ride from home. We lived in a cramped bedroom inside a friend of a friend's house, no better than the inn we lived in before that.

I liked Paul for a whole host of reasons, but most particularly because he didn't speak down to me. He spoke lengthily of stars and galaxies and still somehow managed to bring it back down to earth, to a level of understanding that my younger self could grasp.

He bought me a poster, do you remember? Of the Helix Nebula, after a conversation on how there are universal patterns that can be found in all things big and small: your thumb print, for example, mirrors the groves on wood.

The Helix Nebula, Paul said. *God's eye.*

You broke up with him three days after he told you he loved you. You said he wasn't your type.

What would you think of Tom now, I wonder, Mama? When I talk to him, he listens. And when he talks to me, it feels like seeing the Helix Nebula again for the first time. I'm awestruck, hanging on to his every word. There's so much wonder in this world and he is one of them.

In another life, you married Paul and survived your hurt. I would have called you both to tell you that I've found him—the boy in whose eyes I see the universe.

There are universal patterns that can be found in all things, big or small.

But I turned him away. I turned him away, Mama, because you told me that all men cheat, that all men want is your body, and they stop wanting you when you age. Because Kate thought I'd be stupid in love, and then got left behind by a man she thought was different.

Mama, you taught me that love had to be earned so that when I met a boy who gave his love to me so freely, I didn't know what to do.

But I can't keep blaming you. It had been my choice, my weakness. And this shame—this hurt and this chasm between us—is my cross to carry. It is my fault, my doing, my choice.

A choice that I fear I'll regret making the rest of my life.

Tom

When Nell doesn't show up for work, I try to tell myself it's a good thing. I hold on to my anger, try to fan its flames into a forest fire and burn down whatever affection I felt for her. But it's no good. All it does is make me miss her more.

I try calling myself pathetic. A girl says all of that to me, and all I'm worried about is whether she's doing okay? Pathetic. Absolutely pathetic.

But there's a part of me—the part that's gorged itself on romcoms and happy endings over the past few months—that tells me it isn't over. That she just needs time. Whatever she wants to be at the end of it, I'll accept it. As long as we stay in each other's lives. Pathetic or not, that's my choice. All I know is I don't want to run like I did last time. I want to be right here, where she knows I'll be when she's ready. Where she knows to find me.

I busy myself with work at Roger's behest. "It'll be good for you," he says, "to keep moving."

The last person on our list is Walter, who I'm surprised to learn lives in Windmere, in a gated estate on top of a hill. He'd always seemed so unassuming.

As I drive past the gates and onto the curved gravel driveway, I'm struck by the wish that Nell was here to see this with me. These things weren't nearly as nerve-wracking with her around. I'd been spoiled by her presence.

The house itself is less manor, more mansion: sleek, all white, boxy, and modern with its tall glass windows offering a peek into its interiors. It reminds me of the photo of Vanguard Properties' headquarters in Hetford that featured in the brochures sharks used to give us. Impersonal, wiped of any and all character.

A man in a valet's uniform pulls the car door open for me and takes the keys. I'm led into the house by a statuesque woman with blonde hair tied in a bun, the color so light it's nearly white.

She leads me to the living room, where she says Walter will be with me shortly.

In the meantime, I take in my surroundings. All white everything, save for the eclectic art piece here and there. A black stone fireplace across a black console table with framed certificates displayed on top. I approach to inspect it.

Walter's our newest book club member, and thus remains somewhat of a stranger to me. Like Louis, he enjoys a lot of Philosophy books, but prefers French philosophers like Baudrillard and Derrida. He often requested books in the original French text; Roger said he was learning French, and that was about all I knew of him.

There were multiple awards and tokens of appreciation, but none that catch my eye more than the one front and center: the Real Estate Personality of the Year, awarded in 2018 to the CEO of Vanguard Properties.

"So sorry to keep you waiting."

I turn, and there he is. Walter Grant. Head of the same company trying to buy out the bookstore.

I can't believe I didn't put two-and-two together sooner.

"Your name, please."

Walter crosses his legs and places both hands on his knee. "My name is

Walter Grant. I was the former CEO of Vanguard Properties, but last year I retired and now I would consider myself more a philanthropist than anything."

My blood boils. I have half a mind to ask him to stop sending his men to us and bothering Roger with selling, but I try to maintain a level of civility.

"Who's in charge of Vanguard now?"

"My son, Wesley." There's pride in his eyes. It's hard to miss.

I can't help myself. "Is he the one sending all those sharks to the store constantly, trying to get us to sell?"

Walter sits up a little straighter. My words hang in the air between us. Finally, he says, "Yes."

At least he's not acting like he didn't know about it. "Is that why you started showing up at the store?"

"Initially," he says. His voice is gentle, patient. It makes me want to take the silver sculpture on the coffee table and throw it out the sliding doors that lead to his pool. "My son expressed his frustration over Roger's refusal to sell. I told him I'd have a look and see whether there's anything I can do."

I remember. The first day he came to the store, Roger was out on some errand. Walter waited three hours for Roger to return and left with his first purchase from us: Jean Baudrillard's *Simulacra and Simulation* in its original French text.

"So, you've been coming back ever since to butter Roger up," I say, trying my best to keep my tone even.

"Not at all." He uncrosses his legs and relaxes into his seat. "The first time I met Roger, I was clear about my intentions. He asked me to come back on Thursday to attend book club and see for myself why he refuses to sell. Then he asked me if there was anything I'd been wanting to read, so he could check your stocks and see if he could give it to me. I insisted on paying, of course. Do you remember what I got?"

"Baudrillard," I say. Roger told me all about it. It took me a while to wrap my head around it, Baudrillard's claim that we've replaced all reality and meaning with symbols and signs, that human experience is a simulation of reality.

"First edition," Walter says. "From his own collection."

That I didn't know. Roger kept his own personal collection of books separate from the store, books that he told me he'd never sell unless for good reason.

Walter regards me with a smile. "I assure you, Thomas, that I have no ill intentions. I've seen for myself the value Second Chance Books brings to its community. I see it every week."

"Then call the sharks off," I say. "Tell them we're not for sale."

Walter stares at me intently. I shrink under his gaze. Even retired, I sense some of the power he once wielded—*still* wields. He must have been a force to be reckoned with in his prime; growing up, there was always something being constructed in my neighborhood care of Vanguard Properties.

"Okay," he says at last.

"Okay?"

"I'll talk to my son."

"Really?"

He chuckles. "Yes, Thomas. Really."

I stand and hold out my hand. Walter shakes it.

I leave his house feeling lighter, until I reach for my phone and realize I can't call Nell to tell her the good news.

"Roge," I say as soon as I step into the bookstore and hang the car keys behind the counter. "I can't believe you didn't tell me Walter owned Vanguard Properties. This whole entire time—"

"Sit down, Thomas."

I'm stunned by the seriousness in his voice. Silenced, I oblige.

"I've been meaning to talk to you," he says, "but I couldn't find the right time. You were hurting over Nell, and I didn't want to add insult to injury."

I furrow my brows.

"Walter called me and told me what happened." He draws in a breath. "I think it was in bad form. To ambush him like that when he welcomed you into his home for entirely different reasons. Not for business."

I don't understand. I thought he'd be happy. He was always complaining about the sharks, and after everything Mildred revealed to me about the bookstore's history, I thought now more than ever he'd want to keep the memory of Cecilia and his love for her alive.

I was only trying to help.

"I'm sick, Thomas. There's no other way to put it. The doctor gave me a few months left."

All the world stops.

"What?"

"Cancer," he says. "Late stages. I'll save you the gory details."

"No," I start to say. I want to know. I want every last detail. There must have been a mistake. Roger's the healthiest old man I know. When he laughs, you see youth in his eyes; bits of his younger self shine through.

"No, Tom," he says, cutting me off. "I know it's hard to believe, but it's true. We've run every test. Tried every procedure."

All those times he was out for hours at a time—is that where he was? At the hospital?

I look at him and suddenly I see it: he's so much older than I remember, and his eyes are tired. I've been so caught up in Nell that I'd neglected to notice the signs.

"I want to sell the shop," he says, "so I can leave you with something good."

"Something good?" I echo. This shop is better than something good. It's the best damn thing in my life. And with Nell gone and Roger in his final days, it's the only thing. He can't take it away from me. "Where am I supposed to go?"

"Wherever you want to go," he says. "I'm leaving it all to you." He pauses. "Well, most of it. I intend to leave some money for Nell."

I swallow the lump in my throat. "Does she know?"

He nods.

"Since when?"

"The morning after you went out with your friends."

When I found them talking. When she looked at me funny. The whole week after, I convinced myself she'd fallen for me. But no—she felt sorry for me. Then I went and told her how I felt and put her on the spot, all because I was kept in the dark.

"I don't want money," I say. I intend for it to come out strong, but instead it sounds more like a plea. "This is my home."

"You can't live like this forever, Thomas. I want more for you and I'm running out of ways to give you that."

"Then why didn't you tell me sooner?"

"Because I knew you'd be upset."

"So you're kicking me while I'm down?"

Roger draws in a deep breath. He drops his gaze to his lap, and for a second I worry that something's wrong. That I raised my voice too loud and now he's ill. Finally, he looks up at me. There are tears in his eyes. I don't know if I've ever seen him cry.

"I'm sorry, Tom. I was trying to protect you, but I see now that I could have handled it better. I should have been honest. I should have given you the truth and the choice to make of it what you will. But son—"

"Don't call me that." Not now. *Not when I'm on the edge of losing you.*

Hurt flashes across Roger's face. "Thomas," he says. "Please. Let me do this for you. I can't go unless I know you're taken care of."

I've cried more in the past few weeks than I have in years, and suddenly I'm crying again. "How much time?" I demand. "How much time do we have left?"

"Until the end of the year," he says. "January next year, if we're lucky."

The tears fall in quick succession. I bite my knuckle to keep myself from screaming.

Roger pulls me into his arms. "I'm so sorry, my boy," he whispers, rocking me back and forth. "I'm still here. I won't let anything bad happen to you. I promise."

But the worst has already happened. I've lost Nell, I'm losing Roger, and soon, I won't even have the bookstore.

Nell

As if things weren't bad enough, Kate asks me to accompany her to the doctor because she isn't feeling so well. She won't tell me any of her symptoms, just that she wants me there for support. It's frustrating, not knowing if there's anything I can do to help make things better, but I know better than to push for answers because it'll only stress her out and make her feel worse.

In the waiting room, I busy myself by looking for part-time jobs. With summer ending, I won't be able to work full time, but it'll be foolish of me not to acquire a source of income.

It's all I can do to keep myself from spiraling.

The baby's not due for another two months. If Kate's not feeling well, then surely that's not a good sign. What if there are complications? What if—

No. I can't think like that. If something's wrong, the doctors will find it. They'll handle it. Kate is stressed enough as it is. I have to be strong for her. If something is wrong, I know she'll break, and if both of us are broken, how are we meant to move forward?

Us Garcia girls stick together. This pain won't be forever. In a few years, the baby will be going off to kindergarten and Kate and I will look back on this time and laugh.

Phew, we'll say. *We really thought we were done for.*

My phone beeps with a reminder.

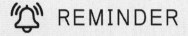

🔔 REMINDER
_____

Interview w/ Walter!!! Don't forget!!!

My heart drops to my stomach. I check the time. Tom is probably there now, setting up the camera, asking our questions. Maybe he's even brought Paulina for back-up.

Fucking Paulina.

I chastise myself for my bitterness. It's not her fault I turned him away. My guilt and my self-sabotage is on me. If they end up together, then good. Tom deserves someone who is good for him. Someone who's been true and honest and motherfucking perfect for him this whole time.

Not me. Never me.

Kate emerges from the doctor's office, a hand on her protruding belly. She offers me a pained smile when our eyes meet.

"How'd it go?" I ask, rising to my feet to hold her arm and help her towards the exit.

"Everything's fine," Kate says. "The doctor says I'm just stressed. So close to the due date and all. First time mother jitters, she called it. It's fine. We're okay."

Somehow, I don't believe her. But I don't say anything. Instead, I ask if she's hungry.

Kate beams at me. "Starving." She smooths her hand over her bump and adds, "Aren't we, little one?"

The diner is empty when Kate and I arrive. A waiter with a paper hat is mopping the linoleum floor by the jukebox playing Ella Fitzgerald. We slide into a booth by the window and Kate hands me a greasy, laminated menu.

We love this place. We used to come here all the time with Henry.

"Do you miss him?" I blurt out as my sister peruses her own menu.

Kate draws in a breath. Her eyes soften and she nods. "Every day."

"But you deserve better," I tell her. Shouldn't she be happy that he's out of her life? That is to say, shouldn't *Tom* be grateful I'm gone?

"I think we're all capable of being better if we want to be." Kate returns her gaze to the menu though her eyes appear to glaze over its contents.

"Which he doesn't," I say.

"No. I guess not."

I gnaw on my bottom lip. I try to distract myself with deciding whether I want bacon and eggs or sausage and pancakes.

No dice. My stomach grumbles, telling me I want both options.

I guess it's just as greedy as my heart.

"I'm sorry," I finally say, setting my menu down.

Kate smiles at me. "Don't be," she says. "I'm glad we get to talk. I feel like I don't see you enough these days, even more than when you'd go to work. I miss you."

Guilt rises like bile in my throat. I'd been hiding out in my room, curled under the covers the past several days. I can't find it in me to face my sister, much less the world.

"I miss you, too," I mumble softly.

"Have you spoken to Tom?" she asks. Just hearing his name lights a fire in me. I extinguish it in my mind, never mind that it burns.

"No."

"Why not?"

"Because last time we spoke, I made sure he'll never want to speak to me again."

Kate's face crumples. "Oh, Nell."

I look away, trying to catch the waiter's attention in hopes he'd save me from my sister's pity. "It's fine," I tell her. "Better that way."

"I thought you liked him," Kate says.

"I do." The truth tastes bitter on my tongue. *Another good thing ruined by my touch.*

"So why deny it?"

Well, that's the million dollar question, isn't it?

I draw in a deep breath. "Because," I say.

Because I'm not Paulina and will never be Paulina, no matter how hard I try.

Because I like him so much it hurts.

Because I'm afraid.

"Because he deserves better," I say. "And no amount of trying will undo what I did."

It's that simple.

Tom

A few days later, at the bookstore. The door opens and in comes Kate, her brows furrowed, her free hand pressed against her stomach.

"Kate."

"Hi, Tom," she greets, smiling. I step out from behind the counter and let her pull me into a hug. I burst into tears. She squeezes me tightly and says nothing. Only smooths her hand on my back between my shoulder blades.

I pull away when Roger emerges from his room. I sniffle and gesture towards Kate.

"This is—"

"Nell's sister," Roger says. "The resemblance is uncanny." He extends his hand towards Kate. They exchange introductions and Roger leads her to one of the tables.

"To what do I owe the pleasure?"

Kate smooths her hand over her bump. "Well, I'll be frank with you," she says. "My sister looks like she's had the life drained out of her. She hasn't gone to work in weeks. She told me everything, but I just—I wanted to hear it from you two. She told me she left but I just... It's not that I don't trust her. It's just—why would she do that? You know? She's not a quitter. So I—

well, I have to know. Did she do something wrong? Was she fired?"

Roger chuckles. He pats Kate's other hand on the table. "It's nothing like that, I assure you. I—" His eyes slide over to me. I know what he's thinking. It's not my place to say.

Kate twists and meets my eyes. My cheeks flame.

"I was an idiot," I tell her.

"Meaning?"

I tell her what happened. About Paulina and the practice dates Nell and I went on. About my confession. How—if I could take it all back, I would. I would swallow my ache and my longing for her, because her friendship is more than enough for me. It's not a consolation prize. It's more than I could ever deserve.

Kate's eyes well with tears. Roger reaches into his pocket and hands her a handkerchief.

"This is all my fault," she mutters. "I let her down. I—"

Roger pats her hand. "Your sister is a smart girl. Give her time."

Kate blows into the handkerchief. She's sobbing now.

"Everything will be alright," Roger says, and I don't know whether he's talking to me or to Kate.

I'm lying in bed when there's a knock on my front door. Startled, I roll off the mattress to see who it is. Roger usually just calls me on the phone when he needs something, and it's not like Nell's randomly going to have a change of heart after some time apart. *I wish.*

I'm not sure who I was expecting to see on the other side of the door, but it's certainly not Paulina.

"Roger told me to come up," she says, a sheepish look on her face. "Can we talk?"

I'm in no condition to talk. I'm in a ratty old shirt and boxer shorts. If I'd known she was coming, I would have changed into something decent.

Still, I step aside to let her through. When we sit on the couch, I cover my lap with a throw pillow.

"I wasn't sure whether to tell you," she starts. "But I figured you deserved to know. Do you remember Sharon's aunt, Jane?"

I shake my head.

"I told you about her. She works for Vanguard Properties? She was the one who said they were building an apartment complex where you guys are. Anyway, we were at her house last weekend, and she was ranting about this girl she'd employed to work at your bookstore to convince you guys to sell. I mean—it could have been anyone, but I thought I'd ask all the same."

No. No way.

"I asked her if the girl was named Nell, and she was surprised that I knew. I figured you'd want to know she's not who she said she was. I know this store means a lot to you, and I'm so sorry you had to find out this way."

Paulina's brows are knitted together in concern. She reaches out to touch my knee, but I jerk it away.

She's lying. She has to be. There's no way Nell would do that to me. To Roger. She might not love me, but I know she loves the store.

"Tommy?" Paulina's voice is soft, gentle. I know she means well, but God, things were bad enough as they were. Did she really have to go and try and make things worse?

No, that's not fair. She thought she was helping. She's just being a friend.

"I think you should go," I blurt, standing to open the front door.

Hurt flashes across Paulina's face. Nevertheless, she does as she's told, stopping only as she stands in the doorway.

"Will we see each other again?" she asks.

With all the hurt, anger, and confusion raging inside of me, I allow myself to be completely and totally honest with her. If nothing else, at least I gave her that.

"I don't know," I tell her. "I don't know."

Our eyes meet. It's crazy to think just several weeks ago, just one look from her could send me into haywire. Now I feel nothing. Only a restless desire to go see Nell. To ask her if it's true.

Paulina gives me a curt nod and walks away. I watch her stop halfway down, then turn to look at me. "Call me if you need me, okay?"

She knows I won't call. I nod, but even without our saying it, we know this is goodbye.

After a quick shower, I head downstairs. I find Roger sipping coffee and reading C.S. Lewis' *A Grief Observed*.

"Did you know?" I ask him.

"Know what?"

I tell him about what Paulina told me. His lips tighten in a line. He nods. "Nell told you?"

He shakes his head. "I just figured."

"How?"

Roger opens his mouth to speak then clamps it shut. "I don't know," he says. "I just had a feeling. She came looking for me that day, and I'd never seen her before in my life. She knew my name. She didn't know anyone else in book club. It just made sense."

That settles it. I stuff my phone into my pocket and grab the car keys.

"Where are you going?"

"To see Nell."

"Thomas—"

"No. I have to talk to her."

My knuckles turn white from how tightly I'm gripping the steering wheel. As if by chance, Nell is returning from a walk when I near her house. When she sees me, she tries to run, but I'm in a car and there's nowhere she can go that I can't find her.

I roll my window down. "Nell! *Nell!*"

"Please leave me alone," she hisses.

"I need to talk to you."

"There's nothing to talk about."

I park the car against the curb and hop out. "Is it true? You worked for Vanguard Properties?"

She stops walking. Slowly, she turns to face me, wearing a look of guilt and shame.

There's my answer.

And to think, after Walter's interview, I wished I could tell her that we had someone from the other side with us all along.

How could I have been so stupid?

I step back, horrified. "You were there to convince us to sell? Really?"

Tears spring from her eyes.

I hate it.

I hate that even now, I want to scoop her into my arms, to wipe those tears away and tell her it'll be okay. *I'm not mad. I'm sorry. I love you.*

But I hold firm. I don't reach out. I don't touch her.

God, I want to touch her.

"Tom—"

"How could you?"

"Tom, you have to understand—"

I shake my head. "No. No, you don't—you don't get to make me understand anything. I see it clearly now. You—I was just a pawn to you. You didn't care about me. I trusted you. I *fell* for you. And this whole entire time, you were lying to me."

"Tom, please," she cries.

"So you knew? You knew this whole time that Walter—fucking Walter owned Vanguard Properties?"

"What?" she gasps. "No. No—Wesley—"

"Wesley is his son."

To her credit, she looks surprised. But I don't believe her for one second. If she could lie for me for as long as we've been reunited, she could be lying about this, too.

I back away from her, from my own heart, breaking right in front of me. I came here, hoping against all hope, that she would tell me it wasn't true. That Paulina had her confused for someone else. That everyone was wrong about her, but not me.

I wanted, so desperately, to be the only one who was right about her. That she was the Nell I knew, the Nell I loved: honest, upstanding, and hardworking. Not a liar. Not a shark.

But she is not my Nell. She never was.

My face screws up in disgust. I feel my heart breaking over and over again. "I never want to see you again."

"Tom—"

"Goodbye, Nell." I turn on my heel and don't look back.

No matter how much I want to.

I drive the country road to Henwick, the town I grew up in, a place I never thought I'd ever step foot in again. It's less sleepy than I remember, its cobbled lanes paved over, its rural charm turned distinctly modern.

Gone are the closely built buildings in the town center, the reason for the yearly fire safety and prevention classes in school. In its place are boxes of red brick and glass windows, soulless architecture and eyesores.

It's funny how you can leave a place swearing you hate it, only to mourn it as it once was and think it better—perfect, even—in memory.

I call Finn and ask him to meet me at the park where we used to hang out. I ask if I can sleep over, and he tells me I can stay as long as I like. He doesn't ask me what's wrong, and I'm grateful for that. I don't know how to begin explaining everything anyhow.

Roger calls me incessantly. I tell him I'll be back next week. That I just need time to process. He begs me to take care of myself and to send updates. I worry, for a second, that life might take him away from me while I'm gone. But I can't keep living my life in fear of losing what I love, or who I love. Fear hasn't kept me from losing them anyway.

Nell

I'm a coward. There's no other way to put it. I should have gone after Tom, or showed back up at work. Begged him to stay, to listen. But I don't deserve good things in life. I don't even deserve a Way Out anymore. I'm a terrible human being who deserves to rot in hell.

In the morning, I stare at my letter of resignation in my hands, addressed to Roger, contemplating how to best send it when I hear Kate calling. I set the letter aside and go to her room, where I find her hunched over and staring down at her legs.

"Kate?"

She looks up at me, grimacing. "I think my water just broke."

We rush to the ER. There's no time to talk. I take the emergency bag Kate had packed, call a taxi because I can't drive for shit, and pay him extra to drive as quickly and as carefully as he can. I call Annabel, even if it's the middle of the night, who then calls Louis and Mildred, to meet us at the hospital and help.

God, I don't even *know* what kind of help we need. It's not like all of us can cram into the delivery room and push the baby out for her. I'm in such a state of panic I can hardly think.

Kate hands me her phone. "Call Henry," she says. "Tell him the baby's coming."

I watch, gobsmacked, as the nurses wheel my sister to the delivery room. Annabel takes Kate's phone from me and begins to dial Henry's number.

"Wait—"

Mildred takes my hand and sits me down.

"But he—"

"He is still the baby's father," Mildred tells me, smoothing her hand over my hair.

"No," I say, surging forward. Louis and Mildred hold me down. "Let me go! I should be in there with her!"

"Henry's on his way," Annabel says.

"Everything's going to be alright," Mildred says. My heart is hammering inside my chest. It's too early. Way too early. Kate said the doctor told her she and the baby were fine. Was she lying to me? Did she just not want me to worry?

I've lost everyone. Everything. I can't lose Kate, too.

Tom

Finn and I have spent the last week getting high and shooting the shit, getting drunk in pubs and then going home to drink some more.

Tonight, we're at the playground near the school we grew up attending, talking about everything but what really mattered.

The town has changed so much since I left—I spotted a few Vanguard Properties signs during my drive over. When you leave home, a part of you expects it to stay the same. But you return and life has gone on without you. Everything's different. You, especially. You become a missing piece to an entirely different puzzle. I suppose this is because we've found home elsewhere. In someone else, even.

Finally, Finn asks me what happened. Why I'm here again. So I tell him the truth. I tell him that Nell's been lying to me. That I didn't like Paulina half as much as I thought. He's quiet even after I finish my story.

"Finn?" I say. "Say something."

"Sorry," he says, swaying in his swing seat. "I'm just trying to wrap my head around it all."

He sighs after some time. He leans his weight back, the gravel crunching beneath his feet as he kicks his legs out.

"What?"

"You can't keep doing this, Tom," he says.

"Do what?"

"You can't keep running away when shit gets hard."

I open my mouth to speak, but the sound of more gravel crunching underfoot causes us to look up. Standing there is my father. And Roger. I stand up.

"Thomas," Roger says.

"How'd you know where to find me?" I blurt out.

My father shrugs. "This was your favorite spot as a kid. I just had a hunch."

My heart clenches at the memory. After my mom left, my dad used to take me here to pass the time. This was before he met Yvonne, when the world shrank to just us my father and I.

"How'd you get here?" I ask Roger.

"I took the bus."

Fuck. He's too old to be traveling this far. "Are you insane?" I cry out. "You couldn't have just called?"

"Kate's water broke," Roger tells me. "I had to come tell you in person and—"

My body moves without my instruction. My heart races, my mind spins. "Already? But she's not due for another two months."

"I know," Roger says. "Listen, Thomas, I know. Which is precisely why I came to see you. Nell could use your support right now. No matter how badly it ended, I know she'd want you there."

I don't have it in me to argue. I know he's right. I want him to be right.

I miss Nell. Now that the anger's subsided, I don't care if she doesn't love me back. I don't care that she was originally there to convince us to sell the store. What I felt for her—that was real. I don't need anything else to be. She made me feel seen, and that was enough for me. She was a friend when I needed one, and now it was my turn to reciprocate.

My father holds up his car keys. "I'll drive."

Nell

When Henry arrives, I stand to—I don't know. Slap him in the face. Gouge his eyes out. *Something.* But instead, my mouth falls open then closes. Opens, then closes.

"She's inside," Annabel says, and calls a nurse to lead him in.

"Have you had some sleep, darling?" Mildred asks. I shake my head.

"You should go home," I tell her. "Get some rest."

"I'll be alright," she insists. "But you—" She cups my face and frowns. I feel the tears stinging in the back of my eyes. "Oh, honey. You look like you haven't slept in ages."

I snort and she laughs. I don't know how to tell her that she's right; I haven't had a good night's sleep since I yelled at Tom and essentially told him to fuck off.

"Have you heard from Roger?" I ask.

Mildred shakes her head.

"Did you know—"

"Of course I do," she says. "His doctor's my son-in-law. There was no hiding it from me."

My face crumples and I start to cry. "I feel like an asshole. I promised him

I'd take care of Tom."

"What happened?"

I tell her everything. About my mother, about Kate and Henry even though she must already know. About Tom, and how easy it was to fall for him despite all the roadblocks I put in my way.

"I love him," I say, shocking myself from how easily it slips from my mouth. "I love him so much, but I can't, and I shouldn't, and my sister is giving birth and who knows if she'll survive and—"

"Let me stop you there," Mildred says, squeezing my hand. "Your sister is going to be alright. She's receiving the best care in the world right now. That baby is going to come out plump and healthy, and we're all going to spoil it rotten. Yes?

"Now, on the subject of Tom: Eleanor, I have been divorced twice and dated many-a men in my time, so I don't say this lightly. But there is no reason—there is never any reason to stop you from loving someone. Fully, deeply, and as truly as you like. Love—"

"—is always worth the risk," I finish for her in a murmur, remembering Roger's words.

Mildred nods. "That was Cecilia's motto. We all doubted the bookstore, you know? But she believed in it. She loved it. And that made it worth the risk."

Annabel takes my hand and squeezes it. "Nelly," she says, "I'm going to go home because my sister needs to get ready for work in an hour, and nobody can watch the twins. But Louis will stay and keep you company, okay?"

I glance at Mildred.

"You should go," I tell her.

"But—"

"Get some rest," I say, "and bring back some apple pie later."

She smiles at me and plants a kiss on my forehead. "Everything will be alright, darling," she says. "Just call if you need me."

I don't know who calls her, but Daphne comes running into the waiting room an hour later, a frantic look on her face. I stand and she pulls me into her arms, hugging me tightly.

"I came as fast as I can," she says.

"How'd you know?"

"Finn's with Tom, so they called me and—"

"Tom called?"

Daphne nods. "He and Roger are on their way."

Tom

I help Roger into the passenger seat. Finn and I settle into the back.

It doesn't matter anymore if Nell hates my guts; I want her to know that I care, at least enough to give her the chance to tell me to fuck off a second time.

Roger coughs and I lean forward to check on him and make sure he's okay. He waves me off and holds on to the grab handle on his side.

I meet my father's eyes in the rearview mirror. I can tell he wants to talk, but I shake my head. *Not now.*

After dropping us off, my dad promises to return in the afternoon. I tell him we'll talk then. Right now, I've only got Nell on my mind.

In the waiting room, Nell sits with Daphne and Louis, who appears to be dozing off in his seat. Roger coughs again, and they all turn to look. Louis stands to greet us and offers his seat to Roger, but Roger waves him off.

"Eleanor," he says, and Nell's face crumples. She rises and runs straight into Roger's arms. He pats her back soothingly.

When Roger releases Nell, he lets out a breath and says, "Okay. Who's hungry?" Three hands shoot up in the air immediately. Daphne's, Finn's, and Louis! It's like they rehearsed it.

Roger cants his head towards the door. "There's a donut stall in the cafeteria with really good pretzels."

"Pretzels?" Daphne echoes as she follows him out. "At a donut stall?"

Nell and I watch them go. It's only when the doors swing shut behind them that I gather the courage to meet her eyes.

"Hi," I breathe.

"Hello." I scan her face for any signs of emotion: relief, worry, anger at my being here. I want her to tell me how she feels so I know what to do, how I can help her, but instead she shrinks into herself. Ducks her chin and keeps her gaze fixed on the floor.

I want to reach out and touch her, to let her know I'm here, she's safe, no harm will ever come to pass. Instead, I sit next to her and keep my mouth shut.

We don't have to talk. I'm happy to just be near her.

Roger and the gang return, carrying white paper bags filled with donuts and pretzels.

A few hours pass and still no news. I offer to drive Roger home and come back for Nell, but he tells me that if anything were to happen to him, it's best he's already in the hospital than anywhere else. Plus, Finn promises to never let him out of his sight, to which Roger rolls his eyes.

Nell insists on staying, but she yawns nearly every ten seconds, until Daphne forces her to leave and Nell finally gives in.

I lead her to the bus stop and let her take the window seat. I sit next to her and still don't say anything. The last thing she needs right now is for me to put my foot in my mouth again.

We hit the road and she turns her head to look at me. The weight of her gaze is heavy on my skin. I glance at her but look away immediately. She's too beautiful, and I'm just a man. It still hurts.

"I'm sorry," she says, shocking me. "About everything. And for saying what I did when you said what you said." Her words hang heavy in the air between us. Like a balloon filling with water; any second now it'll burst and wash us away. I hold my breath, keep my eyes locked on hers, trying to figure out the best way to respond. Then the corner of her lips tugs upwards. The balloon pops. We burst into laughter.

"Could you be a little more specific?" I tease.

"Don't be mean," she says. "I hardly have any sleep."

I smirk. "You were saying?"

The comfort between us returns, and I tell myself I'm okay with it. This—our friendship—is enough. I'll take it over not having her in my life any day.

"That's it," she says. "I'm sorry. It was low of me to bring up when Paulina rejected you. And I didn't mean any of those other things. I was cruel. I was afraid. I went about it in all the worst ways, and if I could take it all back, I would." She takes my hand in hers and squeezes it. It feels, for a moment, like she's taking my heart and stitching it back up together. "You're a great guy. Any girl would be lucky to have you. Even before our lessons, I knew that." She chuckles. "If anything, *I'm* the one who needed the help."

"I forgive you," I say, because Roger told me it's important to say that rather than to tell a person it's okay. Because what Nell said to me wasn't okay. It was mean and it hurt me. But I forgive her.

I don't ask her if she really didn't think she could be the girl *'lucky'* enough to have me. It had nothing to do with luck. Love is a choice, and I can't make her choose me. Even if my heart sings her name, over and over again.

She tells me about her job at Vanguard Properties, how she stumbled upon it after a former boss at a restaurant had been disgusting to her. I'm overcome by the urge to find this guy and crush him, make him pay.

"Fuck him," I say. "But I'm really glad you found us."

She chuckles, gazing forlornly at her lap. "Me, too."

"Roger told me the truth," I tell her after some time. "About his cancer."

It hits me that this time next year, Roger won't be around. I'll wake up and he won't be downstairs doing his daily crossword with a pen instead of a pencil and telling me to go do this or that. He won't be there to call me stupid in the same breath that he feeds me some pithy line and calls me his boy.

His laughter, so common that I once thought it irrelevant, not worthy of documenting, will be lost to time. I will forget how it sounds—hearty, sincere, so joyous you can't help but laugh yourself upon hearing it—but never how it made me feel. *Never.*

There's a chance I might not even be at the bookstore anymore, that it will become a place accessible only in my memory. Time will dull its details, now sharp in my mind's eye, tomorrow a vague vision.

I clench my fists. I don't want to lose Second Chance Books, but something tells me I can't keep swimming against this current. There's no forgetting home, but it isn't enough for me to remember just the big, sweeping details like the green walls, the wide windows, and wooden shelves. I want to keep the little things, too: the creaky floorboard in the second aisle from the back, the scratches in the doorframe from when I'd carry boxes of books into the store.

Already it feels like trying to wrap my hands around water. It slips through my fingers. It's futile to even attempt.

Nell places her hand over mine on my lap. "I'm so sorry. I couldn't tell you. It wasn't my place. I—"

"It's fine," I tell her. And I mean it. "I just—I know now is probably not the best time, but I need to know. Is that why you were so sweet to me? After our night out with Daphne and Finn? 'Cause you said no girl brings a guy homemade lunch unless she likes her, and you started bringing me lunch, so I thought, at that time..." I let my sentence trail off.

Nell squeezes my hand and doesn't say anything. I take it as a yes.

"I'm sorry I misunderstood you, then," I say simply.

"It's not your fault. I should have communicated better."

So that settles it then. Nell and I are just friends. Nothing more, but at least certainly nothing less.

I walk Nell to her front door. She unlocks it and steps inside, leaving it open for me. I stand there, peering in, uncertain, until she returns with a questioning look on her face as if to ask, *aren't you coming in?*

The house is small. Typical. A yellow sitting room with a worn couch and a television maybe a decade old. A worn paperback sits on the coffee table, a receipt tucked between its middle pages.

The strangest thing about this place is that there are no photos hanging on the wall, not even cheap art you can find at any charity shop in town. It's as if they've just moved in—or were in the process of slowly moving out.

Nell orders me to take off my shoes by the door and pads barefoot into the kitchen. She asks me if I'm hungry and I say no. She heats me an egg tart from the fridge anyway.

I eat it gratefully while she showers upstairs. When she comes back, she's dressed in a baggy shirt and shorts. Her hair is soaking wet. She gestures for me to follow her, and together we climb the stairs.

Her room is cramped; there's only space for a small mattress, a bedside table, and a stack of books on the floor. She picks a notebook up from her bedside table and tosses it to me.

"What's this?" I ask. I flip open the cover. Her handwriting is neat, always in script, just like in the notebook she filled with her notes on romance, and I know now that she really only writes in black ink.

"You wanted to read something I wrote. So here you go." She shrugs. "The reason I never showed you before now is… well, you'll see. It's a story I wrote in freshman year. The project was to rewrite one of the oldest things we've written that we can find. That one's about you."

"Me?"

Nell rubs the back of her neck sheepishly. "I mean, I guess now's as good a time as any to tell you I used to have a crush on you."

Her words are a sledgehammer to my stomach. I can't breathe. I can't think. I can only blurt out a pathetic little *"When?"*

"I mean, always," she says, averting her gaze, cheeks reddening as she rests one finger on the edge of her dresser and presses down hard as if to concentrate all her energy there. "I thought it was obvious. I was so jealous of Paulina, I didn't know what to do with myself while you were on dates. I—"

She draws in a sharp breath. Drags her teeth across her bottom lip. My eyes linger there, watching that plump bottom lip swell, trying my hardest not to think of how it would feel pressed against my own. "Anyway, a lot of my stories are about friends who end up together."

My heart seizes in my chest. "Why are you telling me this now?"

"So that you believe me when I say I truly never meant to hurt you. I was just—" She draws in a breath. She tells me everything then: about her financial troubles, how she's lived her whole life just one accident away from destitution; about her worries about Kate and the baby, everything. "It's not right for me to say I had no choice, because I could have just not taken the job. But the moment I realized what was at stake, Tom, I swear to you, I—"

I drop my gaze to the notebook. "You wrote love stories about me?"

She still won't look at me. She lifts her gaze towards her reflection in the mirror, and I stand there, stupidly, desperately, wanting to fall on my knees and grab her by the waist and pull her to me. Press my cheek against her stomach. Hear her tell me she loves me.

"Yeah," she says, dropping her gaze to the floor again. Her cheeks are dusted a light pink. "I did."

Look at me, I think. *Please look at me.* Is she telling me this because she still liked me? Or is it because she's over me and it's just a funny little thing to mention now that it's passed? "And in your stories..." I ask, "you and I—we ended up together?"

"Usually."

"Usually?"

"The ones I finished, anyway." She sits down on her bed, one leg folded over the mattress. She pats the space in front of her, and I plop myself down there. "That was—" She shakes her head. "I'm over it now. I promise it won't be an issue between us."

Oh.

"You should try your hand at reading futures," I tease despite my racing heart.

"Almost futures, you mean," she says. "Ones where I almost get it right, but mostly get it wrong."

We share a laugh. Hers more genuine than mine.

It can still be our future, a hopeful voice in my head—no, in my heart— says. *It's not too late.*

But I know it is. She's made up her mind. Why else would she feel comfortable enough to tell me all of this now?

"I'm really, really sorry, Tom," she says to me, taking my hand and squeezing it.

"I know," I tell her. "Me too."

I return to the hospital and all but collapse into my seat next to Roger. Louis had gone home, and Finn and Daphne were napping next to each other.

"How's she doing?" Roger asks.

"Good," I tell him. "I made sure she ate before she went to sleep. I told her I'd call and pick her up as soon as something happens."

I think about Nell, curled up on that mattress on the floor, her chest rising and falling steadily. I wouldn't have left had she not insisted before falling asleep that I should go back, be her representative while she catches up on some rest. To stay felt like an intrusion on her peace.

I think of the circumstances that have brought her back in my life, circumstances I didn't know about and judged her for, but now feel an overwhelming urge to protect her from.

I want more for you, Roger's voice echoed in my head. *And I'm running out of ways to give you that.*

Roger pats my knee. "Good lad."

I tell him that we talked about what happened. That she and I agreed to go back to being friends. That that's all we ever were, all we'll ever be from now on. I tell him that when I told Nell I'd finished the interviews, she said we were missing three more: hers, mine, and Roger's. And Roger says he agrees.

"After the baby comes," he says, "we should film them in-store."

"I was thinking," I tell him, "about the store." On the ride back alone, I thought about how big of a help it would be for Nell and her sister, to have that extra income from the sale. I imagined, rather reluctantly, my future without Roger. Where would I be? What would I be doing?

I don't know the answer yet, but I know Roger's right. Wherever I end up, it's not going to be the same place I'm in now.

Roger cants his head to the side and looks at me intently.

"Let's sell it," I tell him. He sits up, stunned. "But," I add, "we split it evenly. Me, you, and Nell."

"I'm leaving my entire estate to you," Roger says. "Not that there's gold in there or anything. I'm not worried about me."

"Then me and Nell," I say. "An even split, right in the middle."

Roger nods. "I can do that. I can definitely do that." He takes my hand and squeezes it, already looking lighter, happier, as if my agreement had taken ten years of baggage off his shoulders.

"What made you change your mind?" he asks.

I shrug. "Just something you said."

Roger leans back in his seat and chuckles. "I'm glad something stuck to that stubborn brain of yours."

Nell

I knew, the moment I laid eyes on Tom, that no amount of apologizing or penance would make up for the way I'd treated him. The words I'd said, because it turns out I'm a coward bogged down by the weight of her sins when faced with everything I've ever wanted. *Unlovable. Unworthy. Undeserving.* It was easier for me to hurt Tom than to love him and risk getting hurt myself.

What a fool I was.

As I curled under the covers and fell asleep, I couldn't shake the feeling that I didn't deserve his forgiveness. His friendship. His *love.*

I was cruel. I was vindictive.

And *yet.*

Love is given, not earned.

Even at my worst, even after coming face-to-face with the part of me I hated the most—the part that got angry when she really was just scared, the part that was prone to lashing out like a cornered cat—he still thought I was worth forgiving. Worth loving.

Whatever good he sees in me, I will spend the rest of my life striving to live up to.

Tom picks me up just before noon, with good news that my sister made it out okay and the baby was healthy. They named her Zara, and she weighed six pounds and seven ounces. When we peeked at her through the nursery window, all the love I had to give poured out of me. Never again was I going to doubt love's existence, and whether it was within reach for us Garcia girls. Zara is proof that love exists, in this family and in this world.

Happy endings—they exist, too. All that pain, all that suffering—it was all worth it, now that Zara's here. I promise myself to be the best aunt to ever live; she won't have to go through anything Kate and I did. I'll make sure of it.

I once thought that love was simply a phenomenon. It's not. It's the ultimate source of life and all being. It is essential to human existence.

Annabel returned with the twins, and she and Louis carried them on their hips so they could see baby Zara. Mildred came back with apple pie—as requested—and we all ate it in the waiting room so Kate and Henry could get some rest.

Finally, a little before three p.m., Henry emerges from their room and calls on me. We're silent as we walk down the hallway together, and my head swims with all the things I want to say—no, *yell* at him. We stop in front of the door and he turns to face me.

"Nell," he says. "I want to apologize to you. I didn't treat your sister the way I promised both of you I would. I shouldn't have left. I panicked. Kate was frustrated with me, and I thought I would be doing her a favor to just get out of her hair. I was wrong. I should have been there to help. I know that, and that's why I tried to speak with you at the bookstore because Kate wasn't answering any of my calls and—"

I clench my jaw. "An apology doesn't magically absolve you of your sins, Hen."

"I know." He draws in a deep breath. "Kate and I have agreed to co-parent and seek counseling for our relationship. And we wanted you to hear it from me, so you know that I—"

I push him aside and lock the door shut behind me. My sister jolts in her bed.

"You're getting back together with him?" I cry out.

"Nell," she says calmly.

"Are you out of your mind? He left you when you needed him most." He left *us.*

"He didn't leave on his own accord," Kate says. "I made him."

What? I stumble back a step, stunned by this revelation.

But does it matter—really matter—in the grand scheme of things? "He still left," I don't so much as say as spit out.

"I know that. Which is why we're going to therapy."

"But—"

Kate holds up a hand. "I don't expect you to understand, Nell. But it's different now. We have a baby. I want her to have a better life than I did. Than *we* did."

"And she can have that," I say. "But not at your expense, Kate. Henry—"

"He hurt me," she says, nodding. "But I love him. And he loves me. And we both want to give it a try. I don't expect you to understand, or even approve, but Nell, why are you so angry about this? I thought you'd be happy for me."

"Happy?" I echo. "Why the hell would I be happy for you?"

"Because I'm finally getting the life I wanted, Nell. Because I just gave birth. Because my husband wants to come back. Because we're finally going to be a family." Even though there are tears in her eyes, I'm too angry to cry. Because she's leaving me again. She's starting—no, *started*—her own family and leaving me behind.

"So what am I?" I demand. "What about me, Kate? Am I not family?" *Am I not enough?*

"*Of course* you're family," she cries. "You'll always be my baby sister. I *love* you. What are you—"

"You *love* me? Or you're obligated to me? Those are two different things, Kate."

"How can you say that? I took you in, I practically raised you, I—"

"But you left first. You left first, Kate, and you told Mama I was becoming stupid in love, do you remember? So I swore to myself—I swore I would never make the same mistakes Mama did so you wouldn't think I'm stupid. So you'd come back.

"But you didn't. The state had to find you and surrender me to you, and by then, you'd already started a new life. I didn't fit in. But I kept my promise, didn't I? I studied hard. I closed myself off to love. And when Henry left you, I didn't rub it in your face. I didn't say, *now who's stupid in love?* and I'm not saying it now."

There's a hole in my heart and from it spills out every single one of my deepest, darkest, most selfish insecurities. I can't stop them from pouring out of me even if I tried.

Kate's face screws up. "You just did."

"Shut up," I tell her, fighting the urge to laugh. "I closed myself off to so many things and took on so many jobs I didn't want to so I could help you and I never expected anything back, because you're my sister and I loved you even when you didn't love me."

Kate and I are sobbing now. She holds out her arms to me, and feeling every bit stupid with love for her, I climb into her bed and let her squeeze me tight.

"Ow. Careful," she says, and we adjust into a more comfortable position.

Finally, she says, "I have always loved you, Nelly. And I'm so sorry I left you with Mama. I shouldn't have done that. But Nell, you are the smartest girl I know. You can never be stupid in love. I was just—" She chuckles. "I was just projecting. I was worried about you, but I didn't go about it the right way. I'm sorry."

I choke out a sob and burrow into her neck. "I told Tom to fuck off because I was scared to turn out like you and Mama."

She bursts out laughing, even through her tears. "That's fair," she says. "But Nell." She lifts my chin with her finger and looks directly into my eyes. "I wouldn't have made it this far if it wasn't for you. Every single time I felt like giving up, I looked to you. *You* are proof that love exists. Forget about what Mama said—and I know she said a lot. I should have protected you from that."

"You were only trying to protect yourself," I murmur.

"But I had a responsibility to you. As your older sister," she says. "Love exists, Nell, and it's the most beautiful thing on earth. Forget about everything Mama and I have ever said about it—"

"Even the fact that it exists?" I tease.

"Everything except that," she says. "And just because it didn't work out for Mama—and possibly for me—doesn't mean it won't work out for you. If there was one thing Mama got right, it's that she never gave up on love. Even when the world let her down, time and time again."

I sniff and snuggle closer into my sister. It feels like a weight has been lifted off my shoulders.

"I'm sorry," I choke out, breaking into another fit of sobs.

"Stop crying," Kate says. "You're making me—God, I'm crying all over again." She squeezes me tighter. "I love you. I forgive you."

Relief washes over me. She doesn't hate me. She's not leaving me. Us Garcia girls stick together forever and ever.

"Roger's sick," I tell her after some time. "He's thinking of selling the bookstore."

"I know," she says.

"You do?"

"I went to visit the bookstore. Tom was crying over you."

"Shut up," I say.

"I'm serious!"

I look up at her and there's not an ounce of worry in her eyes.

"I want you to focus on school," she says. "Henry's promised to move us to a bigger place so you could more space, and I made him swear to cover your tuition."

I laugh.

"What?" she says. "It's reparations. I'm not *that* stupid."

"I love you, Kate," I tell her, closing my eyes and breathing her in. My sister, my ate.

"I love *you*, Nell. Now get off me and tell Tom you're sorry."

I pull back to look at her.

"If you don't," she says, her brows knitting together, "then you're really stupid in love, and no amount of crying to me is going to change that."

Tom

The papers have been signed, and the sale finalized. Walter convinced his son to pay more than the store is worth and offered me an internship at the Cultural Center he's chair of—with the condition that I return to school and finish my degree in History so I could work at the museum as a curator. I'd be stupid not to take it, but there's still Finn and the band and the endless possibilities, the many open doors that waits for us if we get back together.

Music is my first love; a part of me will never rest until I know I've given it my best shot. And even then, even if the industry wants nothing to do with me, I'll still write my songs. Still fiddle around on the guitar and the piano.

Nell's returned to work to help pack our things, donate books to schools and charities and shelters so they won't have to end up in a landfill, just like in her pitch to Vanguard Properties. I like to think that part of the bookstore will always exist that way, outside of our memories.

We take turns interviewing each other for the film and then edit the documentary for hours in my empty flat. We settle into a comfortable friendship, and though sometimes I catch myself wanting to touch her neck or kiss her lips, those feelings are fleeting and I go back to loving her the way she'll let me.

As friends. Nothing more, nothing less.

We hold a book sale for the remaining books. Everything half off. We print fliers and set up a booth at the Artist's Market with Abigail. Mildred and Roger stay back at the shop in case new, converted customers want to have a look at the other books we didn't bring with us.

This chapter of my life is ending and I'm nervous for what the future holds. More precisely, I'm afraid of what life will be like when the inevitable comes and I lose Roger. But I know—I'm lucky enough to know that I won't have to go through it alone.

I'll have the book club members, and Finn, and Daphne, and Nell. Always Nell. In whatever shape or form, I know that to be true. She doesn't have to say it; her eyes make all the promises I want to hear.

And the love Roger has shown me—I'll always have it, too. He'll live on through me and Nell and everyone whose life he's ever touched. I'll never be alone ever again.

Nell and I are packing away the rest of the books we weren't able to sell or donate to drop off at a charity shop in the city when we go later this month. It's strange, to see the shop so empty, the once overflowing shelves hollowed, like someone had taken my heart right out of my ribcage. There's no life here. It's just another place.

The bell over the shop door rings, startling us from the comfortable silence we worked in. Standing there by the counter is my father, whose lips are pressed together in a thin line.

Nell throws me a cautious look. I give her a small nod, and she excuses herself, walking straight out the door to give us some privacy.

"Hi, dad," I say.

"Hello, Thomas. How are things going with the—" He gestures around the shop.

"Good," I say, if only because I don't know what else to tell him. Second Chance Books has been home to me for the past five years; I'm not even close to ready to say goodbye to it, but I don't have a choice. I'm just holding on to the hope that what waits for me on the other end of goodbye could be just as good—or even better—than life here at the bookstore.

My dad gestures towards one of the chairs. I nod. We each take a seat, me fidgeting, him with his fingers locked together, his elbows resting on his thighs. I hold my breath as he opens his mouth to speak. I don't know what to expect. After the night he drove us to the hospital, he's been texting more frequently to check up on me, but we haven't properly spoken outside of that. I brace myself for the possibility that this could end badly. That, without Nell to interfere and send him out, we'll have a repeat of our fight five years ago.

"I'm sorry I didn't come see you sooner," he says.

Okay, I wasn't expecting *that*.

My dad keeps his gaze fixed on the floor. For someone who rose to fame singing rock songs about his feelings and championing emotional intelligence in men, he was never really affectionate towards me or open about his feelings in private. I can tell this is difficult for him, so I keep my mouth shut.

"I tried, but your girlfriend didn't want me around, and I figured she was speaking on your behalf." He chuckles. "A firecracker, that one."

I should correct him, but I don't. *Your girlfriend*, I think. *Nell.* Imagine that?

"I have a lot to be sorry for, and you don't have to forgive me. But if you'd let me, I'd like to make it up to you. Or not make it up. I'd like to make it right. I haven't been a good father to you. When you were born, that first time I held you, I promised myself. I promised—*'Michael, you are going to be better than your father'.* And still. Still I failed you in so many ways that my father failed me, and—" Here, his voice cracks. "I'm so sorry, Thomas. If you could ever find it in your heart to forgive me—"

"That night," I interrupt him. "When you were inducted to the Hall of Fame. Greg was showing the guys pictures of Paulina naked. You remember Paulina?"

My dad sits up, his teary eyes sobering instantly. "Andrew's daughter?"

I nod. "Yeah. Greg's ex-girlfriend. My former friend."

"Is that—"

"Yeah."

Dad presses his fist against his mouth. His knuckles turn white from the tension.

"I was trying to do the right thing," I tell him. "And all I've ever wanted—all I've ever needed, dad, is to know you were on my side."

"If I'd known—"

"I tried to tell you."

"Yvonne said—"

"Well, that's the problem, isn't it?" I snap. "You'd take her word over your own son's." All the pent-up anger I'd suppressed over the years surges out of me. "After Mum left, you said it would be us against the world. And then you met Yvonne. And Yvonne has Greg, so I was bumped even further down the list."

My dad's face hardens. *There it is,* I think. I knew this was coming. I don't give him what he wants—in this case, forgiveness—and he gets angry with me. He doesn't care about me or how I feel. He doesn't care to actually make amends. He just wants to feel better about himself. To know that he did the right thing.

And then his face falls. He nods. "You're right," he says. "I'm sorry for that, too."

"Really?" I blurt out.

My dad chuckles. "Why are you so surprised?"

Because you've never apologized to me a day in your life? Because we've spent the past five years estranged? Because I was convinced you didn't care about me in the slightest and were happy to live your new life with Yvonne?

"You are my son," he says, "and I should have put you first."

I slump in my seat, defeated. I was prepared for a fight. I was ready for fire and brimstone. I wasn't ready for *this.*

"Yvonne and I are getting divorced," he says. "And I don't want you thinking that I've only come around because I don't want to be a lonely old man. It's nothing like that. I've been talking to that boss of yours—"

"Roger," I say.

"Roger." My dad nods. "He called me up a few months ago. Said he was sick and he was worried about what would happen to you when he's gone. I was like, what the hell do you mean? He's my son. He'll be fine. And he told me, *'well, you haven't been much of a father to this kid. I have.'"* My dad chuckles. "That was about as rude of a wake-up call any father can get, and I'm damn glad he gave it to me."

I picture Roger on the phone, tearing my father a new one. I can't help but laugh.

"I don't want you to worry about him," my dad says. "I'm making sure he's getting the best care possible. I owe it to him, for all that he's done for you. For stepping up when I hadn't."

My vision blurs with tears. There's still so much to say, so much to talk about, but I start with the truth. "I missed you, Dad." Admitting it feels like releasing a breath I'd been holding this entire time. Hearing him say he missed me back? Like a inhaling fresh air after being trapped in a cramped, windowless room. He hugs me tightly, and I feel like a little kid again, like a boy who's just lost his mother, afraid of losing his father, too.

When we pull away, we're laughing. He hands me his handkerchief and I wipe my eyes with it.

"Finn and I are thinking of getting the band back together again," I tell him after we've calmed down a bit.

"Are you?" he says. "Well, you're welcome to rehearse at home any time you like. I've just renovated the music room, so—"

I shake my head. "If it's alright with you," I say, "I'd like for us to figure this out on our own. No pulling strings for me either." The easy way to stardom would be to ride my father's coattails. But I don't want stardom. I just want to make music.

My father smiles and pats my cheek. "Of course."

The bell rings again. We turn to find Nell poking her head into the store. "I can come back later," she says.

"No, no," my dad says. He doesn't recognize her. "I think it's time I meet my son's girlfriend."

To my surprise, she doesn't correct him either.

Nell

Before any of us expects it, it's the last day of Second Chance Books. Though we still had two weeks of summer left, Roger wanted to end things on a high note, on the same day we're meant to celebrate the book club's anniversary. We've all gathered in-store for the last time to watch the documentary and say our goodbyes—perhaps not to each other, but to the store that's become our home away from home. To an era that is quickly coming to an end.

Everyone's here: Mildred and her family, Annabel and the twins, Louis, Bobby, Walter, Finn, and Daphne. Henry and Kate are busy taking care of Zara but call us on FaceTime to wish us well.

Even Tom's dad shows up. He still thinks I'm Tom's girlfriend, which made for a pretty funny—if awkward—short conversation (he invited me to visit Henwick with Tom and was already asking about my holiday plans). What's even funnier is the way he ducked into the room as if afraid of any potential fanfare; we all couldn't have cared less even if he wore a bright neon sign that read I'M SO VERY FAMOUS AND IMPORTANT!

The tables and chairs are set up no different from a typical book club meeting. There, the chairs in front of the platform on which the projector Walter had loaned us stood. To its right, the wooden round tables lined up in a row, bearing the weight of more dishes than we can eat. Mildred's apple pie, Kate's suman pinipig (prepared by yours truly!), cold cuts and cheeses, and so much more.

Except for the bunting flags Annabel helped me put up, and the balloons Louis and Tom blew up with their own breaths, it looked like all the other Thursday nights we've spent here before. Like tomorrow, it will be business as usual.

"Eleanor!" I break from conversation with Daphne to approach Roger. He introduces me to a tall woman whose cheeks were already reddening from the wine, her vermillion lipstick a pop of color against her pale complexion.

"This is my friend, Kirsten, from Clover Press." Kirsten extends a hand towards me. It takes a second for me to process what's going on. I stare dumbly at her hand before Roger clears his throat and I remember to take her hand in mine and shake it.

"It's so charming to meet you," Kirsten says, her piercing blue eyes a contrast to the warm smile she's giving me. "Roger has told me many great things about you."

"You remember what we talked about?" he says to her.

"Of course." Kirsten reaches into her clutch and procures a business card which she hands over to me. "When you're ready, send me your CV through e-mail. I'm looking forward to it."

Roger winks at me.

"Now, Kirsten, have I introduced you to...?"

I take my cue to leave. I stumble back towards Daphne, who has struck up a conversation with Mildred's grandson, Xavier. He was not—contrary to what I expected—a child with a penchant for apple pie but a grown man with sleeves of tattoos on either muscular arm.

"Who was that?" Daphne asks me.

I stare at the card in my hand.

KIRSTEN OLINSKY
EDITORIAL DIRECTOR
CLOVER PRESS

A smile spreads on my cheeks. "If I play my cards right, I think she might be my new boss."

Daphne takes the card from me, scans it quickly, and then squeals before throwing her arms around my neck.

On-stage, Mildred clears her throat. She casts a shadow on the screen. Her hand is lifted to shield her eyes from the direct light of the projector.

"Everyone," she says, "to their seats, please. Elderly first. Save one for me, Walter, yes, thank you." I follow Daphne and Xavier to the back of the crowd where Xavier's sister, Quintana, is chatting with Finn.

"Now, as you all know, our lovely Thomas and Eleanor have been working on a documentary to mark this lovely occasion." Cheers erupt from the crowd. Daphne claps her hands in my face. Tom stands off to the side of the platform, his laptop casting a blue light on his chest. When our eyes meet, the corner of his lips turns up into a small smirk. With two fingers, he gives me a salute. I salute back and immediately feel embarrassed by how uncool it felt to do.

"The time has come for us to watch said documentary, and—"

"Get on with it!" Roger yells from his seat, eliciting laughter from all of us.

"Oh, alright, alright," Mildred says as she ambles off the platform towards her seat. "Tom, please."

On cue, Tom presses play on his laptop and sets it aside. A gentle melody ushers in the opening scenes: a montage of old photos of Roger, Cecilia, and Mildred in the early days of Second Chance Books, interspersed with clips of the bookstore during golden hour. Mildred's voice fills the room: *My name is Mildred Douglas—and that's my maiden name, mind you. I've been divorced twice and the second time around, I was like, no more. That's that. Next time I fall in love, we don't need to get the government involved.*

A low rumble of laughter erupts from the crowd. I tear my gaze from the screen and watch Tom approach.

"Hi," he whispers under his breath.

"Hi," I say back.

"Mind if I stand here?"

I shake my head.

By the time we reach the end of the film, we're all crying. Daphne is clutching my arm, whining that I should have warned her it would be a tearjerker. I tell her even I didn't know that it would be; Tom had done a wonderful job filling in the gaps when I wasn't there. He saw us all in the best light and stayed faithful to that vision. When my face came up on screen, I wasn't mortified. Instead, I saw myself how he saw me: patient and kind and beautiful in the deepest sense of the word. Beyond skin deep. Beautiful as in *loved*.

And then there was the music. He never told me he'd composed songs solely for the film. Each one was more moving than the last; it was as if he'd bottled up all the love everyone felt for the store and spilled it on his keyboard and on the strings of his guitar.

I want to congratulate him, but a crowd forms around each of us. Mildred cups my cheeks and kisses me on each one. Annabel envelopes me in a warm embrace.

Before I know it, it's time to say goodnight to my friends and goodbye to the store forever. Roger hitches a ride with Louis, who's meant to drop him off at his new home at the hospice where we all promise to visit him every day until he tires of us.

I linger after everyone's left, helping Tom tidy up.

"I really liked the songs you made," I say after some time.

He stacks the chairs and offers me a brief smile. "Thanks."

"Where are you going after this?" I ask.

"Back to college," he says. "Finish my degree in History. Maybe work on the band." He tells me about the internship Walter offered him, assisting in the media department of the Cerulean Cultural Center. "Some films are being produced and he thinks I could help with the research and stuff."

"That fits you," I say. Neither of us brings up the fact that Roger will spend the rest of his days at the hospice instead of here. Even though we've known for days, it still hasn't sunken in. It still doesn't seem right. "But where will you live?"

"With Finn," he says, "for a little bit. Until I can get my own place." The sale had fattened our wallets, but Walter had also enlisted the help of his advisors to help us manage it. Invest it in the proper places so it grows. So far, the only things I've spent it on is my tuition—Henry insisted on paying, but I told him to spoil Kate instead.

I picture Tom in a new apartment, coming home after school having met new people, new girls. Living a whole new life without Roger. Without *me*.

Overcome by a desire to not move into that reality—a reality where he and I are ever apart—I speak before I think.

"Stay with me," I blurt out.

"What?"

I swallow the lump in my throat. I want to cup his face, to kiss him endlessly, to apologize for my ever having thought him an idiot when he was the smartest person I knew, when he was smarter than I've been and ever will be.

I clamp down on every voice in my head screaming at me to stop, you're making a fool of yourself, you're going to regret this. I push past the pins and needles, my heart racing in my chest, and take a step forward.

"Stay with me," I repeat. "As in, move in with me. We're moving to a new place. Bigger. And I'll have my own room, so you and I can share. Henry's desperately trying to make it up to me and Kate, and it's really funny—you should see it—so we'll save on rent until we can find our own place and live together—alone, together—and it'll be fun, like a sleepover every night, and we can have Finn and Daph over a bunch, and maybe some other friends—new friends, when you make some because you will, because you're so charming—and what I'm trying to say is *I love you, Tom. I love you.*" I'm breathless now, but I can't stop. I can't hold back. Not now. Not when it's all I've done my whole life.

"I have loved you since the moment we met, and I'm certain even before that. Like I was put on this earth for one thing and one thing only and—and it's you. To love you. I've just been too busy fighting it, too cowardly to tell you the truth. But I was never happier than when I was with you, going on pretend dates, driving in your car, watching romcoms, and interviewing the members. And when you gave me your jacket, I knew—of course I knew, I'm not an idiot—"

He reaches out a hand and brushes my bangs away from my brows. Tucks my hair behind one ear.

"Tom—"

"Your hair's grown longer," he says.

My hair? Really? He wants to talk about my hair when I'm in the middle of my grand confession?

He smiles at me, and I realize his hand is still on my face.

"I love you," I say, breathless, desperate. My eyes plead with his to give me a response. Any response. Yes, no, maybe.

Instead, he leans in, his lips mere centimeters away from mine. "Say that again."

I'll say it over and over for the rest of my life if he lets me. "I lo—"

Tom closes the gap between us, kissing me deeply. My stomach flips, falls right through to my center, my aching core, arousing in me a dormant desire now evolved into insatiable hunger for this taste—*his* taste. It should be impossible, that his soft lips could kiss me with this much fervor, this much ferocity, as if he too had stumbled in the desert for decades and in me found his long-awaited oasis.

But there he is. There we are.

His arms snake around my waist and I press into him, my fingers tangling in his curls. The pads of his fingers dig into my skin, sure to leave a mark. I want him to. I *need* him to. I want to wake up tomorrow morning knowing I'm his. Knowing he's mine.

Tom lets out a low groan. He backs into the counter and maneuvers us upstairs, where the only things left are his mattress, the couch, and some empty shelves. I whine pitifully at the brief break between our touching, clench my fists around the fabric of his shirt, but he's quick, quick, quick, pulling me back into his arms, making it right again.

"I love you," I say again, in between kisses that light me up in flames. He pants against me, his breath hot in my face. I know immediately that I will never get enough of this, that I will never have enough. I will spend the rest of my life wanting this, needing this, loving him. He is my heart and soul, his arms my home.

He sets me down on the mattress and settles himself between my legs. I meet his tender gaze and give him an encouraging smile. *Yes, yes, yes. Forever yes. I am yours as you are mine. Take me and make it so.*

He kisses my jaw, all the way down to my neck where he sucks gently on my skin. I arch my back into his touch.

Mine. He is all mine.

I slide my hands under his shirt, smoothing them over the soft, warm skin of his waist, his stomach, his chest. He pulls away to tear off his shirt, eliciting another whimper from me.

"I know, I know," he coos, helping me out of my own clothes. Whatever complaints I have die in my throat when our skins touch. We melt into each other: mouth-to-mouth, chest-to-chest, a tangle of arms and legs, two halves made whole again.

"I love you," I say, one last time before we give ourselves to each other.

He smiles at me, gently, affectionately, and presses a chaste kiss on my lips.

"I love you, too, Nell. More than you could ever know."

And the rest is history.

Roger

TOM: Okay, Roge. We're rolling.

ROGER: *[clears throat]* Ready? Okay.

Hi, my name is Roger Fitzgerald. I've been the owner of Second Chance Books for—wow, over thirty years now. That's nearly half a century. I didn't realize. *[laughs]*

By the time you see this, you will have heard countless stories from our customers about the store and its history—both the objective, such as when it was founded, how, and why; and the personal. Anecdotes of when someone found it—which I've noticed seems to be when they're in dire need of love—or how.

I've asked to do my interview differently. Or rather, asked to not do an interview at all. Instead, I want to take the time to thank all of you. For having been with me through this journey. For supporting Second Chance Books even through the toughest of times. For believing, no matter what, in the power of love and literature and its ability to change lives.

In the morning when I wake, I think of my wife, Cecilia, whose dream it was to open this store. When I visit her grave and bring her flowers, I tell her all about you. About how much the store has grown beyond our wildest imaginations.

To Mildred, who I inherited as a best friend and a sister long before Cecilia died—thank you for the strength you've given me all these years to keep going. To keep fighting to keep Cecilia's dream alive.

To Ingrid, and Sam, and children—for not giving up on Mildred when she needed you most. I don't know where any of us will be without her spirit and strength, and it is from you four that she draws that same strength from.

To Louis, whose many thoughts and ideas on literature and philosophy I enjoy so greatly, even when you drone on and on past the point of my patience.

NELL: *Roger!*

ROGER: *[laughs]* I'm kidding, I'm kidding. Where was I?

To Annabel, and children. For giving me the chance to be a grandfather who was also sometimes Santa. The joy you have brought in my life will forever be cherished.

To Bobby, for your determination and resolve. Six years sober! The world is infinitely better with you in it.

To Walter, for saving us from dire straits—both ways. You have my deepest gratitude.

And to Thomas. I thank God and Cecilia every day for sending you to me when they did. You are the son I've never had, and you have been my guiding light these past five years. All I do, all I've done, is all for you.

And last but not least: to Nell. The final piece to our puzzle, the most wonderful addition to our family. Your strength, your patience, and your perseverance has paved the way for us, has given my dear Thomas and I hope for the future.

May you find the love you seek and so immensely deserve, and may you never forget your promise to me.

To everyone. This might be the end of Second Chance Books, and farewells are imminent. But my hope is that when all is said and done, the lessons we learned, the laughter we shared, and the love we felt for one another lives on in each of us.

When Thomas was seventeen, I took him to my hometown to see the field where the first Cerulean settlers lived. I watched as he stared, stupefied, at the empty field and tried to picture it bustling with life.

"Where does it go?" he asked. "All those memories. What happens when the last person who remembers it dies?"

I've thought about it long and hard, and it's only recently that I've come to a conclusion.

We are, all of us, the result of a long history of someone, somewhere, loving another and choosing to act on it. Love, after all, is more than a feeling. It's a choice. And I have been so lucky to have been blessed by your respective choices to love me, to love this store, and to show it by showing up every Thursday the past how many years for book club.

And I have loved each and every single one of you with the ferocity and tenderness with which my wife had loved me.

Let's keep choosing to love one another, so that some day, someone who needs it will feel the echoes of our love, transcending time and space and giving them the strength to go on.

Thank you, again, a million times over. Thank you, thank you, thank you.

Was that alright?

NELL: *[smiles]* It was perfect.

Epilogue

Tom

Nell is bent over the vanity in our bedroom, applying the nude lipstick Daphne had bought her just last week. She's a sight for sore eyes in her periwinkle dress, and when I step up behind her, she spins around and pushes me back, a warning look in her eyes.

"Keep your hands to yourself, please," she teases. I hold my hands up in mock surrender and back away, only to nearly trip over the fat, calico cat we adopted from the shelter and the reason for Nell's needing to take her antihistamines daily.

The doorbell rings. "I'll get it!" I call out, giving *my girlfriend* more time to finish getting ready. It thrills me that I get to call her that. *My* girlfriend. *Mine.*

Today, we're hosting a housewarming party in our brand new flat in Hetford. I purchased it so Nell wouldn't have to spend a single dime and put all her money towards her savings. For as long as I can help it, and even long after that, I'll make sure she'll never have to worry about anything ever again. About going hungry. About not having a roof over her head. I will go through hell and back to give her a home.

I pull the door open to reveal Daphne, carrying a box of cake, and Finn, holding the neck of two bottles of wine in each hand. I step aside to let them in, and when Nell emerges from our room, Daphne squeals and shoots past me to pull her into a one-armed hug.

"Hey, man," Finn greets. We've offered to let him stay with us when his contract ends with his roommates—rent-free—so this is just as much his housewarming party as it is ours.

The flat fills with familiar faces: Kate, Henry, and their baby—who, aside from her button-nose, unfairly looks like her father. Annabel and Louis—who have since made it official—and the twins. Xavier and Quintana, on Mildred's behalf (*"I'm too old for your parties!"* she said, though she did send us an apple pie). Bobby's there, too, as well as my father, though Roger and Walter couldn't make it. That's fine; we're visiting Roger tomorrow, fully intent on telling him about today.

Hosting a party is a lot more work than book club, which Walter now hosts at the Cultural Center—just until the library he's renovating in Newbury re-opens, which has been named after Roger. I sneak into the bedroom for a break, only to find Nell already there, leaning against the vanity again and staring off into space.

"Nelly?"

She looks up and grins sheepishly. "I just needed a second."

I approach her and stand right in front of her. Her hair's grown longer, a little past her shoulder now, and her bangs swoop to the side. I tuck a loose strand behind her ear and kiss her—just because I can.

"Can you believe this is happening?" she whispers against my mouth.

With my eyes drooped, I shake my head, our noses brushing in the process.

"We're having a housewarming party. You. And me. In our own flat. That we own."

I chuckle at the shock in her voice.

Her hands settle on my hips and squeezes. "We should probably get back out there," she says. *We should.* Instead, I shake my head, too entranced by her smell, her touch, to move.

"Five more minutes," I murmur, which she laughs at. I love our friends, I love our family—both found and biological. But in my head, I'm already speeding to the end of the night when it's just the two of us, slow dancing in the dim light to a smooth song playing on the record player Roger gave me.

This is it. This is what I want the rest of my life to look like. This is what the rest of my life will look like.

"Tommy," she says. I dip my head and kiss her neck, making her gasp. Since we've gotten together, I've enjoyed learning all the different noises I can get her to make.

"We should—"

I smooth my hand up her skirt and lift my head so I can speak against her lips. "We should what?"

Her eyes meet mine. For a second, it feels as though it could go either way. Between the two of us, Nell has always had more restraint.

And then she throws her arms around my neck, crashing her lips into mine.

I thought so.

Acknowledgements

A million thank you's to my beta readers: Gabby Jusoy, Yumi Briones, Vaishali Denton, and Shamee Tomawis. Your comments helped sharpen my writing, improve my ideas, and polish the manuscript. Thank you for your patience in reading the earlier drafts and seeing the potential in Second Chance Books.

To my editor, Julian Baet, whose insight and passion for this novel took my little story to the next level. Any errors left are my own.

To Richard Siken, who gave me permission to quote his poetry with proper attribution.

A special mention to Alyne & Mabel Ypil, for your friendship, support, and cheerleader-like energies that encouraged me to keep writing. I still think of when I sobbed after a brutal poetry workshop in college and you guys hugged me and offered me love. It kept me going and I wouldn't be here today without your kindness.

To Jay, for being one of the first people to believe in and love Nell. Your writing inspires me and my brainchildren. Thank you for giving me the space to explore all the goofy little ideas I have with you, for being patient when I disappear to write, and for reminding me how one eats an elephant

(idiom, not literally!)

To my best friend, Jamila Geronimo, whose unwavering faith and support in my writing helped me through roadblocks—both during writing this novel and all the ones that came before it. I wouldn't have made it this far without you (and your constant reminders to take a break). You told me to follow my gut, so here I am!

To Nic—my lover, life partner, and best friend rolled into one. Thank you for everything. Your support, your patience, your willingness to brainstorm and let me bounce ideas with you. For having faith in me and my writing even when I didn't. Your existence fuels my writing: you are so beautiful, so loved, and so precious, and the world has to know. If we're remembered for anything long after we're gone, I hope it's for the fact that we were here, and for that short period in time, we loved.

And finally, to you: for reading my book. Loved it, hated it, didn't care for it—however you feel, I appreciate the time you put into letting me tell you a little story. Still, I hope you had fun. Maybe we'll see each other again in my next book? (Fingers crossed.)

About the Author

Carina Gaskell is a full-time author of cozy romance novels and cat mom to three rowdy cats. She currently resides in Metro Manila, Philippines, and is engaged to her partner of 7 years.

Newsletter

If you enjoyed Second Chance Books by Carina Gaskell, sign up for the newsletter to stay updated on upcoming books!

carinagaskell.carrd.co

Printed in Great Britain
by Amazon